"That's who I am,

"I stay here because land stays. [...] and looked up to the ridge. "You're the wind, Grace."

"Loud and noisy and creator of migraines?"

"Strong enough to knock a man flat." He could admit to that easy enough. It was the next part that choked him up. "And always on the move."

She turned her mouth downward, not disagreeing.

He reached across the table and pulled one of her hands into his. "I'm not going anywhere, Grace. That wasn't so great for us fifteen years ago. I'm hoping that this time it's different."

Dear Reader,

At last, the third and final story in my miniseries A Ranch to Call Home—Grace and Hawk's story. You briefly met them in the first book, *A Family for the Rancher*, and what polar opposites! Feisty and impulsive, Grace has held a high-powered life in the city, while Hawk, reserved and sacrificing, has struggled to keep together the multigenerational family ranch deep in the foothills of southern Alberta. I loved bringing these childhood friends back together—they really are made for each other!

A special thanks to Don and Myriam Wilson. As residents at the Calgary Stampede OH Ranch, they graciously instructed me in the ways of cowboying and ranching in southern Alberta, including its history and traditions. Myriam's tour into the back pastures brought us into view of a special herd—wild elk! Any mistakes are mine only.

And thanks, as always, to you for kicking back with my book in hand. If this is your first experience with me, hello—come see me on my website, mkstelmack.com. And if you are reading me again, you've made my day.

Take care, y'all!

Best,

M. K.

HEARTWARMING

A Family for His Boys

———

M. K. Stelmack

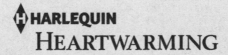

If you purchased this book without a cover you should be aware that this book is stolen property. It was reported as "unsold and destroyed" to the publisher, and neither the author nor the publisher has received any payment for this "stripped book."

ISBN-13: 978-1-335-47576-3

A Family for His Boys

Copyright © 2024 by S. M. Stelmack

Recycling programs for this product may not exist in your area.

All rights reserved. No part of this book may be used or reproduced in any manner whatsoever without written permission except in the case of brief quotations embodied in critical articles and reviews.

This is a work of fiction. Names, characters, places and incidents are either the product of the author's imagination or are used fictitiously. Any resemblance to actual persons, living or dead, businesses, companies, events or locales is entirely coincidental.

For questions and comments about the quality of this book, please contact us at CustomerService@Harlequin.com.

TM and ® are trademarks of Harlequin Enterprises ULC.

Harlequin Enterprises ULC
22 Adelaide St. West, 41st Floor
Toronto, Ontario M5H 4E3, Canada
www.Harlequin.com

Printed in U.S.A.

M. K. Stelmack writes historical and contemporary fiction. She is the author of A True North Hero series—the third book of which was made into a movie—The Montgomerys of Spirit Lake series and the Ranch to Call Home series with Harlequin Heartwarming. She lives in Alberta, Canada, close to a town the fictional Spirit Lake of her stories is patterned after.

Books by M. K. Stelmack

Harlequin Heartwarming

A True North Hero

A Roof Over Their Heads
Building a Family
Coming Home to You

The Montgomerys of Spirit Lake

All They Want for Christmas
Her Rodeo Rancher
Their Together Promise

A Ranch to Call Home

A Family for the Rancher
A Family for Thanksgiving

Visit the Author Profile page
at Harlequin.com for more titles.

**To the ranchers of the foothills,
for keeping the tradition alive.**

CHAPTER ONE

GRACE JANSSON TOUCHED her house key to the lock, and from inside came a distinct thud and scrambling. A break-in. She'd lived for fifteen years in Calgary, a major city a short two-hour drive away, and never once had been a victim of property crime. Yet two months into her new life in the remote foothills of Southern Alberta and some perp had selected her for a home invasion.

Or maybe an animal. Maybe she'd left the back door unlocked, and a deer or raccoon had pushed its way in. She had swept out deer droppings and carried out a swallow's nest when she'd moved in.

A chair scraped across the floor. A long scuff mark across her newly polished wood floor. Definite human activity.

She whipped out her phone to call the police. A piercing howl broke from inside, followed by yipping, and then a smashing and tinkling of fine crystal. Her mother's vase.

The little, thoughtless stinkers. The tenor of their voices gave away their youth. Probably not much older than her toddler-aged nephew and six-year-old Sadie.

Inside, abrupt silence fell and then the pounding of feet. Oh no, they weren't.

She raced to the back of the house, her feet slipping on the slushy March snow in time to spot a small boy dart out the back door. He caught sight of her and, not stopping, called over his shoulder. "Saul! Hurry!"

The second boy burst out, but Grace was there to grip his unzipped jacket. He froze, and then screamed, "Amos!"

Amos tore back and grabbed the hand of who must be his twin. The familial likeness to each other and to their father was too much.

"Hey, listen—"

Amos used the edge of his hand to chop on her grip. Ineffective, but it hurt. Well, if he saw her as the enemy, she might as well play the role. She pulled Saul against her, taking him into both arms. He didn't resist.

"Leave me alone," she said to Saul's defender, "or I will feed your brother cookies while you watch."

He stepped back, but his scowl remained. "You don't have cookies. We checked."

"Including the cupboard above the fridge?"

Amos looked over at his brother, whose shoulders sagged. "It was too high. I couldn't reach,"

Saul said. His near-black hair curled at the ends, just like his father's.

"That's okay," his brother said. "Who puts cookies there, anyway?" His hair was even curlier and longer, and right now, hair length was the only way she could distinguish the twins. They both wore the same blue shirt jackets, blue jeans and snow boots.

"Someone," Grace said, "who battles her impulses. Now, can we agree that if I release your brother, you will both come inside like gentlemen and partake of cookies and juice?"

"And then we can go?"

"And then I will release you into your father's custody."

"Dad's not around."

"Then, to whoever is taking care of you."

Saul dipped his dark head. Dirt smudged his neck, and Grace resisted the temptation to rub it off. Amos fixed Saul with a warning look.

"Please tell me someone is taking care of you."

"Uh," Amos said, "you better just call Dad."

He seemed to assume that she had his father's number, as if everyone would know who he was, and probably in this community, everybody did.

She knew that the boy's last name was Blackstone, that he was twin to Saul, that their father's name was Hawk Blackstone and that her new home was the old homestead of the Blackstones' before Hawk and his parents moved to their pres-

ent location on the adjoining quarter more than ten
years ago, leaving The Home Place to gather dust
and bird nests, it would seem. Word from her father was that Hawk's parents had moved into town
when Hawk had brought his bride there to live.

She also knew things Amos didn't. Like how
she and their father had once been good friends
until fifteen years ago, but that in the past six
weeks or so since she'd formally occupied the
place, neither had renewed contact. Which only
went to show that back when she was eighteen to
his twenty, she was right to think that he would
move on.

But she had his number. Mateo, her sister's
husband and Hawk's former employee, had insisted she have it in case she ever needed help. As
Mateo recited it, Grace had finished it for him.
Hawk had not changed it in the past fifteen years.
He didn't care for change. Her complete make-
over of his fourth-generation home place over the
past year probably had him grinding his teeth.

"I intend to call him, but right now, let's as-
sess damages."

The twin whirlwinds had ransacked the place
she'd originally planned as her weekend home,
but now was her full-time residence and location
of her bed-and-breakfast. Kitchen cupboard doors
were flung open, potato chips strewn across her
granite countertops, and there was a huge sticky
spot on her tiles from spilled juice. All six of

the specially upholstered chairs restored from the original were missing from around the dining table.

The boys had dragged them into the living room, which had sustained the worst damage. A dozen or so of her quilts, productions created over the course of the past fifteen years, her comfort and her pride, were now stretched and bridged between furniture, stuffed under chairs and strewn across her floor.

"Do you realize," she said to the boys captured in her hands, "that if you two were adults, you could end up in jail for this destruction?"

The eyes of both boys widened, and Grace mentally kicked herself for scaring them. That was Hawk's job, not hers. She could play the stern but forgiving neighbor.

"This was our place first," Amos argued, "but then you moved in."

"Because I'm the owner. I get to do that, according to the law."

Amos twisted at her grip on his wrist, but she held on. "It's still our place."

"In that case, why did you wreck your own place?"

"It's not wrecked. Everything is just…moved."

Saul's hand in her other grasp twitched. "There is the glass thing."

At the base of the bureau, bought by her great-grandfather, lay her mother's crystal vase shattered into a million pieces. And gone with it, the hands-on reminder of the years of bouquets she and her sister and her father had brought home to her. The dandelions and weeds with stems so short her mother had tamped them in with a damp towel. The sunflower cut from the garden for her birthday. The dozen roses on Valentine's Day. The Mother's Day bouquets of tulips or daisies bought from saved allowances. Gone.

Gone like her mother. Broken glass. Broken neck. Both accidents. In both cases, she hadn't been there to prevent them.

"You're right, Amos. Most everything was just moved. By you two, and you two are going to move it all back." With her help. She couldn't see them ever properly folding a quilt.

Saul pointed at the remains of the vase. "And that?"

"That I will take care of." She'd sweep up the worst now, and would likely find bits here and there for weeks, months after. That was the nature of breaking something this precious. You could never be sure of finding all the pieces. "But first, I'm calling your father."

AT FIRST, Hawk ignored the incoming call from a private number. Creditors and collection agencies had sneaky ways of contacting him. He tapped End Call and turned back to loading cartons of eggs into his grocery cart. Now that his father had moved back from Ridgeview after his mother's passing last year, he household easily went through a dozen a day. His father suggested they buy chickens, like when Hawk was a kid. "It will teach the boys responsibility, like it taught you."

Responsibility hadn't come from tending chickens; he'd been born to it. As an only child, it had been on him from the time he could spell his last name to uphold the Blackstone legacy. Outside of the twins, he had done a poor job so far.

"And where are those boys of yours?"

Hawk looked up from his eggs. Irina Sandberg. She and her teenage granddaughter, Amy, lived across from the old Blackstone homestead. He did a hard mental check. From where Grace Jansson lived.

"At home with Dad. I thought it would go easier." Last time, with the boys, he had spent as much time taking out bags of candy and boxes of sugary cereal as packing in the items on the list. And a good thing. Easter chocolate and candy lurked at every twist and turn.

"And how is Russell?" Irina and Russell had known each other all their lives, and she and his mom had been fast friends.

His phone buzzed. Again, the private caller and again, he cut it off. "Good, good. You know Dad."

Irina, slim and level with the third grocery shelf, stood with a bag of potatoes and a carton of milk and a ham in her shopping basket, yet she carried it on her arm as if it were a tiny purse. She seemed to expect him to elaborate, but he didn't know what to say that wouldn't give away his secret worries about his dad's health.

"He keeps busy. With the horses and the boys."

His phone buzzed from the same number. He would let it go to voice mail. Maybe they'd leave him alone if given the opportunity to leave a message.

Irina tapped the bag of coffee beans, also in her basket. "Tell him to come over for coffee anytime."

It might be a good outing for his dad. He had not been himself these past weeks. He would stop one job, start another. Perhaps he needed to get out of his head for a while. "I'll let him know, Irina."

His phone pinged a notification and then rang again. "You might as well get that," Irina said, sidling away, "if you want any peace."

She was probably right. He swiped up on his phone screen. "Hello?"

"Hawk Blackstone?"

The lesson he'd learned was never to give the caller your identity. "Who's this?"

"Grace. Grace Jansson. Do you remember me?"

Well, it wasn't as if he could have avoided her forever. He forced out a steady exhale. "I do."

"That's good, because I have visitors you might know. Amos and Saul."

Why had his dad taken the boys there? "You should say hello at least," his father had complained in February when she moved in.

"Same distance for her to come here as for me to go there," Hawk had countered. A whole half mile.

His dad had let it go, as he had a lot of things lately.

"I see."

"So." Grace drew out the one word long enough to have said ten. "I thought that, as their father, you might be interested to know that your children are wandering about the country on their own."

What? "They're supposed to be—" What did it matter now what should be? "Are they okay? They have hats, jackets?"

"Fully equipped, but hungry. The conscripts are disassembling the fort they made of the living room before they receive their rations of cookies and juice. But they are unscathed after their skirmish with enemy forces."

When they were kids, he and Grace, sometimes with her younger sister, Haley, and her childhood friend-now-husband, Mateo, had played out elaborate scenarios of forts under fire, besieged castles, ransacked temples. Two minutes into their first conversation in more than a decade, and it felt as if he and Grace had never parted.

Except they had. "Is the enemy holding them for ransom?"

"One demand. Pick them up in person. Come alone."

"Give me an hour. I'm in Diamond Valley right now."

"That's only thirty minutes away."

He needed to find out what was going on with his dad first. "I have an errand I was hoping to take care of."

"Fine. Any longer, and I will cut their hair." Amos erupted in the background with a panicked cry.

"Can you put Amos on the phone?"

"I thought you'd never ask."

There was a shuffling and muttering, and then, "Dad?"

"Amos. I'm coming to get you, but you and Saul need to stay put. Promise?" He didn't like to bind them at age five to their word, but he couldn't have them turn into runaways, either.

"Promise."

With Amos's buy-in, Saul would also comply. "And, Amos…why did you run off on Grandpa?"

"We didn't. I said we were going for a walk and he said okay, so we did. We got permission. We did nothing wrong."

Sometimes Hawk envisioned Amos making that same defense before one authority figure after another in his future.

Amos's voice dropped. "Hurry. I've seen the scissors."

For a second, Hawk contemplated delaying his arrival, just to see if Grace would inflict the arduous ritual on the twins, first encounter with his boys notwithstanding. Once when she was ten to his twelve, she had pulled out the electric trimmer from the barber's kit from the bathroom vanity and waved it at his bushy head. He had agreed to a one-inch trim, but she had put on the wrong attachment and plowed a buzz cut from tip to crown before she realized her mistake. To stop her tears, he told her it suited him fine in this hot weather and to just give his whole head an army cut. She actually had the gall later on to tell him it had all worked out for the best, hadn't it? And because it was only hair, he'd agreed.

"Sit tight. Be good. Keep your promise." A little late for the first two orders, but wasn't three the lucky charm?

He called the land line to the house. His dad had a phone, but the two were rarely together.

"Hello?" His dad sounded as steady as ever.

"Hey, Dad."

"Hawk. You left town yet?"

"About to."

"I see we're nearly out of milk. Do you mind picking some up?"

His dad didn't seem troubled that he hadn't seen the boys in a good hour. "Dad, are you—"

"I was putting together some milk and cookies for the boys when I saw we're getting low."

Hawk walked down an empty aisle to gain a little privacy. "Dad, are you aware that the boys walked on their own all the way over to The Home Place?"

"A walk? Saul asked to go on one a while back. I didn't think they'd go so far. I guess it will be a while before they are back."

What was the matter with him? "Dad. They are five. You can't leave them alone outside. There's still snow on the hill. The same hill bears and cougars take."

There was a long pause and Hawk could hear his father breathe deeply. "I'll go get them," he mumbled.

"No, stay there. I already arranged with Grace that I would pick them up."

"Grace? You talked with her?" His voice brightened.

"She called me to say she had the boys."

"Well, that's good," his dad said. "Be sure to thank her for me."

That was appropriate if Grace had penned a wandering calf, but he was talking about his grandkids. Something was definitely wrong with his dad. Of all the other things going wrong in Hawk's life, this one scared him the most.

FIFTY-EIGHT MINUTES after talking to Hawk, a black crew cab truck rolled past the window where Grace and the twins sat at the kitchen table, and parked on her new gravel pad next to the house. The first occupant of her guest parking spaces, though not the one she'd expected.

"Dad!" It was about the tenth word Saul had said to Amos's ten thousand. And after taking his twin's lead during the entire visit, even letting Amos select the cookies to eat, he was the first out the kitchen door, Amos right behind.

She reached the door in time to see Saul vault into Hawk's arms. Hawk stood, holding Saul, his free hand opening to take Amos's. The arrangement happened so quickly and naturally that it must be habitual.

The three looked like they belonged in a picture gallery of country living. Hawk, lean and strong in his cowboy hat and jeans, and, tilted into him, the boys with their dark swirls of hair and bit of baby chubbiness.

She felt like an outsider, and, well, she was. No one from the community had dropped by since she had moved in.

Yes, she could've come to his place. It hadn't stopped her nearly three years ago when she'd come to tear a strip off Mateo after he'd deserted her sister, Haley. Back then, her sole purpose had been to persuade Mateo to leave the Blackstone Ranch and return to Haley. The only words she and Hawk had exchanged were to convey her dismay overthe sale of The Home Place. She had left, determined to find a way out for Hawk. Her father had come up with the solution when he bought the place and turned management over to her. Hawk had got much-needed cash, and she, thanks to her dad, had prevented her favorite piece of land from falling into stranger's hands. And no, she was not a stranger. At least, not to the land.

Hawk walked with the boys toward her, across the snow-pocked grass. Maybe, just maybe, the snow might melt in time for her first guests booked for the Easter long weekend two weeks from now.

"Thanks for watching over the boys," Hawk said.

"My pleasure." It was. She had next to no experience with kids, outside of her nephews and niece, almost three-year-old Jonah and his baby brother, Jakob, plus six-year-old Sadie. Young kids, but the responsible adults in their lives had never made the mistake of actually leaving her alone with them. "I've never taken care of kids on my own before."

"I'm sorry this was your introduction. Amos, Saul, what do you say?"

"Thanks for the cookies," Amos said.

"Thanks," Saul said to Hawk's shirt collar.

"And what about making a mess of her place?"

"But we cleaned it all up," Amos said.

"Except for the vase," Saul said and received a glower from Amos.

Hawk's lips thinned, and Grace spoke hurriedly. "That old thing? Don't worry about it."

Hawk held her gaze, and she forced herself to shrug and smile. The last thing she wanted was for Hawk to feel indebted to her, especially over an accident. She was the last person on earth to judge someone for careless impulses.

"Boys, what do you have to say for yourselves?"

Saul turned his head to Grace. "I'm sorry for wrecking your place."

"Me, too," Amos conceded.

"Apology accepted."

With his load of boys, Hawk turned to the truck. "Thanks again."

That was it? No small talk about the spring winds, the cost of doing business, how she was settling in or who was not taking care of his kids when he wasn't around?

She couldn't let it go.

"Wait." She came down the porch stairs. "I have one more demand before I release the kids." Saul looked worried; Amos, curious.

"They have to try out my play pit." She pointed to a clump of poplars, among which she'd set a barrel, stumps, a hammock, a rope lashed between trees. "Fifteen minutes, and then they have to give me their honest opinion."

"Come on, Saul," Amos said.

Saul looked at his dad. "You can choose,"

Hawk said. "You can stay with me or go with your brother. I'll be here, either way."

"Go with Amos," Saul whispered.

"And there are toys in the storage bin," Grace called after them. "It's for guests with kids," she added for Hawk's sake. "I'm opening a bed-and-breakfast. In time for the Easter long weekend. I'm calling it The Home Place."

If he recognized the name as the casual reference the Blackstones made to the old homestead, he only gave a careful nod. "Easter is in two weeks? It's still the middle of March."

"You haven't seen the chocolate bunnies in the store?"

"That's no guide. Christmas goes up in October."

He had a point. "This year the moon has decreed that Easter comes at the end of March."

"Okay."

"I remember us playing in the trees when we were kids, so I added some equipment."

"Okay."

"I would show you around inside, but there's no taking eyes off those two."

"Yeah." He dragged his hand down his face. "Thanks again."

She noted the strain around his eyes, the tension across his shoulders. Back when they were kids, she would have nudged his shoulder, needled him until he let loose with whatever was bothering him. Usually horse related. And then she would impart advice or try to fix it herself. She couldn't stand to see him upset.

And she still couldn't. "That's three times, Hawk. I know you appreciate what I did. The question is, why did I have to do it?"

He gave her a wary look.

"Look, it's me you're talking to. I'm not about to sic child protective services on you. I can see that the boys think the sun rises and sets on you, but come on, Hawk. What gives?"

He looked at his boots. "Miscommunication between Dad and me, that's all."

There was a mountain more, but experience had taught her that Hawk could avoid questions like birds dodged vehicles. "Your dad lives with you now."

"He moved back when Mom passed a year ago."

"I heard," she said. Hawk's mom had been an endless source of iced tea and clean clothes and warm smiles for Grace during her summer stays. The Blackstone and the Jansson ranches were five hours' drive apart, but Grace had never experienced a second of homesickness under the care of Hawk's mom. Grace had bawled for days when her dad told her that cancer had taken Angela. "I am sorry."

"Yeah, it's been hard on dad," Hawk said.

"I guess it's good having him around. An extra hand, right?"

"It's under control," Hawk said.

That comment was odd. "I didn't say—"

He sighed and rubbed his temple. "Look, Grace, I know you mean well, but we haven't really talked for nearly fifteen years. Why start now?" He took a step away from her. "Amos, Saul, time to go."

In other words, mind your own business. Something she'd never been good at, but he had a point. He didn't want her in his life, and she had no reason to be.

"What did you think of the play pit?" she asked the boys as they rejoined their dad.

"It's cool," Amos said and Saul smiled. He had a different smile, both happy and uncertain. As if asking for permission to feel joy.

"Can we come play here tomorrow?" Amos said.

"No," Hawk said, swinging Saul into his arms. He took Amos's hand. "What do you say?"

"Please don't thank me again," Grace told Amos. "Or else I will give you that haircut here and now."

Amos clamped his mouth shut. Hawk turned his dark eyes on her. "I'll take my chances with the haircut, and say it again. Thanks, Grace."

She had got his thanks more times than enough, but not a single answer to what was happening in his life. Seeing him so stressed had stirred up her old desire to set things right for the man she had once considered her best buddy.

A dangerous impulse she had to resist. She had never been any good at going half measures. When Hawk had angled for more than friendship fifteen years ago, she had made a clean break from him. She couldn't pursue her legal career and a life with him. All-in or all-out. She had flung herself into her career, and her driven personality had won her cases but not the support of her coworkers. Hawk was right to slam on the brakes to any renewal of their friendship.

"I should be the one thanking you," Grace muttered to Hawk's retreating truck.

CHAPTER TWO

"YOU CAN TELL your husband I finally met his old boss yesterday," Grace said as she studied quilt patterns on her laptop, her phone on speaker beside her at the dining table. She usually had no problems envisioning her next quilt, but she was struggling this time around. She lacked a theme.

Haley gasped and Grace thought it had to do with her news, but her sister's next words set that to rest. "Jonah, let Mommy pour the milk."

"I do it, I do it!" Her nearly three-year-old nephew's insistence drilled into Grace's ear, even with the phone an arm's length away.

"I think Mateo and I made too big of a deal about Jakob drinking from a sippy cup on his own," Haley muttered to Grace. "Jonah now figures that he needs to outperform his six-month-old brother."

"Boys," Grace said, "and their messes."

"You talk as if it's lived experience."

Grace described her encounter with Hawk's twins that had Haley gasping again, this time with laughter. Grace didn't mention the vase.

"How is Hawk?" Haley asked, laughter still in her voice.

"Oh, you know him. Hasn't changed a bit."

"Uh, you were going off to university when you last saw him. I'm sure he has changed."

"It hasn't been that long. I saw him three years ago when I came down here to talk to Mateo."

"Yes, thank you, sister. That was so helpful."

"You two are married now, aren't you?"

"Please don't overestimate your role in that outcome. Okay then, three years. I haven't seen him in that time either, but Mateo has. He says that he looks as if he's carrying the weight of the world on his shoulders."

Hawk hadn't smiled, hadn't engaged in small talk and had moved as if dragging cement blocks. "He's definitely carrying a load."

"Does he just have the one hired hand?"

"I don't know. He didn't say."

"Mateo said that his father lives there now, so I guess he helps with the boys."

"He wasn't yesterday. I don't know what happened. Hawk didn't say. He didn't say much. Mostly thank you and goodbye."

"I'm sure selling his breeding stock is eating at him. I think Mateo would hand it all back to him tomorrow, if Hawk asked, but—"

"Wait, what did you say? He's giving up his breeding stock?"

"You know that. Mateo bought a colt a year ago."

"One colt. One. Hawk has got—what?—fifteen, twenty horses. He's still breeding them." Grace hovered over a complicated pattern for a spiral quilt. But was it challenging enough?

Haley was silent, too silent.

"Okay, what's going on?"

"I don't know. But he himself brought up the idea to Mateo when they talked last month. He has a mare ready to foal, and I think the understanding was that maybe Mateo would take it over."

"No. Hawk loves breeding horses. That was the whole point. Doesn't he have this awesome reputation? Why would he give it all up?"

Haley sighed. "You know, Grace, not everybody can lead the supercharged, successful life you do. Jonah, drink at the table."

If only her little sister knew how wrong she was. But hey, thirty-four was a wonderful age to launch a new career. Maybe she could get a sideline with quilts. Run classes or something. "Money, then? I thought his problems were solved once he sold the home quarter to Dad."

"That was three years ago this fall. Expenses could have piled up again." Haley sighed. "Look, Mateo and I are just speculating. Mateo doesn't want to press, because he thinks it's not his business. You, however..." Grace's sister let her voice trail off.

"How is Hawk's business mine?"

"Because you two were besties growing up. And now that you're there right beside him, I don't know why you haven't gone over there yourself."

Grace closed her laptop window. "Because I have no reason to. Because I'm trying to mind my own business." And because Hawk didn't want her meddling in his affairs. "And anyway, I'm the new kid on the block. He should come see me first."

"That doesn't sound like you. You have made a career out of getting into people's business."

And that had turned out horribly. Not that Haley or anyone knew. They all thought she was on a sabbatical from the law firm and would return in September and manage the bed-and-breakfast from there with local help. She would have to manufacture another lie to stave off questions she couldn't bear to answer.

"I'm launching another one, as you know. One built on letting people escape from their business for a little while. Anyway, how are our niece and baby nephew doing?"

She was referring to Brock and Natalia's children. Natalia was married to Brock, her dad's hired hand, really the son he'd never had. They all lived on the Jansson Ranch with their four-month-old, named Daniel, and Sadie, Brock and

Natalia's niece. Sadie was adopted by them, after her widowed father died in a drowning accident.

Haley was not to be deterred. "Tell me you're not the least bit curious about Hawk's life and I'll drop it."

"Of course, I'm curious, but that doesn't mean I'm going over there to snoop around."

Haley let out a sigh. "It's not snooping, Grace. It's remembering that you two were the best of friends until life happened. And he could really do with a friend right now."

But what kind of friend would she be?

After the call, Grace walked over to the kitchen window, the one facing Hawk's home place. They were more or less a straight half mile apart. A long slope coming off the prominent ridge to the west blocked the view, the same slope that the twins had walked to get to her place, or they had come along the flat road. Either way pointed to their determination. Amos's, at least. Saul had likely gone along because his brother told him to.

Yes, she was curious. But after yesterday, she was also worried. Curiosity she could ignore. Worry was harder. And more dangerous. *Worried* had got her fired from her job and forced her to retreat out here in the dead of winter. Renovations were already well underway then, so there was power and a new furnace.

She loved this part of the world. It affected her bone-deep: its wind, its sweeping curves, its timelessness. But it was also where her mother had died. A death she could have prevented if she'd kept her word.

Her mother had come to the Blackstone Ranch to visit with Hawk's mother for a week. Grace, in her third year of university, was supposed to drive out for the day from Calgary to go horseback riding with her mom while Hawk's mother attended to local volunteer commitments. Except, then her mother called to tell her to pack an overnight bag, that Hawk's mother had invited Grace to stay the night, that they would have a big supper and that Hawk would be there. It would be just like old times. Grace had come up with an excuse fast to back out completely, wanting to avoid the awkwardness between Hawk and her from her solo visit there two summers ago.

But her mother had divined the real reason. "Oh, Grace, can you not move on from that? He has."

She had really not wanted to go then. Yes, she expected Hawk would get over her and date other girls. She just didn't want to see that in action.

Her mother had been disappointed. She had hoped they could camp out at the old Blackstone place. She had been trying to persuade Angela to convert it into a bed-and-breakfast. Maybe with trails behind the house up to the ridge. With Blackstone horses. She could have used Grace's powers of persuasion. Grace had said that the homestead wasn't going anywhere, and perhaps another time?

Except there hadn't been one. Her mother had gone riding alone. And ended up on a rocky ledge with a broken neck and the horse with two broken legs.

It might never have happened, if Grace had not broken her promise because she simply had wanted to avoid discomfort. She should've faced it head-on.

She was now. She'd driven out here the day after getting fired from the firm and woke up the next day committed to fulfilling her mother's dream of turning the place into a bed-and-breakfast. In less than two months, she'd sold her city condo and landed her first of three bookings. But Hawk was one confrontation she must avoid for the good of all.

Yesterday had already shown that, with him, she couldn't resist poking her nose where it didn't belong. Despite their friendship…sure, she would stick with that term…melting away, she didn't trust that once involved, she could maintain her distance.

The following Monday morning, the local county office emailed Grace the links to the application for her permit. Pages and pages of paperwork, all to judge whether she could have a horse trail that already existed and just needed upgrading.

There was no use arguing the point. She had achieved junior partnership in five years because she quickly learned which battles to pick. That afternoon, she wrapped herself in winter gear and headed out to tramp along the trails. The sooner she roughed out the basics, the sooner she could start filling in the blanks.

It was slow going in the lingering snow among the trees, and then when she emerged from the trees, the ceaseless foothills' winds snapped against her lined jacket. Grace tightened her scarf and checked her phone fitness app. She had walked three-quarters of a kilometer, or as the app happily informed her, .447 of a mile.

"I hope you appreciate what I'm doing, Mom." No, she wouldn't blame her mother. She kind of liked to set herself against the wind, feel it scour her face.

The trail thinned from here to the ridge, if memory served correctly. At the top, there was the main trail that ran along the twenty miles of the ridge, with a view of the Rockies to the west. She could see the short, thin spire of the cairn to mark the spot where her mother had fallen to her death.

After busting through wind-packed drifts, Grace took a breather behind a familiar boulder. Every creature knew this rocky outcropping provided the best shelter for rabbits, coyotes, calves. And for a boy and girl resting from their play.

She looked down and across to the Blackstone

spread. The cattle were in the corrals. Black Angus mostly. A rider cut away a cow from the herd. Cow and horse walked to an open gate. Hawk. It could be him. The cow walked easily into a smaller pen containing a shelter. Probably a cow ready to calf. The old cycles of ranch life.

She hadn't forgotten all that, despite the decade and a half of city living. She'd grown up on a farm, and that sense never left, even if her family wasn't there to remind her. In a couple of months, right where she stood now, the same cattle would graze.

That was another issue to deal with in her report. She would need to speak to Hawk as a local rancher. Get him to sign off on his cooperation. No time like the present.

Maybe she could sweeten his compliance with a deal to rent horses from him to use on the trail rides.

She turned to head down the ridge to the Blackstone Ranch and dropped to the ground. Pain shot through her ankle.

She struggled to her feet, but her ankle screamed, and she retreated to the boulder.

"Great," she said aloud. "Now what?"

HAWK SPOTTED GRACE making her way up the hill, her red parka inching across the snow swept pasture. What she was doing? The wind was bad enough. Mix that with the snow. She should be down at The Home Place.

Then the red spot ducked behind the boulder. Twelve minutes passed before it emerged, moved and then returned to the boulder. A quarter of an hour passed. Hawk drew out his binoculars from inside his coat. His father's trick. Good for eagle watching and finding lost calves.

Grace had taken off her boot and was examining her ankle. As he watched, she hobbled a couple of steps and then collapsed back down.

Nathan, his hired hand, was forking hay to the cow.

"Can you take it from here?"

The nineteen-year-old scanned the calving pen with the five cows. "Depends on how long they take."

"I won't be long. Back in an hour or two."

He saddled Wildrose, and they reached Grace in less than a half hour. She could've watched his progress the entire way, but she didn't speak until he reached her.

"You used your binoculars, didn't you?"

"Not much red out here this time of year."

She pointed at her outstretched leg. "Did your binoculars show I wrecked my ankle?"

"You seemed to favor it."

"You come to rescue me?"

She made it sound as if he was trying to be a

hero. Far from that. He was just being responsible. "If that's what you want."

"Yes. I want very much."

He swung down. "You need help to get up?"

"Considering it's my left ankle that's broken or sprained or whatever, and that's the one that I use to mount, then yes."

That meant putting his hands on Grace, wrapping an arm around her waist to support her. Brief contact, but when it came to Grace, hot enough to burn. "You can mount her on either side. I'll bring her closer."

"Or," she said, "since you bothered to come all this way, you could lend a helping hand over to the horse."

Exactly as he feared, she clutched him the instant he was within reach and he had to put his arm around her. She hopped and teetered along, bumping up against him. Even through the thickness of their jackets, he could feel her curves. It was going to be the longest fifteen feet of his life, unless—

He lifted her in his arms.

She gasped, her face right there next to his. Her blue eyes were wide with surprise, her cheeks pink from the wind. But there was a brightness in her expression, as if this was all just fun and games. "Hawk, what are you doing?"

Trying to put as much distance as he could between them, ironically. In answer, he set her down on the right side of Wildrose.

Grace took her cue, put her foot in the stirrup, and swung herself up. Wildrose didn't shift, good horse that she was.

"Are we riding double?"

"I'll walk."

He started off, leading the way back.

"Aren't you worried about twisting your own ankle?"

Better a twisted ankle than sitting close to her. "I know what I'm doing."

They angled down off the ridge. He could have her back at her place within the half hour, and then he would be back in the saddle. All was quiet, except for the rattle of the harness, the hoofs on the ground, his own tread on the snow. But he could feel her sighs, the little breathy noises. Grace was building up, like a wind before a storm.

And then she hit. "Aren't you curious about why I was hiking around up here?"

"Your land, your business."

"When has that ever applied to this part of the world? Everybody is up in everybody's business."

"I'm not."

"You know, I believe that. But I am more than happy to share."

He marched on, his eyes on Grace's earlier tracks.

"As you know, there is quite a nice network of

trails through here. I thought to run rides along here for my guests."

Where would she stable the horses? Keep the feed? "That's a whole new operation."

"Yeah, but Mom wanted it."

The Blackstones hadn't mentioned Miranda in years, definitely not in the year since his mom had died. It was as if the cairn was only a heap of stones. "She planned to talk your mom into converting The Home Place into a bed-and-breakfast with trail rides."

"First I heard of that."

"I don't think she got the chance," Grace said softly. "Anyway, now I have the chance to carry out Mom's vision. I'm halfway there with the bed-and-breakfast. Now the trail rides."

They had reached a flat spot just before the trail entered the trees, a good place to talk. A good thing, because he had a thing or two to say. "My cattle run through here."

"I know. That's why I thought we need to talk first. My application passed first reading at the county, but now I need to meet with ranchers to find out their level of support."

"I'm not supporting anything that interferes with the cattle."

"I didn't say it would."

"How could a bunch of city folk traipsing up and down the hill not affect the cattle?"

"There are several scenarios."

He waited. Let the lawyer in her worm her way through this.

"A fence, for instance."

"Through bush and into rock. And then what about the elk and deer?"

Grace didn't even pause, as if she had already known what his objections would be. "No fences, and the guests ride at designated times."

"And who is going to teach time to the cattle?"

She gave him the same bleary-eyed look he no doubt was giving her. "It's not as if the cattle are in the same place all summer. They start off here in May and June, but by July you will have driven them north of the river. I could run trail rides then, during the peak periods for me, and there won't be any conflict."

A fair argument. The county had granted her request for a bed-and-breakfast. The Home Place had already undergone the biggest change possible. Gone from being a home to a place of business. The only other bigger change was when his dad's grandfather had come up here from Montana to cowboy on a ranch of an absentee Englishman and put down his own claim. Back then, The Home Place amounted to a one-room cabin with a ribbon of smoke rising from the chimney. A picture of it sat on the mantel with his great-grandfather outside on his horse. "That might work."

She gave him her special smile, the one where

her left eye scrunched up into a half wink, as if they were sharing a secret. "See? That wasn't so hard."

He walked on. It was too cold for these boots. "I haven't agreed. I'll have to think it over."

"Of course," she said. "I would have fallen off of the horse in shock if you'd agreed on the spot. There's one more thing."

With Grace, there always was.

"I was wondering if I could rent horses from you for the rides. I can pay for the gear, and for your time, of course."

"How many do you need?"

"I'm not sure. Three or four, likely."

He only had two horses he trusted to have untrained riders on. She was riding one, and the other was due to foal in July. "I don't have any to spare."

"If I bought some, would you be interested in boarding them?"

And have Grace coming over on a more-or-less regular basis. His dad and the boys would be thrilled. As for him— "I'm not, but thanks."

"Why don't—" She cut herself off. "All right," she said. She was backing off, exactly as he wanted her to, only he felt a little empty. It came as a relief when she spoke again.

"I want to make the trail a kind of memorial to Mom. Are you okay with that?"

Memorial? "How do you plan to do that?"

"Not much, I suppose. Have it named on my website. Maybe a sign at the front, a plaque. Just something to show she came from around here."

Miranda's dad had been Diamond Valley's pharmacist, and all the family had returned to Montana when he'd retired. Only Miranda had stayed in Alberta. There was a picture of her and his mom on the mantelpiece, and over the years, he had more or less slid that image of her over the sight of her when he'd found her after her fall. "I always wish her well when I find myself up there," he said.

That sounded stupid, and he was about to explain himself when Grace murmured, "Thanks for doing that."

He gave a quick nod and resumed his walk. Ten more minutes through the trees and they would be at the back fence of the homestead, then back to the cattle.

"How are Amos and Saul?"

"Good."

"Home with Russell?"

"With their aunt." He didn't bother adding that the aunt was the boys' mother's sister. Gemma was, well, a gem for taking the boys. Except that she led a busy life, too. He glanced at his phone. He would barely make it back in time before having to run into Ridgeview to pick them up. He picked up his pace. Hopefully, Nathan could handle the cows.

"I like your boys, Hawk." Grace spoke almost dreamily. "They're…interesting."

"How so?" Hawk had never heard that word attached to the twins. It usually didn't get any more complimentary than "energetic."

"I don't know. It's hard to explain. They look a lot alike and they are inseparable, but they both have their own distinctive personality." She sighed. "I can see that they are a lot of work, and I can see how they are worth every minute of it."

Hawk swallowed. It was what he thought when he was about to give up on the ranch, on the day, on cooking a meal. The kids were worth it. He choked out a quick thanks.

"Stop thanking me," she said. "It's not a compliment, just an observation."

They reached the creek at the back of The Home Place. It was still frozen, and only a horse's length across, but one misstep was enough. He turned to Wildrose. "Take your time."

The mare did, probably because she was loyal enough to follow Hawk off the edge of a cliff. She wasn't cutting horse quality, but Wildrose was just as special to him.

As they came up to the other side, Grace did what he had intended and rubbed Wildrose on the neck. "Good job keeping me in the saddle."

He stopped at the graveled parking space in front of the house. "You need to get off here. I don't want to pick stones out of her hoofs." Which meant doing what felt much like chewing on the gravel at his feet. "I'll carry you across."

"Why, Hawk, I do declare," she said in a faux Southern belle accent.

He did not look at her while he carried her to the door, her arms looped around his neck, pretty sure she was looking up at him with that half-wink smile. He set her down and stepped back as if she were on fire. She teetered on her weak ankle.

"The clinic's open until nine," Hawk said. "I've run the boys in a few times when they have had a fever. Amos needed stitches once."

"Why am I not surprised with that boy? I'll take a painkiller and ice it, and see how I'm doing tomorrow."

He nodded and turned, eager to make his escape.

"Hey, Hawk. Thanks for being my cowboy in shining armor."

Back when they were kids, she used to poke him and he'd automatically say, "That hurt," even when it didn't, even when they grew older and he wished she'd lay more than a finger on him. Fifteen years later, she was poking with words, and it still didn't hurt and he still wished for… more. The first time alone together, and he had her in his arms. Twice. Armor was exactly what he lacked around her.

He counted it a minor victory that he kept walking and let her have the last word.

CHAPTER THREE

AMOS AND SAUL rode up on a pony, just as Grace was about to start the egg hunt for her five child guests on Easter Sunday. The parents of both families looked on as she, with an Easter bunny puppet as an MC, prepared to give the count-down. The older kids, eleven and ten, crossed their arms to show their disdain for childish pur-suits, even as they eyed viable locations for caches amid the remaining snow banks and open grass. The three younger ones bounced like bunnies, baskets swinging.

"Just a minute," Grace said, and approached the twins. "You two run off on your grandpa again?"

"Not Grandpa. Amy," the one in front said. They were again dressed identically in jack-ets and boots with fresh matching haircuts. She would have to rely on their behavior to tell the difference. He dismounted and the other followed. The first one to get off handed the reins to Grace, as if the pony was now her problem. Amos, then. "We're going back, so we're not running away."

"And we didn't come alone," Saul explained. "We came with Greta, and once she kicked a cougar."

Amos had his eyes on the kids and their baskets. "What's going on here?" He spoke in the high-handed way of an adult.

The right thing to do was place a phone call to Hawk, and get the boys picked up. She was still kicking herself for flirting with him two weeks ago. She had enjoyed teasing him far too much. What would she have done if he had taken the bait and flirted right back?

He had sent her a simple text confirming that he agreed to trail rides based on their conversation, and she had sent her acknowledgement via text, too. Yep, both of them were keeping at arm's length, instead of, well, her being in his arms.

But the boys looked so wistfully at the pastel balloons and baskets. They were lonely and bored, and they had come over to see her. Who was she to refuse the black-haired, booted delinquents? Grace looped the reins over the railing. Greta had gray around her mouth and likely didn't care to go one step farther.

"Only if you answer one question and no lying."

They shrugged their agreement.

"Are you Amos?"

"Yes. How can you tell?"

Because Amos rode up front in their little duo. And Saul kept a careful watch. "I have my ways."

She lifted Easter Bunny and spoke in a falsetto voice. "All my eggs have fallen out of my basket when I was running away from a coyote," she explained in a high, breathless voice. "Would you help me find them? I have a prize for the one who finds the most." The puppet pointed to a basket on the top step, dominated by a huge chocolate bunny.

Amos turned to Saul. "If one of us wins, we split it with the other, okay?"

Saul regarded the basket, the competition and, finally, his brother. "We have to share with Dad and Grandpa, too."

Amos shrugged his agreement, and the boys entered the competition. Grace, via Easter Bunny, explained the range of where the eggs might have fallen—not beyond sight of the adults—and that time was a factor, before setting them loose.

"Those two boys look like the real deal," one mom gushed. She wore jeans and a puffed vest, and held a cappuccino. Grace knew not to deprive her urban guests of boutique coffee.

"They are," Grace said, "neighbors from up the road."

"Aren't they a little young to be out alone?" the other mom said. "I mean, shouldn't they at least be wearing helmets?"

Grace's phone rang, and she stepped away to take the call.

"Hello. Um, I was wondering… This is Amy Sandberg, and it's about two boys, Hawk Blackstone's boys. He gave me your number, in case. I am supposed to be, actually I am—"

Grace couldn't let the girl fumble along any further. "I know them. Amos and Saul. They are here, safe and sound. They came on a pony."

"Oh, thank you, thank you. I'll come get them right away."

Amos was engaged in a round of rock-paper-scissors with the two older kids, Easter Bunny's rule for deciding eggs spotted at the same time. Amos gave a fist pump as he won the round.

"Actually, I have an egg hunt happening right now. And there's juice and snacks after. How about I bring them and the pony back in an hour or so?" Her ankle was fine, after two weeks of tender care.

"Uh, it's just that Hawk will be back by then. He went out with Russell. That's why I'm here."

"Perfect. There'll be someone home when I bring them by." If Amy thought she could get the boys back without having to provide an explanation to Hawk, that wasn't happening. Yes, the boys were born jail breakers, but their antics needed to be nipped in the bud.

By Hawk, of course. She would simply return the boys, like a good neighbor.

Amy heaved a sigh. "All right. I—I'll call Hawk."

"Sure," Grace said. "Good idea." See how well that would go for the poor girl.

Saul took the prize, having more eggs than he could count and six more than the next closest, the older girl. The kids got to keep the chocolate-covered eggs they'd found. Grace had a sinking feeling she would pick up shiny wrappers for weeks. She and the crows.

The guests piled into their vehicles soon after with promises of coming again. Little did one mom know her husband had booked a romantic getaway just for them, for their anniversary weekend in July. The lure of trail rides snagged him.

Now, she just had to figure out how to get horses before then.

The walk back over the hill with the boys proved illuminating. She discovered they attended kindergarten on Tuesdays and Thursdays all day, after which they stayed with their aunt and played with their cousins until Hawk picked them up. Their cousins were girls, and bossy. They hung out with their grandpa other days, usually. Not lately, Saul had contributed. The babysitter was okay but hung out with Nathan, the hired hand. That's what she was doing today, when they left. Amos had apparently told her of their traveling plans, but conceded that he hadn't waited to get her attention, which had been on Nathan.

They were coming down the backside of the hill, the Blackstone spread before them when Saul pivoted the questions to her. "Do you live by yourself in the house?"

"Yes, unless I have guests."

"You don't have kids?"

"No."

There was a moment of silence while they absorbed her childless state. It was unusual for women her age not to have children in the rural areas. In Calgary, no one would've blinked an eye.

"Aren't you lonely?" Amos asked.

And here she'd been thinking they were the lonely ones. Maybe she had projected her own feelings on to them. She missed the bustle and camaraderie of the law office, the staff birthday celebrations and the after-hours drinks. She missed the sense of belonging, that her presence mattered.

"Sometimes it's quieter than what I'm used to."

"We could keep you company," Saul said.

"Since you don't have kids of your own," Amos explained, "and we don't see Mom much, anyway."

She turned to face them. "I'm your neighbor, not your mother. I'd like you to come visit me, and then you go to your home. That's it. Are we clear on that?"

The boys nodded, their expressions like kicked puppies. She sighed. "And neighbors keep open doors for each other. You are always welcome at my place. Okay?"

Happier nods this time. Hawk appeared from the horse barn, his mouth in a harsh, flat line.

"Looks as if I have to thank you again." His eyes were on the boys.

Saul looked abashed, but not Amos. "Saul won top prize. Look, a big chocolate bunny, and we got eggs, too! I am happy to share." Amos was clearly trying to talk his way out of trouble.

"All of which I'm confiscating," Hawk said, "as it was obtained by illegal means." He gestured to the candy, and the boys relinquished their winnings. "You take Greta inside the barn. Amy and Nathan are already there to watch while you two brush her down. And then he'll show you how to clean out her stall."

Heads down, Amos and Saul did as they were told. Amy came out of the barn and took the boys' hands. Hawk was still tight-lipped when he turned to Grace. "I'll drive you back." He sounded as thrilled to be alone with her as before.

She was rounding the hood of his truck when the front door to the house opened.

"Grace, is that you?" Russell appeared on the front step. She hadn't seen him since she was eighteen. During her whirlwind drive out for a couple of hours three years ago, he had still been living in Ridgeview with Angela. His hair was mostly white now, and he was thinner. But his smile was just as wide.

"As you live and breathe," Grace said. "How are you doing, Russell?"

"The better for seeing the prettiest girl I know. Come in and have a coffee."

Hawk sucked in his breath. "She has to get back, Dad. I'm dropping her off."

Why was Hawk trying to hurry her off? "Not before I have a coffee with you, Russell. Do you still make it strong enough to risk a heart attack?"

"Not quite," Russell said, holding the door wide. "I'm still around, aren't I?"

Once she was inside, Russell closed the door, right on Hawk following them in. Deliberate?

Inside, the place wasn't exactly neglected but somehow looked unfinished. There was a set of couches but no coffee table and no throw rug on the floor. The kitchen counter had a box of crackers and a jar of peanut butter and three rolls of paper towels at different stages of use. The dining table had letters and envelopes, as if Hawk ran the operations from there.

Behind her, Hawk opened the door. He pushed papers to the far end of the table, and tossed flyers onto letters from the bank. "Have a seat," he said, his voice grim.

His anger with the kids didn't explain his attitude. They'd run off before and he hadn't been that upset. What was up?

IT STARTED OFF well enough. Hawk sat silently while Grace and Russell chatted together. There was a slight blip when Russell asked Grace twice if she took cream and sugar, but she answered a little more loudly the second time. Good, let her think his dad was deaf.

"And how's your father? Why hasn't he come down this way?"

"I ask him that myself."

"It must be at least twelve, thirteen years. Since before Miran—" He broke off, shook his head.

Grace took his hand. "Yeah, I know." Hawk felt thankful for Grace the second time that day. "Dad tells me you two go way back."

Russell grinned. "You don't know the half of it." And then he called up old times, and the tightness in Hawk's chest ease. His dad was as good as ever when he talked about the past.

But it being the way of all conversations, it didn't stay in the past, and during a lull, Grace asked, "So what do you do these days to keep yourself busy?"

His dad blinked and frowned in confusion, just as he had when they had gone on the drive into the mountains that morning. Hawk had wanted solid one-on-one time to gauge his dad's mental acuity. His father recognized where they were, but for the names of neighbors he had known all his life, Hawk had to prompt the answers. His father wondered at the new fence at the Sandbergs', even though they had augured in posts last fall and driven by it once a week since then. He forgot Amy's name. And then had wondered if she was old enough to take care of the kids, even though she had driven herself over.

All signs of dementia, but until that was backed up with an official diagnosis, strangers like Grace didn't need to know. "I keep him busy enough," Hawk said.

Russell's tension eased. "Yep, always something. And the boys. They keep me busy."

"They got away on you a couple of weeks ago."

Russell looked up as if she were about to tell a good story. "Oh?"

Grace paused. "When they walked over to my place."

"Walked to your place? You live in Calgary."

Hawk avoided the look of uncertainty Grace shot him. "She moved into the old home place, Dad. Remember I sold the quarter coming up three years ago to Knut?"

"But aren't you a lawyer?"

It was Grace's turn to look uncomfortable. "I am, but I'm on a bit of a sabbatical. I am living down here full time now."

"I see. Well, the old place needs some fixing up."

Hawk cut in again. "I guess you haven't been there in a while. Grace has fixed it up nice." Not that he would know.

"You should come by, Russell. I don't think you'd recognize it."

"The wiring is no good. You will have to fix that."

"It's all fixed," Grace said.

"Good," Russell said. "Good." He passed his hand over his temple. "You don't mind, I'm going for a bit of a lie down."

Sunday naps had always been part of the Blackstone lifestyle, so Hawk was spared another of Grace's quizzical glances as his father disappeared down the hallway to his bedroom.

But that didn't mean he escaped her interrogation. "Something's going on with your dad."

"What do you mean?"

She gave him the scrunchy left eye, but without the smile. "Russell. He's not himself. Do you know that?"

"He's tired. Mom's passing hit him pretty hard." His dad had started to decline right after. That's why he'd encouraged him to move back, and living on the ranch had seemed to give his dad a boost of energy. But during winter, he had lapsed.

"I'm not talking about his nap. There's more to it. How could he forget that I live here now?"

"I'm not really prepared to talk about Dad with you."

"I'm not sure that you're really prepared to talk about him even to yourself."

She was wrong there. During the entire drive today with his dad, he had also been talking to himself. *Hawk, time to be the caregiver. Get him help.* "I'm not blind to what's going on."

"Then, why did you leave him with the boys the other week?"

He had asked himself the same question more than once since then. "I guess I wanted to believe it was all in my mind. What happened made me realize I couldn't ignore the signs. As you saw today, I adjusted."

"Same outcome. The boys sneaked away on her, too."

"Easy enough to do when your babysitter has her eye on the hired hand. She as much admitted that herself, and that there'd be no repeat, either."

"Ah, teenage romance. First love is the most powerful." She spoke lightly, nostalgically.

Grace had been his first love; he hadn't been hers. She had broken his heart back then, but he was all grown up now. Had loved again and lost again. This latest loss, he still paid monthly support for. "Stupidest, too."

She looked out the window. "True enough."

He didn't want to sit in the past with her, and he didn't want to talk about the present with his dad. He couldn't change one, and he had no idea how to deal with the other.

"Have you talked to your dad?"

"Grace, it's none of your—"

"Business," she finished, turning back to him. Unshed tears stood in her eyes. "I know it. I don't have any claim on you or your kids. But look, Hawk. I care. I care about your dad because he's a good man. And I care about your boys because they're good people, too."

That was Grace. That was why he had once loved her with the strength and foolishness of an untested heart. Because she was a power unto herself. Like the winds that would come off the ridge and knock off your hat and cut to your very bone. All around you, all the time. If Grace cared, there was no force that could turn her.

"Fair enough," he said.

She swiped at her eyes. "Okay, then. So, I was thinking. Since the boys are bound and determined to come visit me, and since I told them that they could, why don't we set up exact times for it to happen?"

"You don't have to do that."

"Hawk, I just said that I cared for them. As neighbors. As my mom's friend's grandkids. I'm not doing you a favor. I'm asking if you would share your boys with me for a while every week."

Of course she wasn't taking on the boys as a favor to him. "All right."

"And you can drop off your dad, too, if he wants."

"He can manage on his own, still."

"I'm not saying that. I'm saying that I am more than happy to host your family. I can do Mondays and Wednesdays since the boys are busy Tuesdays and Thursdays."

"How do you…? Never mind. The boys didn't know that they were up against a legal mind."

Grace bit her lip, looked out the window again. "Yep. They didn't know." There was an odd strain to her voice.

"Missing work?"

She shrugged. "Sometimes. So, Mondays and Wednesdays?"

Grace didn't want to talk about it, and he wasn't about to push her. None of his business.

"I'M ON THAT website of yours. How do I pay for a room?" That was the first thing out of Grace's dad when she picked up his call, that evening.

She was piecing together scraps at her quilting table, hoping for something to click into place. No luck so far.

"What? Are you coming down?"

"Not if I can't figure out how to pay. What's the point of booking online, if there's no way to pay?"

"Dad, I don't have a booking page. What you're looking at is the contact page. You leave me your email and phone number, and then I will contact you. It's a way for me to screen people."

"Oh. I see." It was as much of an admission of fault as she was likely ever to get from him. She had honed her argumentative skills at his knee. Haley said the two of them were constantly bickering because they were the same—brutally honest.

Usually. Grace had withheld her termination from her family, primarily because she couldn't bear the inevitable honesty from her father. He would either scold her or he would take her side and threaten to storm her old office. Exacting and loyal. Great, troublesome qualities.

"When would you like to come down?"

"When will you have me?"

"Weekdays are better. I have openings then."

"Meaning you want to keep your weekends free for proper guests. I can pay."

"Dad, you are not paying to stay. You already paid for the house you'll be sleeping in. Now, pick a day."

"Natalia said that I can come any day, but just to give her a week's notice."

"Natalia has you on that short of a leash?" Grace and Natalia had hit it off right from their first meeting in Natalia's collectible store in Spirit Lake.

"I want to bring along Sadie, but Natalia needs to let her teacher know."

Grace thought of Amos and Saul mixing it up with Sadie and smiled.

"Let's plan for you to stay for a Tuesday and Wednesday. That way, you can be here all day Wednesday when I have Hawk's boys."

"You taking care of Hawk's boys?"

"On Mondays and Wednesdays. Just for the next little while."

"Don't you have things to do?"

"They are five. I can bring them along on errands, and I always have chores to do around here. They escaped over here twice already, convinced the place is still theirs. It's just easier to host them than to fight them."

"Since when did you have a problem fighting anyone on anything?"

"I fight if the cause is good."

"You've taken a shine to them."

"I'm just being a good neighbor. And I like to keep busy." Between the boys and guests, she certainly couldn't complain about loneliness anymore.

"A couple of weeks back, you told Haley you hadn't spoken to Hawk the whole time you were down there, and now you're taking care of his kids. Sweet deal for him."

"I made the offer. I don't mind. They are… fun." Why did she keep defaulting to that word? They were fun, but not the way partying with friends and coworkers had been. More like the fun of projects, of making a quilt—long, complicated, fulfilling and never turning out quite the way you expected.

"What's going to happen when you go back to the city?"

"Oh, that's not for months. It's not a permanent arrangement, anyway. How's life with a newborn? Sleeping through the night yet?"

"I don't know about them, but I am. I'm out in the bunk quarters." Brock had lived in the attached quarters until he and Natalia had married. Then Knut had insisted they switch places. With Haley and Mateo less than a mile away, his days were full of family.

Which begged the question he was dodging. "Why visit now, Dad? After all these years?"

"Because you haven't been there all these years. Now I have a reason to pay a visit."

"You could have visited Russell and Angela. You had an open invitation from them."

"Right, then. Let's say it's about time."

If he wasn't going to say it, then she would. "It's about Mom, isn't it?"

Her dad's sigh was audible through the phone. "You know how I put together all those pictures a year or so ago?"

Her dad had taken over the living room for months, sorting through old pictures, archiving them on the computer and handing over flash drives to Haley and her, with all the pictures labelled and in neat folders.

"I think there were a few missing pictures. And I'm coming down to take them."

Grace could buy that. Her mother had wanted to transform the place into a B and B, and her dad had helped make it happen for her when he had purchased the land. "I guess you can see mom's dream come true."

"You have more to do with that happening than me. I bought the land to help out you and Hawk."

Grace started at how casually her dad linked their names together, as if they were a couple. "Help me?"

Her dad's voice grew distant, as if he'd turned away from the phone. "Oh, you know, I didn't buy it for my health."

"Are you saying you bought it for mine?"

"It's helping you, isn't it?"

Something in his voice suggested that he knew about her work situation. Or she was overthinking this.

"Anyhoo," her dad glided on. "I might stop in and see Russell while I'm out there."

Should she tell her dad about Russell's likely dementia? Russell deserved some privacy, but the two men were old friends. "When's the last time you and Russell talked, Dad?"

"I dunno...around Christmas, I guess. Why do you ask?"

"Just making conversation, is all."

"That's all we did, too. Talked about the old days, mostly."

The old days were Russell's strong suit. Her dad had probably not noticed that anything was amiss four months ago. "Okay, I'll let Hawk know that you're coming down, and you two old codgers can get together."

Her dad grunted at her derogatory term. "I can always count on you not to hold back what you're thinking."

Except she had lied by omission twice. About her firing at the firm and Russell's likely dementia. And if she had learned anything from her legal career, the truth eventually wormed its way out.

CHAPTER FOUR

HAWK DROPPED THE boys off with Grace on the Wednesday following Easter Monday. She'd had a guest staying over on Easter Monday and wanted a couple of days to prepare for them. As he drove away, Hawk looked in his rearview mirror. Grace was pointing out something to Amos and was holding out her hand to Saul. And Saul took it.

More easily and naturally than he did his mother's. The boys had not seen their mother since Christmas, three months ago. She had been relieved when he had obtained sole custody. She had told him as much.

"It's probably for the best, right?" she had said in her soft, questioning way, which had once made him want to give her certainty and take away her fears. Instead, he had only given her trouble. Outdoor living, and then worst of all, kids. Not the one he had talked her into, but two.

The babies had thrown her into a state of shock she had never recovered from. He had put it down to the overwhelming work of newborn twins, and chronic sleeplessness, but when Eva lay in bed through dirty diapers and empty tummies, he'd had to admit that his wife was in full-blown postpartum depression. He urged her to seek help, even arranged for health services to call her, but admitting to her state seemed too much for her. That's when Mateo stepped up, and together, the two men had taken charge of the twins.

One day when Amos and Saul were seven months old, he came in from outside, and the house was unusually quiet. Eva sat in the living room in front of the playpen. Hawk checked on them, as per habit. They were happy enough, clean, sitting up, facing each other.

"Hawk," she said. "I can't do this anymore."

He began to say how he knew it was tough, but it would get easier, and then— She had held up her hand, palm raised.

"Hawk. I don't know much about myself. But I hate my life. I hate this place. You're a good man, but I hate being with you. And these babies… I will never love them. I have tried, but they were your idea. Take them."

She left the next day.

He didn't blame her in the end. There had been warning signs. She had always been reluctant about the ranch, but he'd thought that his love for the ranch would be infectious. He thought he could fill the unidentifiable emptiness in her life.

Grace had reminded him that he was about

to ignore the warning signs with his father. He couldn't put off the hard conversation any longer.

He found his father in the barn, looping rope. Over the years, his father had handled hundreds of miles of rope, but in his hands now, the process was slow, extra deliberate.

"The boys are with Grace," Hawk said.

"Okay."

"It'll give us time to talk."

His dad didn't answer but kept winding rope, as if he had arthritis in his hands.

"I was noticing," Hawk began and stopped. "I was wondering if you are finding things harder than usual."

"Everything gets harder at my age," his dad said. Something he often said since turning seventy on his last birthday.

"I suppose," Hawk said. "I guess I meant things you used to find you could do without thinking. Like, I don't know, making coffee or dealing with numbers."

"I can make coffee. I can count. What are you getting at?" His dad sounded irritable. Mood swings were another sign of dementia.

"You seem to have trouble doing ordinary jobs, and I'm wondering if you'd like me to make you an appointment with a psychologist to figure out what's going on."

"A psychologist? You think I'm crazy?"

"No, Dad. It's just that with age come changes."

"I am an old man. Aren't I allowed to slow down?"

According to websites Hawk had visited last night, people with normal aging memory loss worried about their mental state, while those with dementia denied any problems.

"You don't have to do another minute of work, for all I care."

"That's what you already figure. That I'm good for nothing."

"Dad, that's not it."

"Then, why don't you let me be with the boys?" His dad's eyes were wide with accusation—and hurt.

Hawk stared down at his boots. Old and wrinkled and soft, bought the year the boys were born. "Because last time you had them," he said, "they wandered off."

"One time, one time only, and you take them away."

"You didn't know they had wandered off, that's the problem. What if Grace hadn't been there?"

His dad hung the rope. The loops were uneven, but his dad either didn't notice or didn't care. "But she was there, and that's the point. The boys weren't in any danger. She takes good care of them."

He made it seem as if Grace was always around.

"I am sure she does."

"She's nothing like—" his dad frowned "—that first wife of yours."

Hawk knew it was cruel, but he had to make his father see. "What was her name, Dad?"

"Why? Don't you remember?"

"I do," Hawk said. "I'm not sure that you remember."

"You can't expect me to recall everybody."

"But she was your daughter-in-law for three years. We had Christmases together. There is a picture in the house of all of us together."

Fear flashed across his father's face. And then anger. "I don't have to put up with this." He turned and walked away. "I'm going inside. To make coffee by myself."

Okay, Hawk thought. *Don't push it.* But it was a classic catch-22 situation. He had to let his father come around to the idea himself, because he couldn't forcibly drag him in for a diagnosis, but the nature of the disease prevented his father from recognizing the symptoms.

Hawk prayed his father would come to his senses soon.

THE BOYS TURNED out to be quilters. Well, Saul was. They had wandered into Grace's quilting room, and Amos had latched on to the sewing machine, while Saul had taken up the scissors. She had hung up a few wall quilts, and they had sat—actually, sat—and stared at them. Saul, especially, had studied the patterns and refused to budge, despite Amos's urgings that they go outside. Saul decided he'd rather build quilts, and without his playmate, Amos joined him.

Grace inwardly winced at their hatchet job, but gave them free rein. She could fold fabric later to straighten out the squares. Saul might have spent all day on this art project but, after lunch, had allowed Amos to drag him outside. They wanted her to drop them off early to show her the pen their dad kept them in. What?

"Of course," she had said. "I'd be delighted."

It was a cattle pen on a slope above the corrals where the boys could see everything and be seen. There were bales and toys and an old saddle, hockey sticks and balls in an old metal water trough. And rope. Scraps from around the ranch.

Off in the real corral, Hawk was leading a yearling horse. Was it any relation to Risky Business, the mare that Mateo had bought almost three years ago from Hawk and now showed to good profit?

She waved, and he raised his hand. "Do you want to go see your dad?"

"Nah, we can see him from here," Amos said.

"Rule is," Saul explained, "is that an adult lets us in, and we have to stay here until Dad or Grandpa says we can come out."

"What if you have to pee?" Grace said.

Amos pointed to a spot at a fencing panel. "Dad said to aim between the rails."

Grace sucked in her lips to suppress a smile. "As long as you got a plan."

"Yeah, we always got a plan," Amos said. "You can go now, Grace." He climbed the railings without a backward glance.

Saul stayed behind. "You said we can keep building a quilt?"

"I did. And we will. I promise." Making a quilt with them had not ignited her creative spark, but she had seen it in the boys' eyes, the value of making something out of nothing. And that had thrilled her in a way she had not experienced before. Was this what mothers felt?

"Will we get it done before you leave?"

"I'm not sure what you mean."

"Dad said that you're going back to the city."

Of course. Hawk assumed she had a job to go back to. He had probably heard through Mateo that she was on a sabbatical. Now Hawk was part of her great lie.

"Who knows what the future holds?" Grace said. "I promise you we will finish the quilts long before I leave. In fact, after we make a quilt for you and Amos, we can make another one for whoever you want."

"Grandpa," Saul said. "His has holes so big I can put my foot through them."

"Sure. For Grandpa. You good to play with Amos now?"

Saul smiled. "Yep. You can go."

"I'm going to talk to your dad, but I'm keeping my eyes on you two."

Grace reached the corral fence as Hawk rounded the inside with the yearling. He looked as if they were on a stroll. "All right for me to come in?"

He glanced at her hikers. "As long as you don't care what your boots pick up."

Except for a few replacement boards, this was the same fence from her summers here. She fell into step beside Hawk, the yearling on the other side. The roan gave her a little side-eye, but Hawk, buffered between them, continued on.

"She's a beauty," Grace said. "Light on her feet."

"Gets that from Mama. She has a bit of the Indian pony in her."

"Huh?"

"The secret ingredient to my stock. Picked her up from a horse sale up north. A three-year-old then, and broken to ride but not to cutting. But man, she was fast."

Hawk's face relaxed and his mouth almost twitched into a smile. He pointed with his chin up to the play corral. "Had enough of them?"

"I think they had enough of me. Amos wanted to show me their outdoor pen, and I had to admit that I was curious about where their dad kept them corralled. But as soon as we got here, he shooed me off. Saul did, too, once I promised we would continue on the quilts next time."

"Quilts?"

"Yeah. I've been making quilts since—since Mom passed. It started off as a kind of therapy, and then it just became a kind of passion. Saul, especially, has a real eye for pattern."

"That right?" Hawk said, a shot of pride in his voice. "He always gives things a careful look over."

"He wants to make a quilt for Russell. I was wondering... Do the boys have clothes they've outgrown?"

"Four boxes in their closet. Have at 'er. You short on cloth?"

"Funny. I wanted to make the quilt special. And hold the boys' interest before they turn into horsemen, like all the Blackstones before them."

Hawk's face clouded over. "I hope so." The filly leaned over and nuzzled Hawk's belt. Hawk pushed away her nose. "Go on with you." Then rubbed her neck.

"Kind of a mixed message there, Hawk."

"She needs to know it's okay to make mistakes."

"What's her name?"

"Palette, Pal for short. After her mama, Paintbrush. Dad's choice." Hawk's face tightened, and Grace guessed where his mind had gone.

"How is he?"

"I tried to talk to him this morning."

"I take it that didn't go well."

"He doesn't think there's a thing wrong with him, other than being old."

"Why am I not surprised? Stubbornness is hereditary among the Blackstones."

"An excellent trait to get through trouble. Dad is using it to avoid trouble."

They walked together, their strides matching. "Do you want me to talk to him?"

"Not yet. I'd like him to think it over. It might be hard, coming from you."

Grace tried not to take offense, but— "What do you think I'm going to be, cold and callous?"

"No, I think that you're going to be direct, and my dad doesn't need to hear from somebody he hasn't seen in a dozen years that he's probably got dementia."

Hawk's breath hitched on the last word, and Grace's heart went out to him. How would she feel if her cantankerous dad, the man who was never at a loss for words, suddenly couldn't remember where she lived? If she and Hawk had not gone their own ways so long ago, she might have reached out and taken his hand. As it was, she said, "Okay, I get it."

"You know, we wouldn't be walking this horse today if it wasn't for Dad. He got us into the cutting horses."

"I didn't know that. The horses always seemed to be around."

"Oh, we always had horses. But mostly just quarter horses for riding. But one time, Dad went south to Arizona to a horse show, and he rode a horse that came straight from Metallic Cat."

"That's the futurity stallion, right? Mateo and Haley bring it up about Risky B."

"That's because she carries his DNA. Anyway, Dad got on a trained cutting horse. The trainer gave him a few pointers and then just told him to give the horse full head. Dad said later that it was like riding a tiger. He said he never had a better high. And he swore he was going to bring cutting horse stock to the Blackstone Ranch. Grandpa was still alive then, and them two got into the biggest fight, Mom said. Well, Grandpa did. Dad never raised his voice once. He just kept saying how it was going to be. And then he went into the Blackstone account and cleaned it out. Went down south and bought that horse."

Grace sucked in her breath. "Kitkat Wrapper. I remember her. Your dad wouldn't let me near her."

"Yep, her. She came here as a three-year-old, and Dad brought up a trainer for the summer. Converted a corral into an arena, and when the trainer left, Dad kept it up. She paid off, and then we bred her with good stallions. Some of them were good, really good."

"Where are the rest?"

Hawk pointed over to the small pasture adjoining the barn. "That's it."

Grace counted. "Five? But when I was out three years ago, there were easily fifteen."

"Twenty-one, to be precise." Stiff regret marked his voice.

"What happened?"

"Horses are expensive to keep, especially when— There were bills to pay."

His ex-wife's bills. How could she have abandoned her own children and then expected Hawk to pay for her upkeep? *Stop it, Grace. None of your business.*

"You wouldn't rent horses to me because you don't have any?"

"That's about the size of it."

"I suppose I should be glad it wasn't anything personal."

He didn't comment.

"Okay, was it also personal?"

Hawk looked up to the ridge. "Ah, Grace, when has it not been personal?"

It was her turn to seek answers from the lofty ridge. She was really trying to hold back, to keep their affairs separate, to only do what a neighbor with time on her hands might do. But this was Hawk. The one she had spent the best summers of her life with, when they were as inseparable as the twins were now. She had broken with him completely because she knew she couldn't take him in small pieces. Nothing or the whole cake. The very fact that she was walking beside him right now, and not beetling away, proved that her stiff resolve was ice cream on a hot day.

Hawk cleared his throat. "Anyway, it's not all bad. We produced Risky B, and she was the best from her line so far."

Grace forced herself to focus on Hawk's effort to steer the conversation in a safer, less personal direction. "Was?"

Hawk gave a little smile, and Grace's heart skipped at this sudden glimmer of happiness. "I think this one here's the best yet. I got this feeling."

"What does your dad think?"

"Dad keeps calling her Risky B." Amos let off a holler, and they looked up in time to see him jump off a stack of square bales and hit the ground. Saul ran over, making ambulance noises, and helped Amos to his feet. "Wish Dad was as easy to fix."

Grace gave up. "You're right, Hawk. It is personal between us. There's no going back to our summers again, but we are more than neighbors. Your best horse belongs to my sister and her husband, and she asks me about your state of mind—"

"What?" Hawk pushed up on his cowboy hat, his face flushed. "Haley thinks you know how I'm feeling?"

"Exactly my point. As much as we might throw up fences between us, there are five-year-olds, horses, nosy family and our own memories to knock them down. So how about we not fight it but deal with who we are and where we're at?"

Hawk scratched the filly behind the ears. "What did you have in mind?"

She glanced up at the ridge and back to his dark eyes, watchful and glinting.

"Okay, this is the thing. I feel as if we're family." She rushed on. "Not like brother and sister."

"Given our history, we are definitely not that."

His voice was rough, suggestive of— No. "Anyway, our mothers were best friends, and we lived in each other's homes during the summer, and then Mateo marries Haley, and then he buys your best horse, which is like—I don't know—buying a piece of you, and then I'm living on your land."

"Your dad's land now."

"That's what I mean. It's all mixed up for good, and so we need to figure us out. And until we do, you're not selling any more horses, especially to Mateo. We'll figure something out."

"Not sure you can tell me what to do."

"Hawk, didn't I just do that?"

He smiled, as if they were kids planning a camping trip. "We're one messed-up family."

Wasn't that the truth?

GRACE'S TWO ADULT guests emerged from their car, stretching, and shouting to each other, despite standing beside each other. It was amazing how quickly Grace had become used to the profound quiet of the country. The slamming of their car doors was like bullet shots. Or maybe it was her nerves. Ever since the online booking request had popped up last week, Grace had braced herself for her former colleagues.

"This place is absolutely amazing," Keira said, spinning slowly in all directions. She was the office manager at the firm and had helped assign interns to Grace in the case that turned out to be her last one. Grace had stopped at Keira's office on the way out with her moving box and had apologized for pressuring Keira into favoring her above the needs of the other lawyers in the firm. Keira had merely wished her well and asked her to stay in touch. And when Grace had assumed that Keira was just being nice, had called her three weeks later to ask how she was doing.

As soon as The Home Place opened, Keira had booked a room. And then she had sent a message last week to say that Rachelle wanted to tag along. Grace had swallowed her bile and agreed. Only two weeks after her Easter opening, she wasn't in the position to turn down clients.

"I kind of like it myself," Grace said. "Welcome."

Rachelle surveyed the place with a cynical

smile. Why had she come? Rachelle and Grace had been hired within months of each other eight years ago, and they had become instant rivals for favor in their boss's eyes. They both entered a rivalry the years had not diminished.

The last case had been especially vicious, as Rachelle played all kinds of tricks to undermine Grace's work. But in the end, Rachelle had won. Won, because she was right. Grace had bullied staff and manipulated colleagues to the greater glory of her own case without regard for the firm. Her boss had been right to expunge her toxicity.

But Rachelle's victory still stung. She would take Rachelle's money and bite her tongue, as a delightful host should. And for Keira's sake. She didn't need a reenactment of workplace tension on her miniholiday.

She waited for them on the steps and Keira folded her in a tight hug. "I miss you," she whispered in her ear. "I especially miss your croissants."

Grace laughed and squeezed her friend back, absorbing her positive energy.

She looked over Keira's shoulder at Rachelle with her cynical smile still in place. Grace released Keira. "Hello, Rachelle. Welcome to The Home Place."

"Oh, I wouldn't have passed up this opportunity for the world." Without a word of invitation, she waltzed right in.

Keira's smile faded. "I'm sorry," she whispered. "I know she's not your favorite person."

If only to ease the worry lines on Keira's face, Grace would take the high road. "No problem," she said. "That's all in the past."

Rachelle was standing before the wood stove, her wheeled overnight bag at her feet. Grace had splurged on the pioneer woodstove replica from Natalia's store. Functional, but as Rachelle was proving, also eye-catching.

"Does this actually work?"

"Sure does," Grace said. "I'll be cooking your pancakes on it tomorrow morning."

Rachelle wrinkled her nose. "None for me. I'm strictly keto."

Grace had specifically asked about dietary references on her registration form, and Rachelle had filled in "None." "Then, an extra helping of eggs for you."

"I can eat meat as well. Steak or, if you don't have that, bacon."

Grace fixed a smile on her face. "I'll whip you up something special, Rachelle. Rest easy. How about I show you your rooms?"

When they arrived at the top of the stairs, Keira had her bag in tow, while Rachelle didn't. If she expected Grace to carry up her luggage, she was going to have to sleep in the clothes on her back and spend the day with fuzzy teeth.

"This is your room, Keira."

It was the larger of the two, with a queen-size bed. Russell and Angela's old room. Keira skimmed her fingers over the star-patterned quilt. "Did you make this?" Keira said. "It's absolutely gorgeous."

Mostly sage green, it was bordered in fabric she had specially ordered. "Thank you. I'm fond of it, too. There's an armoire over here," Grace said. "Three electrical outlets."

Rachelle gave a little snort. "Electricity. Yay."

If Rachelle only knew how much brainstorming had been done with the electricians to figure out a way to wirethe place and still meet code, she wouldn't be so sarcastic. No, check that. Not as sarcastic.

"And your room, Rachelle."

She took them farther down, past the bathroom. "A shared bathroom?" Rachelle questioned. "And the shower is downstairs?"

"I'm working with a home old enough to be a heritage site," Grace said. "The plumber and I had to be inventive."

"I think you should have negotiated a better deal," Rachelle said.

Grace couldn't have done better, but she registered Keira's pleading look and only said, "Perhaps so."

Grace opened the door to Rachelle'sbedroom and got the comment she expected. "Small."

"You are right, and that's reflected in the lower rate. But I think the view is first-class."

Rachelle moved to the window, and Grace braced herself for another criticism. How would the view of the greening ridge and a glimpse of the creek somehow not meet her standards? Instead, Rachelle gave a genuine smile.

"Well, would you look at that? A real-life cowboy."

"Let me see!" Keira joined Rachelle at the window, and sucked in her breath. "Oh wow! He's totally how you would picture them. Like at the Stampede."

She turned to Grace. "Do you know who he is?"

Grace dutifully peeked out the window. Sure enough, Hawk had emerged from the bank of trees on horseback. He was looking down, his cowboy hat covering most of his face, his hand loose on the reins as he approached the creek that ran behind her place. He wore a jacket shirt and work gloves, and yes, he looked exactly like he could star in a Western.

"Yeah, I know him. He lives up the road. We're neighbors."

Keira got right to the point. "Is he available?"

"I don't know. The topic hasn't come up."

"You've talked with him, and you haven't found out?" Keira squeaked.

Hawk let his horse edge to the creek crossing, and the horse stepped in. "That's so…incredible," Keira whispered.

Rachelle turned to Grace. "He's coming here. Right?"

"It would seem so. If you two want to make yourselves comfortable, I'll just go out—"

Keira waggled her finger at Grace. "No way are you keeping him to yourself." She paused. "Unless you already have plans—"

Grace waved her hand. "No, we're just— Our families are friends."

"Well then," Rachelle said, heading for the stairs and Hawk, "what's that about all's fair in love and war?"

No, no, no. If Rachelle and Keira talked to Hawk for two minutes, it would come out that she wasn't employed by the firm. She could already see the disappointment in his eyes.

She had to steer Hawk away. She caught up with Rachelle and Keira on the front steps. Hawk had crossed the creek and was coming up across the small pasture where the old paddocks had once stood.

"That horse," Grace said quickly, "sometimes gets spooked. You better let me check with Hawk first."

"Hawk? His name is Hawk?" Keira breathed. "That's so…perfect."

Grace intercepted Perfect Name at the edge of the paddock. "Hey, there."

He looked past her to Rachelle and Keira. "I've come at a bad time."

"A little bit. My guests just arrived and we were about to go out for dinner."

It was four in the afternoon, and his cool gaze said as much. "All right, then. I just wanted to stop by and put my signature on the consent for the trail."

"Okay, that's great." She did not want to pass up this opportunity. He was hard enough to track down, and he had come all this way.

"I can come by another time," Hawk said.

"No, no, I'll just go back in and grab the paperwork."

Hawk looked past her. "Meanwhile, it looks as if I'll be entertaining your guests."

Rachelle and Keira were fast closing the distance, Rachelle a few steps in the lead. Whether she liked it, Hawk was about to get pulled into her old work life.

"Hawk, I'd like you to meet my guests, Rachelle and Keira."

"More than that," Rachelle said, reaching up her hand to Hawk's. "We used to work together at the same firm."

Hawk removed his work glove and leaned down to take her hand. Rachelle hung on for a few seconds longer than she needed to, and Grace fought the urge to whack her hand loose. Keira gave a little wave and giggled.

Hawk's lips twitched. He had attended enough Calgary Stampede events to know exactly the effect he had on the urban bunnies. He glanced at Grace and his smile broadened. Nothing pleased Hawk Blackstone more than to see her riled up.

"Welcome to my part of the world," Hawk said. "Staying long?"

"Only until tomorrow," Rachelle said and added with a seductive purr, "but we're here all night long."

No way was Grace hosting a one-night stand under her roof.

"Grace says you live close by," Rachelle said.

"I do," Hawk said. "I live up the road with my family."

"With his twin boys," Grace said. "I take care of them twice a week. They are absolutely adorable. Anything to help Hawk out."

Grace knew she sounded catty, but she was doing this for Hawk's own good. Neither of them was suitable. Rachelle was too domineering, and Keira was…well, too submissive.

Keira took the hint and dropped her gaze. Rachelle, of course, saw it as a challenge. "Oh, how old?"

"Five."

"Really? I have a five-year-old niece."

"You do?" Keira said. "I never—" Rachelle shot her a look, and Keira shrugged.

Hawk had his laughing eyes on, and Grace knew he would grin all the way back home.

"So," Hawk said to Rachelle, "you said that

you used to work with Grace. You at a different firm now?"

Rachelle blinked and turned to Grace. She could feel heat rise to her cheeks, to the top of her skull and beyond, into a little cloud of guilt above her. Rachelle took it all in, and spun back to Hawk.

"I'm at the same firm. It's Grace who has moved on. Have you managed to find a position elsewhere yet?"

Grace could feel Hawk's eyes cut to her. Could feel all sets of eyes on her. "My position is here right now," she mumbled.

"And what a great place to land in," Keira rushed in. "This is such beautiful country. And the views! And it even smells different. So… fresh! I kept telling Rachelle that on the drive here."

Be quiet, Keira. You're only making it worse. Or from Rachelle's smirk, better.

"Well, I've interrupted enough," Hawk said. "I'd better be getting back." He tipped his hat to Rachelle and Keira, something he and Grace used to do as kids when they were spoofing Westerns.

He gave her a nod, his expression unreadable. She couldn't tell if he was disappointed or angry for leading him on about her so-called sabbatical. Right after her big talk last week about how they were all one big happy family-like group. He'd opened up to her about Russell and then came to sign papers as a gesture of trust and hospitality, and in return, she had lied to him.

"I'll come by later," Grace said. "If that works."

"Sure," he said. "I'll be around."

It was a polite thing to say, but she could tell from the stiffness in his back that she had a lot of explaining to do.

CHAPTER FIVE

GRACE ENDED UP cooking supper for Rachelle and Keira, because the prima donna openly asked Grace to. Keira had rushed to say that guests were served breakfast only, but Rachelle had laughed and said, "Yes, but we're friends. Right, Grace?"

When it was just Keira coming, Grace had planned to cook a meal and they would have a long evening together of gossiping. Somewhere deep in a bottle of wine, Grace would apologize again for her office antics.

"Right," Grace said. "I'll fire up the barbecue and throw on steaks. Grill up some veggies. Will that do, Rache?"

"Wonderful," Rachelle said. "Will the marinade be gluten-free?"

"It'll be everything free," Grace said, "because there will be no marinade."

"Wonderful," Rachelle repeated. "How about we eat at seven?"

And on it went. Would Grace add an extra

towel in the bathroom since the ones there were a little small? Would Grace check for the visiting hours at the local distillery? Would Grace open another wine bottle?

When Rachelle disappeared upstairs to use the bathroom after dinner, Keira sidled up to Grace in the kitchen. "I'm so sorry that I invited Rache out here. She's a diva at work, but I didn't know how much she has it out for you."

Grace scraped Rachelle's meal into the garbage, nearly half a steak. She was not used to eating Grace's proportions, Rachelle had explained.

"It's okay, Keira. I'm more worried that she's ruining your time here. I handled her for nearly eight years, remember?"

"But she's coming on real strong, even for her."

"Rachelle and I were at each other's throats from day one, and I regret that, once again, you are caught in the middle." Grace could hear a toilet flush from upstairs and hurried on. "Listen, Keira, I want to apologize again for how I treated you during that last case. I was always a little pushy, but I went overboard. I don't regret all the work I did for my client, but I regret expecting you to favor me over the needs of others in the office."

Keira raised her hand as if to brush aside the apology, but then she lowered it and took a deep breath. "Yeah, it was…hard. Whatever I did, someone was unhappy. And that meant that I was always unhappy. It's…better now, I admit. Seeing you two together now brings it all back."

Grace felt sick to see Keira's dejection. "Look, I'm the problem. So I'm going to remove myself."

At Rachelle's step on the stairs, Grace called out. "Hey, I was just telling Keira that I have to run over to Hawk's. I need him to sign paperwork, and it's got a ticking clock on it. But here—" she signed the back of her business card and handed it to Keira "—your ticket to half-price drinks at the bar in Ridgeview, the big one with the Western front, Bar None Saloon. Saturday night, there's always a band, and it's shoulder to shoulder real cowboys."

"Really?" Keira said.

"Really. I know the owner." Grace knew the owner because she'd enlisted him into her network of local businesses. "And don't worry about drinking. I will drop you off and pick you up."

Keira turned to Rachelle, like a kid to a mom. "Can we? It'll be fun."

Rachelle crossed her arms. "When will you pick us up?"

"Twenty minutes after you call to say you want to be picked up."

"I suppose we could." She glanced over at her suitcase still parked in front of the woodstove. "I gave blood yesterday and I'm not supposed to lift anything for the next twenty-four hours. Would you mind?"

"Certainly," Grace said. Anything to get them on the road so she could try to set things right with Hawk.

GRACE FOUND HAWK leaning on the pasture fence for the five horses. When he turned at her greeting, his jaw was a hard line and his dark eyes strained. The earlier humor with Rachelle and Keira had vanished.

She drew her hand down her blond ponytail to calm her nerves. "I drove the girls to Bar None for a night on the town," Grace said. "I came out so we could finish our conversation." And confess to her lies.

"Bar None, eh?"

"Yeah, Emmett took it over from his dad, built a dance floor. There's live music every Saturday. Good bands, too. I've gone a couple of times." Back when the winter nights closed in early on her, alone in the half-renovated, memory-heavy home. She rattled on to cover for her nerves, "Emmett was there once, and we came up with the idea of a kind of passport of discounts and freebies for visitors to use at local, participating businesses."

"Emmett always was good at roping people into his schemes." Hawk sounded bitter. Why would—

Grace connected the dots. "Oh, that Emmett."

"Yeah, that Emmett."

A girl always remembers her first kiss, except the aftermath of Grace's was far more memorable. At eighteen, she was still without her first kiss. She and Hawk had driven to the bar on her last night at the ranch before returning to the Jansson Ranch and then to her first year of university. When Emmett had shown interest in her, she sneaked out with him to his truck. A rap on the glass from Hawk had interrupted them.

"Still want a ride home, or you made other plans?"

She had gone back to the ranch with Hawk, and they had their first and last fight together out here in the middle of the horse pasture under a flashlight beam. Why had she kissed a stranger when he had brought her to the bar? Why did he think they were on a date? How could she not have tried with him? She remembered her answer, the one that shut the fight down for good. *Because we are friends, and friends don't kiss.*

He had walked off into the darkness and she'd gone back to the house. She left the next day, with Hawk already fixing fence in the far pasture. Grace covered with a story about how they'd said their goodbyes the night before. Once gone, she couldn't find a way to heal the rift, and her mother's death had kept her away.

She followed Hawk's gaze out to the horses covered in blankets. The yearling held tight to his mother's side. Never too old for Mama's warmth.

Did Amos and Saul miss their mom that way? What was it like to have a mom who wasn't there for you?

"We need to figure out what to do about the cows coming into your yard," Hawk said without preamble. "The fence got so rotten we took it down and let the cattle into the yard, but that won't work going forward."

"I can put it back in."

"For my cattle? That isn't fair."

Except if Mateo was right, Hawk was cash-strapped. Between the sale of her condo and her decade of savings, Grace had money, even after all the renos. But she knew Hawk wouldn't accept money straight out. "How about you provide the muscle? That's more than the materials. Fair enough?"

"All right. I'll be turning the cattle out in the next few weeks, so the sooner I can get at it, the better."

She was adding to his workload, but— "And that horse pen attached to the fence... Do you think you could tighten up the wire, put in a few new posts for the trail horses?"

"You found horses, then?"

"Not yet, but I'm sure something will turn up in the next couple of months."

Hawk grunted. "And if it doesn't?"

Grace hated his pessimism. When they were kids, he had talked about how he was going to have a hundred horses and people working for him and go to shows across North America. "Then I will have a place for them when it does. You draw up a shopping list and I'll order it."

"We can load it on my truck. Saves the delivery charge. And I run the boys into town every other day, anyway."

"They weren't with you today."

"At their aunt's in town. Her daughter's fourteenth birthday."

"And five-year-olds were invited?"

"It was the family party. No doubt she'll have her own friends' party, too. But Gemma and her husband are big on family."

They would be the sister or the brother to Hawk's ex. Another piece of information she filed away. When news of Hawk's wedding had reached her, she had not recognized the bride's name. Eva, her dad had said, had moved with her family from Calgary to Diamond Valley to open a jewelry store.

The cattle were in the sprawling pasture next to the horses, and in the quiet, she could almost hear them chewing their cud. Nathan moved among them with his dog, Doxie Sue.

"Your hired hand seems to fit right in."

"Not bad for a stray."

She settled her shoulder blades against the pipe railing, pulled the cuffs of her sweater over her hands to warm them in the freezing spring evening. "I got to hear this story." She didn't really, but anything to avoid owning up to her lie.

"Not much to it. Amy brought him over, and he says he's looking for work. Willing to work for room and board, and a bit of spending money. We agreed to try each other out, and if either didn't like the arrangement, off he'd go. That was November."

A stranger with unscheduled access to the twins. "But you don't know his background. I mean, with kids."

"He's from Montana and that's paperwork I frankly don't have the time for. Besides, he came with a dog."

"You're telling me that if he's good enough for a dog, then he's good enough to have around kids?"

"She's one smart dog." Hawk rolled his shoulders. "You come here to investigate my help?"

No, but she liked to lean on the fence and talk things over with Hawk. "My dad's coming down on Tuesday. Is it okay if I bring him over to see Russell?"

"Did you tell him about Dad?"

"I don't think I'll have to. Dad will see it for himself. I don't know if he'll say anything to your dad, though."

"Avoiding the truth seems to run in the family," Hawk said, squaring to her. "Does a friend lie?"

Well, here it was. "No, she doesn't, unless the truth is embarrassing. It was kind of my fault."

He looked ready to listen, then his jaw tightened right up again. "None of my business."

"How about you make it yours for a few minutes? I've got no one else to talk to about it."

"What about Haley and your dad?"

"I haven't told them. What about *embarrassing* didn't you hear? On top of disappointing Dad. He tells everyone about me being a hotshot lawyer, and now I'm a glorified homemaker."

"Nothing wrong with that," Hawk said. "Both our moms were that, and neither of us think any the less of them."

"You know what I mean."

"I don't think I do, but go ahead. Convince me." Some of the tension had gone from his body. If her minor tragedy distracted him from his genuine worries, so be it.

"I have developed a bit of a reputation for being a bulldog in civil law matters."

Hawk's mouth twitched. "You don't say."

She glared. "Do you want to hear this or not?"

"You're the one who wanted to talk it out." His mouth was about to split into a smile. She should hate him for enjoying himself, but it was enough that he was.

"Anyway, city council approved my client's small six single-home development in north Calgary. It had taken two years to gain that approval, during which a car accident had taken his wife, leaving him with seven-year-old twin daughters."

Hawk made a sympathetic noise in his throat.

"You know where he's coming from. He had mortgaged his assets to the hilt. He had sold their home to pay for mounting costs, and moved into a tiny one-bedroom apartment. They ate spaghetti most nights."

Grace stopped. There were so many parallels between her former client and Hawk that she had not noticed before. Single father. Twins. Hard luck. She had always thought that she had fought for the man because his cause was just. But three years ago, she had argued against Hawk selling the Blackstone home place, and their father had bought it out of regard for some convoluted ancestral link between their mother and related Blackstones in Montana. Grace had pushed for a solution, but her dad had saved the day. Fighting for her client was fighting for Hawk when she hadn't the power to save him on her own.

"The suspense is killing me," Hawk interrupted her thoughts.

"The city was stonewalling him with paperwork. He couldn't afford my fee, he said, but neither could he afford any more delay. His story hit home for me. Maybe it was the death of his daughters' mother. Sudden, like Mom's. Their lives had changed forever. So I took on the case." She wouldn't admit to the part of how her client's case reminded her of Hawk. That connection was too raw, yet.

"I discovered one council member directly interfering because the developer's homes would ruin her view. I became…intense. I snatched legal interns from their work on other lawyers' cases, and shifted my caseload to colleagues with promises of help and then didn't keep my word. And yes, sleep deprivation made me snippy."

"Remember that time you pulled an all-nighter waiting for a cougar?"

"I protected us."

"Against nothing. Except I got you as mean as a cougar all the next day. So yeah, I sympathize with the staff."

"I thought it was worth the trouble in the end. My client won damages from the city and we had forced the council member to step down amid allegations of personal interference. I bought pizza and beer for the entire office, and while they were kicking back, my boss called me into his office.

"I expected him to congratulate me. Which he did, and then he handed me my notice. I sat there stunned as he explained how I had thrown his entire firm into chaos. I won the case, but had lost the goodwill of the firm. His duty was to the firm.

"'Maybe,' he said, '"you should find an occupation more suited to your temperament.'"

Hawk grinned. "And here you are, a B and B owner in God's country."

"Yeah, look at me. I sent him and his wife an

invitation to come visit at my good-guy price as a way to reach out and try to get back in their good graces. George and Hilda were family friends. He brought me on as a favor to my dad, and I've disappointed them…and my dad. That's the real reason I don't want him finding out."

"What if George and your dad talk?"

Grace dragged her hands down her face. "The terror is real, believe me."

"You want to go back?"

"I don't know where I want to be, but this is as good a place as any to find out where that is."

"So, ask me." His voice was low, dogged. "Ask me for the favor you really came over to get."

"All right. I'm hoping that you don't tell Dad about my job and, by extension, don't tell your dad either, in case it slips out."

"You're going to have to tell your dad at some point."

"I told him I was on sabbatical until September. I've got the summer to figure things out. I guess I want to buy time and get something going for myself so he won't worry that I ruined my life."

"Can't you just look for work at another firm?"

"I can, but—" She swallowed. "I can't swear that I won't do the same thing all over again. And besides—word gets out. I'd practically have to go independent."

"You could set up somewhere else in Calgary."

"I sold my condo."

"Whoa. You really pulled up stakes. But the longer you delay, the bigger the lie in the end. That and I'll have to keep up the lie in front of Mateo and Haley."

"Are you saying you want something in return?"

"No, I don't want anything." He spoke with such finality, it hurt.

"Will you do it?"

"I won't tell Knut."

Grace let out her breath.

"But Mateo is a different story. If he asks me directly, I'm not lying to him. I've got too much riding on my dealings with him to harm it with a lie to save you from putting off the inevitable."

"That's fine." She would just have to make sure that she didn't give Mateo any reason to ask. But wait—

"Too much riding on what dealings?"

He turned back to the horses. In the growing dark, the horses were silhouettes. Outrage and loyalty rose inside her, the same emotions she had felt when listening to the developer's case. If she would lose her job over a guy whose circumstances were something like Hawk's, how far would she go to help the real Hawk?

She touched her hand to his arm. "Talk to me."

HAWK FELT THE pressure of her hand on his arm like the heat of the sun, despite chilly evening.

There had been a time when he had thrived with her around. A cloud had hung over him for years after she had left and never come back, even for a visit.

Now listening to the story of her firing had brought back what he had missed about her. The same Grace pushing the envelope for whatever cause she had set her mind on. Cougars or city hall, she never backed down.

"You might as well tell me, because all I have to do is call up Haley and ask her."

She had him there. She always had him. "I'm thinking of selling the horses."

"All of them?"

"Yes."

"But Blackstone Ranch isn't Blackstone without the horses."

Trust her to cut to the heart of it all. "Didn't you say that our families' businesses cross over, anyway? Mateo would have them, is all."

"But you agreed not to sell the horses."

"You telling me not to doesn't equate to me agreeing, Grace."

"Fair enough, but Haley told me Mateo would rather look for another solution, rather than take your horses."

"Then I would owe him," Hawk said. "And you have no idea how tired I am of owing people money." He had never said that aloud before. Even with Mateo, he had kept it mostly to business. But one conversation with Grace in the near dark, her hand on him, and he was coming apart. He shifted his arm along the railing, stretching the space so her hand might easily slip away. Instead, she edged closer. "It's that bad, eh?"

The automatic halogen light at the barn switched on, and suddenly the two of them were lit up. He bent his head under the sudden glare, the sight of her hand on his arm filling his vision. "It's not good."

"I thought that by selling the home quarter, you would've got back on your feet."

"Other bills came up."

"Like the ex?"

People thought Eva had taken him to the cleaners. He had sidestepped all that, but it was too much for Grace to think that way, too. "Of all the debts I have, I don't begrudge a cent to my kids' mother. She and I made an agreement, and I'll stick to it."

"Even if it means losing the ranch?"

He jerked his arm out from underneath her hand. "You have a knack for tearing me down, Grace."

Her hand fisted on the railing. "What's that supposed to mean?"

"How can you not know, clever lawyer?" He could feel his old frustrations on the rise. That talk about Emmett hadn't helped. Grace had forgotten about that night at the bar, as if it didn't matter that it had ruined their friendship, had ruined his stupid youthful dreams of a life with her. "How about we call it a night? I'll come over to fence. I'll keep your secret. Deal?"

Grace held up her hand. "No way. We're going to hash this out. I have a stake in this ranch, too. It was me three years ago who talked to Haley and Dad about the home quarter."

"Sweet deal for you. You got a piece of Blackstone without having to marry into it."

She flinched, and Hawk didn't blame her. He was hurting and had lashed out at her. He opened his mouth to apologize, but Grace spoke first. "You're right. I didn't. And since I'm now in your life whether you like it or not, how about we deal with this Emmett elephant once and for all?"

"Emmett's not the problem. I never cared that he kissed you."

She cocked her head skeptically.

"Not as much as I cared that you didn't want to kiss me."

"I told you it was because—"

"Friends didn't kiss. I don't need the reminder. Fifteen years later, and I still remember. You were always up for anything, and yet when it came to us, you didn't even want to try one kiss. That's what hurt."

She drew her hand down her ponytail, a kind of self-soothing gesture that pulled at Hawk. "I admit there were times when I wondered what might have happened if I had given in."

The collapse of their friendship had torn her up, maybe not as much as it had eaten at him, but the point was that it had mattered. He caught her hand in his and pulled her close. "And now? Now that not kissing didn't work out so well? Should we try it my way this time?"

Her eyes widened in surprise, her lips, inches from his, quivered.

"Say it, Grace. Say what you have denied us for the past fifteen years."

She laid her free hand on his face, her fingers scraping his stubble. "All right, Hawk. All right."

He kissed her, holding nothing back. And she responded in kind. It took the same effort as pushing away a falling horse, but he pulled away.

"Well, Grace. What are we now?"

GRACE WAS WIDE awake when Rachelle called her at midnight for a ride back. It was almost a relief to pick them up and listen to their tipsy patter about country music and two-stepping cowboys. Anything to take her mind off Hawk's kiss.

And his question. She had not given him a straight answer, had made an excuse about pressing phone calls and paperwork. He had given a little half smile and wished her a good night. He knew she was running off.

Grace brewed a dark roast coffee for herself the

next morning. She hadn't taken more than a bitter, reviving sip before Rachelle descended from on highand plunked herself down across from Grace. Grace hadn't seen her without makeup before. She had great skin, though a little green right now.

"I'll get you a coffee," Grace said. She didn't bother to offer cream or sugar. She and Rachelle had always preferred their coffee strong and black. The staff room reserved all the dark roast pods for them. Rachelle had them all to herself now.

Grace set her biggest mug, filled to the brim with the black potion, before Rachelle. "Steak and eggs now, or do you want to wait for Keira?"

Rachelle groaned and shook her head. Grace sat again, bracing herself for Rachelle's onslaught. Hangover or not, her old rival wouldn't pass up a chance to needle her about something.

It didn't take more than a half-dozen sips. "How did it go with Hawk last night?"

A rather presumptuous question. She and Rachelle had never socialized together outside of the group events, like a Christmas party or Friday staff drinks.

Grace shrugged. "Good. We sorted out issues around land sharing."

"I bet he folded."

Grace bristled. "You know, Rachelle, I settled a whole lot more cases before they went to court than in court. I can negotiate. Believe it or not, I prefer a win-win situation."

Rachelle widened her eyes. "You do know how he looks at you, right?"

Grace took a gulp of coffee, the heat nicely searing its way down her throat. "I don't know what you're talking about."

Rachelle stared at Grace as if to force a confession out of her, and then she peered more closely at Grace. "You really don't know."

Her old office nemesis pushed aside her coffee. "Let me enlighten you. This is how he looked at me." Rachelle gave a friendly smile. "And to Keira." Rachelle's smile widened into something reminiscent of Hawk. "Now, this is how he looks at you." Rachelle's mouth shortened to a tease of a smile, her eyes softened, lingered. Yes, she had seen that look. Just before his lips had closed on hers. But all the time?

"Stop it," Grace said, and Rachelle laughed.

"It's not me you need to tell to stop."

"I think it is. If you could see that he…he has feelings for me, why did you tell him about my firing, then?"

Rachelle set her elbows on the table and leaned across to Grace. "Because I hate liars just as much as you."

Grace blinked before Rachelle's intensity. "Fine. Apparently, he's not as hung up about liars as you and me. He was more concerned about me not telling my family." Why was she confiding to Rachelle as if they were best buddies? "You really are good at getting information out of reluctant people."

"It's why I'm sitting in your office now," Rachelle said.

Her junior partner spot.

"You didn't know? I thought Keira would have told you. About a month after you left, I got my invitation."

It should have hurt. But after last night's kiss, it was only one more confused feeling in an already whirling mix. "Congratulations." It wasn't as hard to say as she thought it would be.

And from the way Rachelle's triumphant smile faded away, she knew it. "I see you've moved on to greener pastures."

Meaning Hawk. One kiss did not determine a future together. Especially a future she wasn't sure she wanted. She wasn't ready to give up her law career and settle in as a simple B and B owner. She wanted…something more.

Who are we now?

Forget that. Who was *she* now?

CHAPTER SIX

As soon as he dropped the kids off at kindergarten on Tuesday morning, Hawk beelined for Grace's place. The Home Place. Smart to use what the Blackstone family had always referred to the old homestead as. It had a nice ring to it. Another linking together of the Blackstones and Janssons.

Of course, their families wouldn't be joined. The wild dreams of his twenty-year-old self weren't going to fall into place because he had finally kissed the woman who had got away. She had run off again, after his question. Not that he knew the answer himself. Today, he was just the guy building her a fence.

He was coming up on the straight before the bend at Irina's place when he recognized her truck coming toward him. He expected to exchange waves, but she slowed and stuck out her hand. He rolled to a stop alongside her open window.

"You're a busy man," Irina said. "I've been meaning to stop in, but I see you coming and going on the road so often I can never say for certain when you're home."

"Coming and going describes my life. What can I do for you?"

"I was just wondering if Grace has talked to you about her plans for your home quarter."

He had sold the land nearly three years ago, and Irina acted as if it belonged to the Blackstones. "You mean the trail rides? Yes."

"You're not going to let her do it, are you?"

"I don't know that I have any objection. She sounded pretty reasonable to me."

"You would think that. You have a soft spot for city girls."

"Grace isn't from the city." Now, why say that? It admitted that he had a soft spot for her. "I'm not sure what the problem is."

"The problem," Irina said, pointing with her thumb behind her to the bend, "is that corner there." Hawk did not have to follow the backward point of her thumb to know she meant the crash site. Like the stone cairn for Miranda on the ridge, a wooden life-size horse, painted roan, stood there now, and soon Irina would set out containers of flowers where the saddle would go. "It's unnecessary. Her whole business isn't necessary. Why do people need to come out here to relax? Let us work our butts off in peace."

There was a time when Hawk couldn't have

agreed more. A pre-Grace time. "I understand, Irina."

"If you did, you wouldn't sign off your support, which you plan to, right?"

Hawk nodded.

Irina lifted a folder from the passenger seat. "And that's why I'm going into town now to request to make a presentation when county sits for a second reading on her proposal. I'm making two. On my behalf. And on behalf of the ranchers' association. That's two against your one, Hawk. She might be a lawyer, but I'm meaner."

Hawk repeated the message to Grace during a lunch break. It was the first time he had stepped inside the place where he'd spent the first twenty-five years of his life since the sale. The house was already the worse for wear then, and while they had taken care to board up the windows and drain out water, a good decade of vacancy had taken its toll. When he had sold the quarter to Knut, he half expected the house to get demolished.

Instead, he stepped into a full restoration. Grace gave a tour of his old home, and he was happy to tag behind her long legs and messy blond twist of hair. She had updated the kitchen and flooring, replaced fixtures, stripped off old wallpaper and painted the walls, and installed new windows. Yet she had maintained the open concept of one living area flowing into the next. She had kept the hardwood flooring in the living room and polished over the scars. Grace had brought The Home Place back to life. He might feel at home himself here, if it wasn't a beautiful reminder of his failure to keep the Blackstone land together.

He rubbed the newel post at the bottom of the stairwell. "You kept this."

"It's smaller," she said. "I had it sanded down before applying the stain. But even now when I make the turn, it kick-starts my day."

"Yeah, I know what you mean. Now two sets of feet hitting the floor do that for me."

"Which reminds me…" She moved into a story about their latest shenanigans, and that carried them right into a lunch of burgers and homemade fries. All very friendly, but he felt a kind of frisson between them that hadn't existed before. She gave him a small, knowing smile and he realized that she'd caught him staring at her.

He cleared his throat. "I met Irina on the road," he said. "She plans to oppose you at the second reading."

Grace straightened. "But why? I followed every regulation to the T."

Hawk didn't relish gossiping about other people. But this was Grace, and maybe some insight might smooth things over for everyone concerned.

"Irina…is scared. Her husband left her with a daughter to raise."

"Lena, I remember her. She was a few years

older than us. I always felt like such a kid around her. Didn't she marry and move away?"

"She did, but it was to the wrong guy. She came back with a little girl. Amy. You met her, the babysitter. But about a year later, not long after your mom passed, Lena was killed out at that corner."

Grace gasped. "That is who the horse cairn in the ditch is for. It's...hard to miss."

"Lena was riding in the ditch, and an RV came around the bend too fast, lost control and hit her and the horse."

The aftermath of that scene still flashed through Hawk's mind. In a quiet country, he had heard the squeal and crush of steel from their place, a full mile away. And then the screams of people, and what pricked up the ears of the Blackstone horses, the scream of a horse.

While Irina rode with her daughter in the ambulance, Russell had put down the horse and his mom gathered up Amy from Irina's house.

"It was a hard day, that one," Hawk said.

Grace frowned. "But what has that to do with my trail rides? They are not on the road."

"There's the issue of increased traffic. It is a dangerous curve, if you're not used to it. But—" Hawk hesitated, unsure of opening up to Grace. She widened the blue pools of her eyes and like a fool, he plunged in.

"Something else you might not know. This

home quarter used to belong to the Sandbergs. They claimed it first. Then, when my great-grandfather showed up a few months later and took up the land here and to the south, the first Sandberg sold half the quarter to him and both their names went on the title. That continued out of habit until Irina's husband died, and she sold the other half to my dad. She needed the money, yes, but she thought she was selling to a Blackstone. And then I sell it to an outsider. I didn't even let her know my plans."

"Why didn't you?"

Because he would have had to acknowledge that he had failed to hold on to the land. As it was, he had disappointed his own parents. His dad had blamed himself. *I poured too much into the horses, and left you with the fallout.* "I honestly didn't know it would bother her."

"But you are not to blame. You did what you had to do. How many times do I have to say that before you believe it?"

Every day of my life, he thought. He looked around at his old home, her new one. She had restored The Home Place—and a bit of the Blackstone legacy. He pushed away his coffee. Time to do his part. "Let me get started on the fence."

A WEEK LATER, Knut and Russell sat sideways to the dining table, their legs stretched out, and talked. They had wandered about the ranch for the past couple of hours, shooting the breeze, and had come in for a cup of coffee. The boys were outside with Amy. Hawk stayed in the background as he did household chores, trying not to appear to be monitoring his dad.

Irina pulled up. Hawk welcomed her in and she called a "hello" to Russell. And there it was, the hand over the temple, the frown as Russell searched for the right name. Knut made the connection first. "Irina. Well now."

Irina's hand fluttered to her short hair, her cheek. "Knut Jansson. Is that really you?"

Knut stood, touched his own gray hair. "It is. Hard to believe. But you haven't changed."

She came over, hand extended for a shake. "Then, you need new eyeglasses."

Russell waved to a kitchen chair. "Have a seat. I'll get you a coffee."

"I can grab that." Hawk could see from the way his dad's eyes darted about that processing a new arrival was already taxing enough. The more people for Russell to sort out, the harder it was for him to track. He hesitated and trailed off a couple of times, but Irina and Knut didn't seem to notice. The two chatted, and Russell frowned and his silence grew longer.

Grace pulled up. He hadn't seen her for more than a week, other than brief exchanges when dropping off and picking up the boys.

"Grace is home," Russell announced.

It was so dead wrong, so patently false, that both Irina and Knut turned to Hawk for confirmation. Irina's look was of disapproval; Knut's of open curiosity.

"A bit of a joke," Hawk said. "She's over here so often."

She hadn't come alone. She held the hand of a little redhead about the boys' age.

"That's Sadie," Knut said. "She's the grandkid I was talking about." As soon as she came inside, she kicked off her boots and climbed onto Knut's lap as if she had full rights there.

At least, that's what Hawk saw from the corner of his eye. He mostly had his eye on Grace. She came in like a fresh breeze, all swinging blond ponytail and fancy blue jeans. She carried a big shopping bag. "Are the boys around?"

"Outside with Amy."

She held up the bag. "I finished putting the border on the quilts and I couldn't wait to show them."

"How many quilts is that now?" Knut said. "One hundred?"

"I lost count. Natalia knows better. She insists I keep her updated. But I don't plan on telling her about these two. These are real heirloom pieces."

"You quilt?" Irina said.

"She can do just about anything," Russell said. "Right, Hawk? This one's a keeper. Not like…" His hand went to his temple. *Don't Dad. Don't.*

"The other one. I forget her name." He lifted his head. "Not important, anyway."

Russell had never approved of Eva, but Hawk had made him promise not to badmouth her in front of the kids. He was keeping his promise, but his talk was making the others uncomfortable.

Grace dove her hand into the bag. "I'm not taking credit for these creations. Amos and Saul originals. The first crazy quilts off the Blackstone production line."

She spread two quilts over the dining table, and Hawk drew closer. He recognized the boys' outgrown shirts and pajamas. Cloth bunched like pebbles in places. "Amos did this one." It was big chunks of color with two-inch ridges here and there. "And this is Saul's." It wasn't bad. There was a kind of pattern there.

"The boy has an artist's eye," Grace said to Hawk. "I'm so proud of him."

He would never have thought his rowdy boys would ever sit long enough to quilt. He had thought she meant a few patches sewn together.

"Thanks, Grace."

"Believe me, my pleasure. Where—"

Amy came through the front door. "Gramma, what are you doing here?"

"Visiting," Irina said. "Is that a crime?"

"No," Amy sighed. "I lost track of the boys."

Russell made a disgusted noise. "Those boys are always running off. Don't worry. They'll come back. You chase after them, and you chase them all their life. I remember when we were that age, and gone all day."

He looked for support to Irina and Knut who were exchanging glances between themselves.

"I keep telling Hawk not to let the boys run the show." His dad was getting wound up.

"I'll go out and check again," Amy said, backing away.

"I'll come with you," Grace said. "Let's go, Sadie. I want you to meet Amos and Saul." She cast a look at Hawk, her expression clear enough for him to read. *You take care of your dad, and I'll take care of the boys.*

His dad turned out to be right, sort of. Grace with Sadie and Amy had barely reached the corrals before the boys came ripping around the house, straight out of the caragana bushes, pedaling their bikes, in hot pursuit of whatever their imaginations had created. He could see Grace and Amy turn at the screaming and start back.

"What did I tell you?" Russell looked around in triumph. "They showed up, not giving a care for the trouble they're causing."

"That's kids for you," Irina said neutrally. She turned to Knut. "I hear you have more than one grandkid."

"Two so far, and two more that feel like my own."

Irina rested her cheek on her hand. "Oh?"

Knut explained how he had two through his biological daughter, Haley, and another two with the man who used to be his hired hand and his wife. Brock Holloway. Hawk knew of him through Mateo. They ranched together, now. Hawk wished he had a partner like that. Close, family even. "Brock and Natalia, their coming together is quite the story."

Irina deepened her resting posture. "I like a good story,"

Was she flirting with Knut? Knut's eyes crinkled, and he gave Irina a soft look over his mug.

Through the open kitchen window, Hawk heard Grace call to the boys about someone she would like them to meet. They detoured to her and he couldn't quite make out her introductions to Sadie. Saul took Grace's free hand, leaving Amos to tuck himself right in front of Grace as they all moved forward together. One kid must have said something, because she stopped in her tracks, threw back her head and laughed.

If he was lucky, she would share the story later with him.

Grace must have told the boys that there was a surprise was on the dining table, because they rushed in, screaming, "Cookies!"

They were brought up short by the quilts, and then they were all over that, dragging them off the table, hiding under them, rolling in them. Everyone, including Hawk, was caught up in their antics.

His dad jumped to his feet. "Hey, watch what you're doing! You're wrecking them. Grace made them for you!"

He reached and yanked the quilt off Amos, but he must have caught hold of Amos's hair too, and Amos let out a howl.

"Shut up," Russell said and pulled on Saul's quilt. Saul spun out of it. "Look at the mess you two made. You two are nothing but trouble."

His dad had never yelled at the boys. He couldn't remember his dad ever yelling. Stern words, yes. That had been enough. This was not his dad.

Saul started crying, and Amos stared in fright at his grandfather.

His dad drew himself up sharply, and he looked about. Irina, Knut with Sadie back on his lap and tucked tight against his chest, Grace, and finally Hawk. Sudden terror welled up in his father's eyes.

His dad left the room without another word. And everybody, including Grace, left within minutes. She looked at him in sympathy, but he couldn't bear to hold her gaze.

His dad didn't come out of his room for the rest of the day. Supper comprised of food being pushed around plates, and it was the quietest bedtime since the boys had started talking. Hawk was walking past his room on his way to his own room at the end of the hall later that evening when his dad emerged. His face was pale and drawn. "You make me an appointment, okay?"

Hawk swallowed. "Okay, Dad."

HER DAD TOOK the lead up the slope the next day, with Grace a few steps behind, the task so much lighter than when she had tramped up the hill more than a month ago.

The three kids—Amos, Saul and Sadie—ran about her dad and Grace, like gophers, whizzing back to them to show off with their treasures or to tank up on the water Grace had packed. They were on their way to visit her mother's favorite viewpoint. And location of her cairn.

"They remind me of you girls and Mateo and Hawk, all running together in the summers."

"The four of us didn't often run together. It was mostly Hawk and me picking on the other two until they went off on their own."

"Well, all that time together paid off."

"For Mateo and Haley."

They had reached the outcropping of rock where she had twisted her ankle. And Hawk had rescued her. She had flirted with him, and why? Had part of her wanted to reconnect even then?

Her dad sat on a flat spot of the boulder. "I suppose it could for you and Hawk, too. You are both free to choose each other."

"Because we're both available, because we ran together when we were kids, because we're neighbors? Because it's convenient?"

Knut held up his phone and took a snap of Sadie and the boys. She was slung between them. Amos had her underneath the shoulders, and Saul by her boots, as they rescued her from what sounded like a fire in the barn. Sadie waved her arms and begged them to save the horses.

"Sounds as if you've already given this some thought."

Grace seated herself on another part of the rock, an edge biting into her butt. "I might have, and that's all I'm saying on the matter."

Knut grunted. "I suppose you have a whole life in the city, still."

Grace turned away, using the kids as an excuse not to look at him. "There is that, but I'll be here often enough."

"Hard to be in two places at once. Hard for the heart to be, at any rate."

Her dad seemed to be gunning for her to move out here. To give it all up. If she did, then she would never have to confess about her firing. At least, not right away. "Would you be okay if your lawyer daughter gave up the city life and became a quilter and B and B operator?"

"What do I care what you are, so long as you're healthy and happy?"

That was about as good of an opening line to

make her confession as any. Except she couldn't be sure that living out here forever and a day would make her happy. Neither could she keep him out of the loop. Her dad and George would eventually talk. She would tell her dad once she screwed up the courage.

A sudden wind slapped against them and Knut tugged his hat down tighter. "I guess we better keep going before we are blown back down the hill."

It wasn't just the wind that slowed their steps as they climbed. Her mother's cairn gradually came into view. No longer just a blip on the ridge, but with form and shape. And remembrance.

The kids had quieted as they drew closer, perhaps picking up on the quiet of the adults. The horse trail, which once ran straight along the ridge, now took a detour around the cairn, like a loose loop in a straight stitch. How many times had Hawk ridden past? He'd kept more in contact with her mother's memory over the decade than any Jansson had.

As they approached, Grace reached out her hands and felt the boys slip theirs in. Sadie did the same with Knut.

"Dad has never taken us here," Amos said.

"He said it's too dangerous," Saul added.

"He's right," Grace said. "Under no circumstances are you two to let go of my hands. There's a drop-off here." A deadly one.

Knut approached the cairn with Sadie. She fastened her attention onto the rock arrangement. "Isn't that a cairn? Uncle and Auntie helped me put one up for Daddy where he fell into the river. Did somebody die here?"

Knut looked over at Grace. So much for a tale of pretty views. "Yes, Sadie."

Sadie twisted to look up at him. "Your wife?"

"Yes."

Saul laid his head against Grace's arm. She couldn't see his face under his hat, but from the weight of his head, he was feeling it. Amos was digging his toe into the grass.

"Okay," Sadie said. "Do you want me to get a new rock for it?"

Her dad rubbed his thumb along Sadie's hand. "I think she'd like that."

She turned to the boys. "Come on. Let's look for rocks. One for each of us."

She scampered down the hill. Amos's hand twisted in Grace's as he stretched to follow her. He stopped. "Can I? Can we?"

"So long as you come back straight to me. Got it?"

Her attention still angled to the kids, she watched her dad at the cairn. The rest of the ridge had a steep but not a deadly drop-off. It was only here at his feet, where some ancient forces had sheared off the rock, that a cliff had formed, and from then on, water and wind had worn away at the face. This horse path, formed hundreds of years ago, traversed by natives, first on foot and then on horseback, and then by settlers, had inches shaved away—until time and circumstance narrowed to one fateful second.

Hawk had discovered the body. And shot the horse.

"Did you ever speak to Hawk about—what happened?" Grace said.

"There wasn't much to tell."

Grace wasn't so sure about that. From the stillness in Hawk's frame when he'd talked about Lena's death, coming a year after her mother's couldn't have been easy. He was probably sparing her father. "Okay."

Her dad lifted his eyes from the cairn, west to the Rockies. It was an immense view. The blue sky with far ribbons of cloud, the long range of Rockies still capped with snow, blue and craggy, rounding into the grassy heave of the foothills. A harsh, unforgiving country of rough rivers and skin-stripping winds. Even now, the wind plucked at them, buffeted her, testing her footing, looking for a way in.

He raised his phone to the view and tapped the screen. So these were the missing pictures he had talked about. "I could always tell when she'd been up on this ridge," her dad said, taking another picture from a different angle. "She'd call and say 'I was up on the ridge' and she sounded as if she'd talked to God. She told me in the morning she was heading up there, and I waited for her call."

"I should have been there with her," Grace said. "She asked and I begged off."

"You still holding on to that?" Her dad lowered his phone, and wrapped his arm around her shoulders and pulled her tight to him. "You can't beat yourself over that all your life. Let it go."

"You're one to talk," Grace said. "How many years has it been?"

"Thirteen years on the day I called to say I was coming down."

"Oh." She had only remembered the month, not the day.

"And you're right. It's time both of us let her rest in peace."

"We're coming!" Amos yelled, even though she had been monitoring his progress the whole time. The kids were making their way back up the hill, slowed by the weight of their burden. Amos carried a rock the size of his head, Saul juggled two jagged ones and Sadie cradled two egg-sized ones.

Grace had them deposit their load well away from the cairn. Knut walked the kids, one at a time, up the hill with their personal offerings, taking a picture each time. Rocks in place, Grace retreated off the ridge with the kids, letting Knut have a moment alone. She glanced over her shoulder, expecting him to still be on one knee at his wife's marker. He had risen and was gazing in the opposite direction to where Irina lived.

Her father might have let go. She looked toward the Blackstone Ranch. She had avoided Hawk for so long—and avoided her own conflicted feelings for him. Maybe it was time to take her mom's advice and move on. Not away from Hawk, but to him. And face up to the one person she had always avoided—herself.

CHAPTER SEVEN

IRINA ROLLED THE wheelbarrow out of the barn, the empty metal chop pails from feeding grain to the horses clanging away, just as Knut pulled into her yard two mornings after the visit with Russell. Poor Russell. What was going on there?

As Knut unfolded from his truck, Irina paused to admire how he was every bit the handsome rancher who had stolen her good friend's heart. He looked around her spread. There wasn't much for him to see. With only her and Amy, and a tractor that worked half-time, they had scaled down to next to nothing. She might have to sell, not for lack of money but for lack of manpower.

Knut approached with a long, easy stride, messing up her heartbeat.

"Irina," he said with the same lift as he had when he had greeted her at Russell's, as if he actually was excited to see her. No wonder Miranda couldn't stay more than a week here before hightailing it back to him.

"Knut, nothing for years and now twice in

three days. I'm honored." She was, too, though she passed it off as a joke.

"Ah well, since I'm down here, I might as well see as many people as I can."

"I didn't know I was on the list."

"It's a long one." His eyes lifted to the ridge that ran along the Sandberg and Blackstone property. No doubt his beloved wife topped the list.

She stripped off her gloves. "I bet. You have time for a cup of coffee?"

"The question is if you got the time. Did I catch you in the middle of chores?"

She had the chicks to sort out and Amy's pet goat. Amy was supposed to take care of that, but she had stayed in town for a high school volleyball game. Nathan was going to drive her back out. "Odds and ends."

"I can do odds and ends. That's all they let me do anymore."

By "they," he was likely referring to Mateo and Haley, and that other boy he considered a son. "Well, in that case, I keep the shovels inside the barn."

It was also where she had the chicks madly cheeping away. "Well now," Knut said. "I should have brought Sadie along. No, better I didn't. She would stuff a couple in her pocket and bring them home."

"I might have done the stuffing," Irina confessed. "I got them with plans to do up the roosters in the fall, and winterthe hens over. But I think I just made myself work."

Irina filled their feed pen. "You want in."

Knut looked at her dog, Lulu, staring between the railings of the pen, her tail in a slow wag. "Won't she—" But Irina had already opened the door and Lulu came in.

"I thought the same myself when she barged her way in the second day. I thought they were done for, but—"

Lulu sniffed the chicks and then lay down on her side. The chicks scampered over and started using her as a jungle gym. "She's the worst dog this place has ever had. She won't bark at strangers, as if it's not polite. I swear she'd show the thief over to the gas tanks and nose out the house key."

"Whereas the one we got at home thinks he runs the place."

"Oh?" And just like that, they fell into a conversation as easy and fresh as the one yesterday at Russell's, while Knut shoveled out the old straw and chicken poo, and she laid out clean straw and checked the heat lamp. They moved on to the goats and the conversation shifted to hobby farms and the cost of everything and her hips and his back. She asked outright what he thought of Nathan.

"I don't think we exchanged a dozen words. Quiet. Good with the stock."

"Only reason Amy babysits the boys is to find time with him, and to be blunt, Sandberg women don't have a great history with choosing men. I married a gambler, my daughter a drunk and now Amy has set her eyes on some kid who can't keep his eyes in one spot. Dodgy."

"Or real nervous around the one woman who holds sway over the girl he's lost his heart to."

"If you're right, I intend to leverage that until she's out of high school with marks that'll take her to university. Hopefully by then, she can see straight to make her own decisions, and he might figure out how to look me in the eye."

Knut twisted the fork handle. "Ah well, that takes courage. Even for a man my age." His voice was soft, amused. What did he mean by— "You could ask Hawk. He's the one who hired him."

"I don't want to bother him. He's got enough to think about, what with—" She waved her hand, unsure she had read Knut's concern about Russell the same way she had.

"He's our age," Knut said quietly.

"Speak for yourself," Irina said. "But yeah, I know what you mean. That's got to be its own circle of hell for him."

"And for you," Knut said. "You are good friends, right?"

She had leaked out a few tears when she had come home the other night. But only a few. Russell's decline would go for a stretch and best to ration out the tears. "Is what it is."

She could feel his eyes on her, and she took a deep breath, afraid she'd open the waterworks right then and there. "Listen, you here about Miranda?"

"Maybe, a little. I went to see her cairn today, with Grace and the kids."

"Best view in the country, Miranda always said."

"It's a good one," Knut said. "I could see straight down to your place here."

"Spying on me, were you now?" The notion didn't bother her. She felt protected.

"No, but it got me to thinking that I was really surprised to see you the other day at Russell's. Surprised in a good way."

She reached up to touch her hair, but her hand touched her beater of a cowboy hat. He couldn't possibly mean—

"Knut, I'm too old to be this confused. Are you making a pass at me?"

"I'm kinda out of practice myself, but I think I am."

"We live hundreds of miles apart."

"For now."

"What does that mean?"

"I don't know. I'm just not wanting to figure out the future when I'm not sure about the next few minutes."

"Fair enough. You know I don't see eye to eye about your daughter's bunk 'n bacon operation?"

"I heard. I believe you two can work something out."

"Huh."

"So...yes."

"What are you agreeing to?"

"That cup of coffee you offered."

"I can do that." Surely, by then, she would have stopped her hands from fluttering like butterflies. The ones in her stomach were another matter.

BEFORE GRACE'S DAD left after lunch with Sadie back to the Jansson place, he hinted she might want to check into Nathan. And when she pressed him, he only said that Irina was naturally concerned since Amy had taken to Nathan.

"Maybe you could run a check on him or something."

"Dad, I'm a lawyer, not a private investigator."

"Still. You could do something through the firm, right?"

Grace bit her lip. "I'm on sabbatical. The terms of the sabbatical are that I don't conduct business on behalf of the firm."

"But this isn't on behalf—"

"Dad, just let it be."

"Everything all right, Grace? Anything you want to talk to me about?"

"Everything's fine, trust me. I already questioned Hawk about Nathan, and he's satisfied with him." Grace didn't think it wise to add that Hawk was using Nathan's dog as his chief character reference. "Listen, I will check into Nathan. And let you know."

He nodded, though his bright blue eyes—the same color as hers—regarded her for a moment longer. He held out his arms, and she stepped into them automatically. His arms weren't as thick and strong as they used to be, but he was still real and strong. Body and mind.

She began her research on Nathan the next Monday during the boys' visit. Over a snack of granola bars and milk, she asked, "Do you hang out with Nathan much?"

"We can't ever find him," Amos said. "He's with the cattle or gone somewhere."

"Him and Doxie Sue," Saul added. "His dog."

"If you see the dog, he's close by. They are both strays."

"Do you like him?"

Amos and Saul looked at each other. "I don't know because I don't know him," Amos said.

"We like you better," Saul said, as if the issue was a popularity contest.

She brought the boys home a half hour earlier than usual. Sure enough, when she pulled up, Doxie Sue barked from the doorstep. Seconds later, Nathan was coming out the door, Amy on his heels.

Nathan sidled off. *Oh no, you don't.* "Uh, Nathan, is it? Hawk asked me to give you a message." She looked over at Amy. "You okay with the kids?"

She was unloading the kids early, but this was important for Amy and the kids. Amy nodded, clearly not happy but resigned. When they had disappeared inside, Grace turned to Nathan, who was looking at the silent door.

"I don't have a message from Hawk," she said, "but I do have questions for you. Care to walk with me out of earshot? Say, over to the corrals?"

He stilled, except for his eyes, which darted about for an escape route. Where did he think he could go? He had no vehicle, not even a horse.

Doxie Sue decided for him. On her own, she began a leisurely trot toward the corrals. He followed, and she fell into step beside him. "How did you meet Amy?"

Nathan pulled his cowboy hat lower. It had bits of straw and grass on it and a hole in the front brim. It looked as if he had stolen the home for a family of mice. "She babysits for Hawk."

"That doesn't answer my question."

"Me and the dog slept in her barn one night, and before I could leave the next morning, she came upon us."

"Not your usual dance or bar or our-parents-are-friends kinda meet," Grace said.

"I told her I would go, but she asked if I wanted

work and said that her neighbor needed help. And then she brought me here."

They were at the horse corrals. Doxie Sue shimmied under the railing and began sniffing at dung in the corral. After apprising the new arrival in the pen, the mares returned to grazing.

Nathan faced her. His eyes were dark brown, a bit like Hawk's. "I work hard. I like it here."

"I bet you do, but no one knows you, Nathan. That's the problem."

"My boss doesn't mind."

"And you don't give him trouble, which is exactly what he doesn't need more of. Me, however, I made a career out of causing it."

He gave her a quick, hard look. She called him on it. "And I bet you're hoping I go back to causing trouble somewhere else."

He had the decency to flick a smile. "I honestly don't mean any harm. I'm grateful for the place to sleep and food and work."

Sometimes the direct question was the best. "What's your last name?"

"Smith."

Grace crossed her arms.

"It's true."

"Are you a suspect in a crime, Nathan It's-true-my-name-is-Smith?"

"Not really."

"Not really an answer."

"I stole some money from my stepdad, but not as much as he's taken from me."

"Fair enough. I'm going to assume from your current living situation that it wasn't enough to count."

He gave a single sharp nod.

The boy was unusual. She could imagine his appeal to Amy. Poor, troubled boy with a soft spot for animals. What was there not to like?

"I won't give you trouble," Grace said, "but if you ever feel like running off again, let us know. Maybe we can give you reason not to. Deal?"

He looked over to where Doxie Sue and the mare had lain down together. "Deal."

Grace waited until late in the evening, when Mateo might finally be putting his feet up, before calling him.

"Okay, what did I do wrong now?" Mateo's question was only half-joking. True, she gave him the gears, never for her sake she liked to think.

"Nothing yet. And that's why I'm calling you. So you don't do something that you think you have to do."

"Okay. I don't know how you got into my head, but go on."

"I don't want you to buy the rest of Hawk's breeding stock."

"Well, we agree there, because I don't really want to buy them. It's mostly to help him out."

"It won't help him."

"Hawk might argue that point. How do you know his mind so well?"

"Because I've known him for longer than you."

"I knew him for the past six years. When you weren't around."

"Yes, I know. I have faults—thanks for pointing them out—but not when it comes to Hawk. You just said that you are only doing it to help him out with money. Is that what it comes down to?"

"And it would expand my operation. It wouldn't be just me buying them up. I'm partners with Will Claverley, right?"

Grace knew Will from her childhood. A good guy, one who would do the right thing. So long as she could persuade Mateo, then he would persuade Will.

"Okay, I know why you want to buy the horses. Tell me why you don't."

"Because he's lost enough. The land, which is like losing his home, he's reduced his cattle herd—and then there's Eva and the money paid out to her."

"What happened there?" Grace said. "And yes, I'm snooping."

She heard the crack of a can open, and Mateo mutter a thanks and then—lovely—the distinct smooch of her sister's lips on Mateo. "I dunno, Grace. She always seemed like kind of shell-shocked. Quiet, and would start at every sound like a baby calf. A few times she came outside and kept looking up at the sky as if expecting something to fall on her. I guess she wasn't made for the ranch."

She didn't sound at all like Hawk's type. You had to be a special breed to make it as a rancher's wife in this country. Tough, independent and never lonely. Like all the Blackstone women. Love must have mushed his brain.

She touched her lips. What had happened to his brain when he kissed her?

"I don't want him to lose any more, either. How about I buy the horses instead?"

"They are not cheap."

"I've got money set aside."

"How much?"

He grunted when she named the figure. "That's good down payment, but I can give him a better offer."

"Withdraw it."

She could hear Mateo suck back on his drink. "I'm not going to withdraw my offer. You pitch yours to him and let him decide. What's so wrong with that?"

She was coming off as bossy and interfering. Exactly how she had treated her coworkers, and look how well that had worked out. "You're right," she said. "There's nothing wrong with Hawk looking at two offers instead of one."

"Whoa, did Grace Jansson just admit she's wrong about something?"

Grace let him crow for a bit more, before interrupting. "But—"

Mateo sighed. "Of course there's a *but*."

"But, like it or not, we're family. And it doesn't make sense for us to treat this like a business deal."

"You're saying that we should combine our money and present Hawk with a single offer?"

"Not exactly." Grace fumbled to explain her half-formed thoughts. "I mean, Mom considered the Blackstone Ranch like a second home, and I'm living on the land, too, and in their old house—" She stopped. Explaining to Hawk had gone easier. "I just think we're all family. Hawk included."

"Uh-huh. In your family scenario, what's Hawk to you?"

"I don't mean family family. I just mean family in a general sense."

"Uh-huh. Like how Haley and me are family?" In the background, Haley gave a whoop and then dissolved into giggles. She said something that had Mateo burst into laughter.

"Haley said that she sees Hawk as a brother-in-law. She wants to know if you view it the same way."

"What are…? I never… I don't mean… That's not right." Grace tried again. "I'm only concerned about coming to an arrangement that benefits us all."

She swore Mateo snorted beer out his nose. "I bet you are."

On principle, she liked to get in the last word, but he and Haley were impossible to reason with in their current state. She ended the call with them still laughing.

CHAPTER EIGHT

HAWK HAD HIS arm up a heifer's birthing canal when Grace came alongside the calving shed. Her flashlight cut across the heifer and him, and then slanted onto the straw-piled ground.

She shouldn't be here. It was tricky enough with heifers on their first calving, without strangers about.

"Can I help?" she whispered.

That was enough for the heifer to decide to lie down. He yanked out his arm in time, just as he was about to unhook the problem hoof. The calf was trying to come out front knees and head at the same time.

He hoped the glare he shot her way was answer enough. She winced and he could see her flashlight bob away, in the direction of the house. Why was she even here at nearly eleven on another night as chilly as their last night-time chat more than two weeks ago?

On his knees now, Hawk reached inside the heifer to continue his work. He hooked his hand on the hoof and eased it forward. There. The second front hoof followedmore easily. And just in time, as the heifer heaved herself back up. Now the calf was in position, the heifer seemed to have fresh energy, and Hawk had little to do except watch as the calf's head and front legs emerged. He broke the calf's landing. Now he just had to hope the heifer accepted the calf. Some heifers took to their calves right away, and a few never did.

A few were like Eva.

"Can I talk now?"

Hawk spun around. Grace had switched off the flashlight, her voice coming from the metal side of the shed. Clearly, what she had to say couldn't wait, in her mind. Still, getting calf and cow together was more important.

The heifer had turned to see her baby, but there wasn't any nosing or licks. She just stared. "She's yours," Hawk said. "Get on with it."

He took a handful of straw and rubbed the calf's nose and mouth to free it of the afterbirth. The calf started and shook its head. The heifer gave a soft moo and leaned forward. A good sign. Hawk stepped back to give her a chance to take over. The heifer sniffed the calf and then licked. Hawk blew out his breath. He'd let them alone for a short while and check back to make sure the newborn was suckling.

In the meantime, there was Grace to deal with.

He tilted his head around to the back of the shed. There was a stiff breeze Grace must have stood in the entire time. She definitely had something to say. Likely, the twins had got her going.

"Sorry I interrupted," Grace whispered. She edged closer to him, just like the night they had kissed. It was her style. She wore a puffed vest over a sweatshirt, and a toque. Her arms must be freezing. May the first had come with a frost warning.

"Is it the boys?" he said.

"What? No, they're fine. I mean, I assume. I haven't seen them since dropping them off. Why? Did something happen?"

Hawk closed his eyes briefly. "No, just trying to figure out why you tracked me down when it's going on for midnight. I assume that it's something that can't wait until daylight."

"Well, it could, but you're hard to track down. I mean, you are always out here, it seems."

The same complaint Eva had made, as if cows worked a neat nine-to-five schedule. "Still have forty-three left."

"How many have calved?"

"The other two hundred and thirty-seven."

"That's a lot."

"Some didn't make it." Seven calves and two cows.

"Oh. I'm sorry."

"The way of it. Look, I still have to see that

the heifer lets the calf feed before I can go inside and grab a few hours of sleep before I start again. What would you like?"

"Mateo and I talked—and he indicated that he's open to the family concept of investment when it comes to your breeding stock."

"Family concept of— English, please."

"It's like you said. We're a messy family, but still family."

She stood close enough for him to loop his arms around her waist, pull her against him, give her some of his warmth. "Grace, we kissed. We are not family."

"Okay, so that area of relations is still a little soft, but generally, when it comes to the ranch, we can all agree that it would be better if the horse breeding was kept here, right?"

"This 'we' include Mateo?"

"Yes. If you could keep the horses, he doesn't mind. Call and ask him."

Great, his ex-employee was bailing him out. "I'm not calling at this time of night. Anyway, I believe you. It's just that—that I need the cash, Grace."

"How much?"

When he named the sum, her eyes darted back and forth and then settled on his. "Okay. I can swing that."

"So now I'm your charity case, instead of Mateo's."

"It's not charity. I want a stake in the horses and boarding for my trail horses. That includes feed and grooming, too."

"Horses you don't have. You're just saying that to make me feel better."

"Do I look like someone in the business of making people feel better?"

Cold to the bone, tired to the bone and his pride ground to the bone, and yeah, she made him feel better. Or, maybe gave him reason to do better. "What kind of stake do you want?"

"What are you offering?"

"Half."

"Done."

She was within striking distance of a kiss again. From the other side of the back wall, he could hear a bleat from the calf. "I have to check on her," he said.

The calf was up on wobbly legs and the heifer was licking its flanks so hard that the calf stumbled a little. Ready for the next step. Hawk nudged the calf forward and hoped that the heifer put two and two together. The calf ducked its head and took hold of a teat. The heifer took a step forward. The calf lost hold, but it was persistent and tried again, and this time, the heifer let it suckle. Her head dipped. Good.

He headed for the house. Grace fell into step beside him.

"Well?"

"I'm not deciding anything at a quarter to mid-night."

"Are you at least interested?"

Yes, he was interested. Not in her money, but in her. In her being on this ranch, in his life, at his kitchen table, there at the end of the day. But he had long ago given up on that dream, and her return had ignited a spark of hope that he was for-ever trying to stamp out. And here she was again, on a chilly May night, throwing heat on it again.

And yeah, he wanted to keep the horses. She knew that, too. Was she doing this for his sake? Did she…care about him? Or was he just setting himself up for another heartbreak?

"I'm interested to know what we are, if you say we're not business partners and I say we're not family."

This time, her eyes shifted back and forth without settling on his. Fine. He didn't know the answer himself, only what he wanted it to be. "Good night, Grace. We'll talk again."

FRIDAY WAS ALWAYS a tricky day for childcare. Neither Grace nor Gemma had them, and Amy was still at school. Usually, Hawk shifted more of the workload to Nathan, while he focused on the boys.

But this Friday, there was the Pincher Creek horse sale. Big enough to draw in horses and buyers from both sides of the border. He had already decided not to attend. He couldn't afford any stock, and what stock he had, he'd promised to Mateo. Or Grace, should he take her offer.

Then, at the breakfast table with his dad, Nathan and the boys, he got a call from his Montana buyer. He wanted to know if Hawk was selling there, and when Hawk said no, he said come on down anyway and we can talk. Meaning there might be a future sale in the works. He couldn't miss this opportunity.

"I'll be there," he said, with no idea how to make that happen.

"That was Grant Sears," Hawk said to his dad. Russell frowned and nodded, and Hawk could tell he didn't recognize the name.

Nathan perked up. "From Montana?"

"Yeah, he's coming up to the Pincher Creek horse sale. You know him?"

"No," the boy said and then shrugged. "I mean, I know of him. Who owns a cutting horse and doesn't know him?"

Nathan dug into his porridge. He was the only person Hawk knew who could eat porridge by the bowlful, layered with whatever was on hand. Today it was frozen berries and walnuts. On other days, days when calving had gone hard the night before, he'd seen him shake instant coffee granules onto the steaming oatmeal. The kid was strange, but man, did he know animals.

"He expects me at the sale today but—" Hawk looked at the boys.

"We can come," Amos said.

"Me, too," Saul said, as if dividing the two of them was ever an option. It would be like using a knife to split a puddle.

"I can't bring you boys," Hawk said. "Too long to sit."

It would also signal to Grant that he didn't respect his time. He could make the boys mind for maybe a half hour, but that would hardly be enough time to catch up on where Grant had vacationed over the winter.

"Do you know if Amy's got school today?" The teachers might have booked a Friday off, as the joke went.

Nathan shook his head. "No, she has two exams today. I haven't seen her all week."

Right. And he couldn't ask Nathan. There were still a dozen cows expecting and two heifers any day now.

Grace. He could ask her. He could ask her outright as a favor or...

He tapped her name on his phone.

"Why are you calling me when I haven't finished my first coffee yet?"

He explained his situation, and before he could properly finish, she said, "Sure. I have guests checking in tomorrow, but tonight's guest canceled. It's meant to be. When do we leave?"

Had he really thought Grace would make it easy? "I meant the boys would stay here, and I would just go."

"But why do we have to miss out on the fun?"

"It won't be fun. A lot of standing around."

"Not my first rodeo, not my first horse sale. Besides which, I'm in the market for a few trail horses. You can be my expert eye."

Which meant bringing the horse trailer. "I don't know if they'll have riding horses there. It's for cutting horses."

"I'll take my chances. I'll pack up sandwiches and snacks for the road. Make sure the boys fill up their water bottles. They like lots of ice."

Grace beside him on the hour-and-a-bit drive and the boys behind in their seats. They would pile out and everyone would think they were one big, happy family. The real kind, not the mixed-up one Grace went on about.

And when she slipped into the truck passenger seat an hour later with the kids in the back, it felt so much like a family he had to grip the steering wheel to remind himself that it was all wishful thinking. Grace slipped waters into the cup holders in the truck console. "I packed a thermos of coffee, too."

"They have a concession stand at these things," he said.

"Which comes with lineups. This way, we eat

on our schedule. Tell me, what's the story on this buyer?"

Hawk threw the truck into gear and they rolled away, hauling the horse trailer. "His name is Grant Sears. A year before the boys came along, I visited the Sears ranch in Montana. Not overly large, but top-notch. The animals were treated like royalty, and the hands had no less than a dozen years of cowboying experience apiece. Then he came up and saw the Blackstone Ranch, and we did business together. He likes my mares, and I like his studs. He doesn't like the actual foaling end, but he's picky about what mares his stallions cover. Which is good for me. That means he asks for higher stud fees, but if I give him a stallion, then I will see that back easy, because he'll automatically buy it."

"Wouldn't it be more efficient for you to have the studs, too?"

"Eventually, yes. But this works for now."

"But you have to depend on a guy in Montana this way."

He might as well admit it. "I depend more than I like on too many people, Grace." He turned to her and added, "And you're at the top of my list."

She set her hand on his shoulder. Her touch constituted a violation of the distracted-driving law. "Good thing I'm so dependable."

Her voice had a teasing lilt, like when he'd carried her to her doorstep back in March. He couldn't leave fast enough then, but now... He offered his hand palm up and she slipped her hand from his shoulder into his waiting hold. He spoke softly so the boys couldn't hear. "You're my good thing, Grace."

"Would you rather," Amos said loudly from the back, "be a horse or a goat?"

"A horse," all three said together.

"Would you rather," Saul said, "live on a mountain or in a valley?"

They settled into the road game, and Grace eventually drew away her hand to pour coffee, but Hawk didn't mind. On the road with Grace and the boys, there was no other place he'd rather be.

"WHAT DO YOU THINK?" Grace said to Hawk, as she rubbed the neck of an eight-year-old roan through the railing of a selling pen. The boys were beside him.

"She's good. But fancy, for just a trail horse. I know the ranch she comes from. They sell cow horses and ropers."

"Out of my league, you're saying."

"I'm saying she'll sell for more than your needs."

Grace didn't care. She simply liked this horse. The moment Grace had started circulating among the pens, the mare had snickered at her and given her head a toss, as if to say. "Come over here. Let's talk."

"Could you use her, too?"

"That's not the point. You could get two decent riding horses for the price of her."

"But maybe I could expand to include guests at your ranch. On special days like when you're taking the cattle out to pasture or rounding them out."

"I'm not letting strangers around the cattle. That's a flat no."

He was right. Too dangerous. The mare turned her head to nuzzle Grace's hand. "Oh, come on, Hawk. I can't just let her go."

"She looks good to me," Amos said.

"Son," Hawk said. "You don't buy a horse because it looks good. You buy for how the horse will fit into the program. And she doesn't."

"What's your program?" Amos said to Grace.

Grace avoided Hawk's eye and said, "This horse."

Hawk shook his head. "Why am I even here?"

"There you are."

Grace turned to take in a rancher about her dad's age in a crisply pressed shirt and jeans, with a spotless hat and cowboy boots. He looked as if he was dressing for the part, except that the lines around his eyes and his thick hands proved that he was the real deal.

Hawk took the outstretched hand as if they were old friends. "Grant. Good to see you."

Grant nodded to Grace.

"This is my—" Hawk seemed stuck, and she couldn't blame him. It was easier to say what they were not. "This is Grace," Hawk said, "and my boys. Amos and Saul."

They exchanged greetings, after which Grace took her cue to leave with the boys. *Time to let the men talk,* Grace grumped to herself. She led the boys over to the picnic tables near the concession stand and fished out their sandwiches.

"I see our husbands found each other." Grace looked up to see a woman about the same age as Irina sit across from her. With her were two girls about the age of the boys. The girls assessed the boys. Saul offered each of them a cookie, leaving himself with none. Amos sighed and gave his brother one of his.

"What do you say?" the woman said to the girls.

"Thanks," they said to Saul.

"I'm Deb, Grant's wife. You must be Hawk's wife. I heard you had twin boys."

Amos shook his head. "This isn't our real mom. This is Grace."

Deb blushed and squeezed her eyes shut. "I'd apologize, if it weren't for the foot in my mouth."

"It's okay," Saul said. "She's like a real mom."

Deb and Grace exchanged quick smiles. The older woman reminded Grace a lot of her mother. The same easy humor, the same perceptive eye, the same long legs.

"This is Amos and Saul," Grace said. "My favorite five-year-olds in the whole world."

Amos rolled his eyes and Saul grinned. Deb introduced her grandkids as she drew out plastic food boxes and opened them up. The older of the two rolled grapes across the not-too-clean table surface. Before Grace could intervene, the boys snatched them and popped them into their mouths. To their credit, they thanked the girl before Grace had to prompt them. A little proud moment to share with Hawk later.

"I understand Hawk and Grant are business partners," Grace said.

"Unfortunately, yes. I'm trying to get Grant to retire, but it's harder work than ranching, I swear."

"Have a kid ready to step up?"

"Both my son and daughter, and their spouses. We couldn't ask for a better transition, but Grant can't seem to let it go. He told me on the way up that he's just here to take a look, and then we get here and he takes a checkbook out of the glove compartment."

"Do people still take checks?"

Deb sighed. "The auctioneers will take Grant's. He's a known quantity."

Unlike her. She was good for the money, but she'd never thought to ask about how the money was transferred. "So, he came with an eye to buying one?"

"Oh yeah. A stallion from the Cross C Ranch. It has lineage from Metallic Cat. He's quality, but he'll need training before he can go into the arena, and our ranch is not geared up for that right now."

But Mateo was. And no borders to cross to breed with Hawk's mares. And didn't Hawk say that getting his own stud was part of the plan?

Deb threw up her hands. "Of course, there's no talking Grant down once he gets something stuck in his head."

"Oh yeah?" Grace said distractedly as she thumbed through her contacts. "I'm sorry, but I have to make a call."

MUCH TO HAWK'S SURPRISE, Grace, with the boys, joined him ringside for the auction. Amos sat beside him, Grace was on the other side and Saul tucked tight on her left. From her bag, Grace produced a tablet for Amos and she gave her phone to Saul. They automatically opened up apps and got to playing, the noise muted.

She winked at Hawk. "Normally, they only get fifteen minutes when I'm catching up on emails, but today is a treat."

He couldn't begrudge her the break. "I've done that myself."

They weren't buyers, but they were sitting in the buyers' rows. "We should move back," Hawk said, "since we're not buying. Unless you still want that roan?"

She shook her head. "You're right. She's too expensive."

"You actually listened to me?"

She shot him a bright smile. "I listen more than you think. But can we stay? The boys are comfortable."

She was right, let sleeping dogs and quiet boys lie.

When the Cross C stallion was brought into the ring, immediate tension ran through the buyers. The horse was the highlight of the show, and for good reason. A bay, the stud circled the ring, his head high and with a light, athletic step that marked him as champion material. Grant had agreed earlier to give Hawk access to the horse. Maybe, one day down the road, he might be able to bid on a quality horse like this himself.

The bidding started. Grant Sears and another buyer Hawk didn't recognize raised their bidding cards. Hawk's head was half-turned toward them when from the corner of his eye, he saw the flick of a bidding card.

It was Grace. The auctioneer acknowledged her card, and raised the bid.

"What are you doing?"

"Shush." Grace waved her hand at him. "I'm trying to concentrate. These auctioneers really do talk fast."

"You can't do this."

"Why not?"

"I told Grant I wasn't bidding against him." Not in so many words, but he had assured his stud supplier that he was sticking to his mares.

"You're not. I am." She raised her card again.

Hawk risked turning in Grant's direction. The older rancher was shooting daggers at him. "Grace," he said through gritted teeth. "This is my reputation."

"I didn't know, okay? And this is in play. I need to get this right or I'll never hear the end of it from Mateo."

"Mateo is in on this?"

"As if I know the first thing about this. Mateo already knew about the sale and the horse. He wants to do the training, and yeah, maybe he'll breed down the road. This has nothing to do with you."

Amos had picked up that Grace was bidding on the horse in the ring, because when the auctioneer acknowledged Grace's card on the next round, he gave a whoop and fist pumped the air.

Hawk took hold of his arm. "Not a sound, boy."

Amos shrank down. Hawk himself felt like doing the same under Grant's glare. "You do this, and Grant won't allow his studs to cover my mares."

"I'm sure you can talk to Mateo about that."

She was determined and nothing would change her mind.

The third buyer had backed out, and now it was down to Grant and Grace. They were bidding ten grand above the top price Hawk had expected. The Cross C owners were leaning forward. How much money did Mateo and Grace have, anyway? Their pockets couldn't be as deep as Grant's. And he was rich in US, not Canadian, dollars.

Then, from the corner of his eye, he saw Deb touch Grant's arm and speak to him. When the raise came back to Grant, he shook his head and kept his card down, though from his stiff back, he didn't like it.

"Sold to Grace Jansson of Pavlic Ranch." She had used the name of Mateo's ranch then, salvaging his reputation somewhat, though he doubted Grant would see it as anything other than a partnership between Grace and the Blackstone Ranch.

Right after the auction, Grant marched straight for Hawk. "There's the law, and then there's the spirit of the law," he said bluntly.

Grace had gone to make payment, and the boys were stuck tight to his side at his order. Hawk couldn't agree more with Grant, but they had both assumed that Grace was with Hawk, while she, as always, had acted independently.

"I spoke for myself," Hawk said. "And she acted on her own."

"Did you know what she had planned?"

"If I deny it, would you believe me?"

The older manopened his mouth to counter when his wife came alongside him, two little girls trailing behind. "You know, Grant, not getting your way every day is not a bad thing. Aren't you on about the grandkids sharing?"

"With each other, not with others," Grant burst out.

Deb laughed. "The last thing we need is one more horse."

She acted as if buying the horse was a lark, which maybe for them, it was. She steered Grant away. Now he could focus on dealing with Grace and her new purchase.

THE TRIP BACK from Pincher Creek was as silent as Grace had expected. She had decided not to make a peep until Hawk spoke first, and he didn't seem too intent. Instead, he drove a good ten kilometers under the speed limit, no doubt in honor of the precious cargo.

Her new purchase rode quietly in the back, and she rode quietly in the front. For once, he could do the talking. Amos and Saul were nodding off in the back, their heads bobbing like unstrung puppets.

"You know where I'm going to keep him?" Hawk said suddenly, making her start.

"You've got lots of pens."

"None good for a stallion. Not of his quality. I can't have him getting in with the mares."

"What does it matter? Don't we want them breeding?"

"I don't know. That might be a question for Mateo. Or do you two have it all figured out?"

"Don't blame Mateo. He didn't know until I called him from the sale, but he had half thought of coming down himself. It became a kind of no-brainer for us."

"And neither of you cared to clue me in."

"Mateo did, but I wanted to surprise you."

"Surprise me with what? The cost of feed, a new pen, another animal to groom and ride?"

"I will pay for that, okay? Besides, the horse needs more training, so Mateo will probably take him, anyway. Hate me or not, this is the right thing for all concerned."

He finally turned his eyes from the road. "Wasn't it that kind of thinking that got you fired, Grace?" His voice was light, but with a thread of taunting.

"I got justice for my client."

"And lost your job and your reputation. Was it worth it?"

"No," she said, "it wasn't. But this is."

"This is just you turning me into one of your cases. You should go back to lawyering. You got what they call in the arena a lot of *try*."

"I've got more than try. I pulled it off."

Hawk shook his head, sighed. "That's exactly what I mean."

"Can you not just say 'Look, Grace, I don't entirely approve of your tactics today, but you got us a quality horse that I can build an outstanding future on. Thank you. And oh, thanks for taking care of the kids, too'?"

"So, you did buy it for me? Not for you and Mateo?"

"What difference does it make? You and Mateo have a partnership already."

"And you just got yourself a buy-in here, and I never agreed to any of it."

"Is that the problem? You wanted to be consulted?"

"Yes, Grace, yes. Didn't you say that I'm part of this big family you keep on about? I like to think that I can be open-minded. You don't have the same confidence in me."

He was right. Once again, she had bullied her way into his affairs, made assumptions about him and dragged them into a fight. She pressed her hands against her thighs. "I'm sorry, Hawk. I should have talked to you."

He didn't say anything, but she thought his grip on the wheel eased a bit. It gave her the courage to add, "I have a world of confidence in you, Hawk. That horse in the trailer behind us proves that. I believe in your breeding. I believe you know how to get the best out of horses.

I know it's in your blood. You are the one with no confidence."

His grip tightened right back up. "You're right. I don't. Not anymore. Not with you around, pointing out how I don't supervise the kids right, how I should get Dad treatment, which, by the way, is happening next month, and then I find out from Nathan that you've been asking him questions. You've been gone all my life and now—now you decide to show up and take over. What gives you the right?"

They were approaching the highest hill of the ride that lifted them to the top of the foothill overlooking their valley, and the horse adjusted to the sudden steep incline, his motions rippling through to the cab. While Hawk was attuned to the horse, Grace twisted in her seat to check on the boys. They were both out like a light, their heads against the headrests on their booster seats. Each had their fingers touching their dad's cowboy hat in the seat between them.

Today she had more than babysat. She had mothered them. Fed them, wiped their faces, reminded Saul to avoid biting on his loose tooth, consoled Amos over not having any loose teeth and kept her mom radar on at all times. They hadn't seemed to mind one bit. They'd followed along and taken her hand from time to time as if she really was their mom.

It was a role she had jumped into. And today,

she had jumped again into a partnership with Mateo on a horse. And she could concoct whatever excuse she wanted about good investments and interest in the kids, but at the heart of the matter, she had wanted to help the man sitting stony-faced beside her.

Because she cared about him, maybe even... No, she wasn't ready to go there yet.

But she was eroding Hawk's belief in himself. She had gone too far, and she didn't know how to stop herself.

They descended the long hill into their home valley in silence. At the turn into Blackstone Ranch, Hawk turned on the flashers and pulled the unit into Park. "I'm still waiting for an answer."

She turned in her seat to face him. "I don't have the right. I screwed up, Hawk, but that's what I do. I push, I interfere, I act before I think. I'm not the good thing you said I was. And you probably regret saying that now."

He reached across and took her hand. "I don't. A good thing isn't perfect. I'm still annoyed with you, but I have to admit I'm excited to drive this horse onto the Ranch. It's a big deal that would not have happened if you hadn't acted."

"So I'm forgiven?"

"I don't have a choice, because the alternative means you're not part of my life, and I couldn't forgive myself if I let that happen again."

His dark eyes had warmed and settled on her lips. Was he aiming to kiss her again? Last time had ended in a question she finally could answer. "I think I know who we are now, Hawk."

"Yeah?"

"A couple of good things."

He grinned and lifted up their hands, bringing hers to his lips. "I'll buy that," he said, "any day of the week."

CHAPTER NINE

HAWK WATCHED THROUGH the open barn doors as the boys ran ahead of his dad to Katzmobile's pen. Since the horse's arrival three days ago, his dad had come out in the mornings to feed the stallion a carrot or apple while the boys observed. The small ritual helped repair the rift between his dad and the boys after his explosion two weeks ago. The psychologist's appointment wasn't until next month in early June. Another month of keeping a close eye on him…and then what?

"You'll be run off your feet with your foal by then," Hawk said to Paintbrush. Her milk bag had swollen in the past few days. She was still a little early, but calendars were only a suggestion when it came to animals—and humans. The twins had been born six weeks early by an emergency caesarian. That threw Eva further into a depression that she had never fully recovered from.

Another layer of remorse. Grace wasn't the only one who was pushy. He could see himself in her.

No, he could see himself *with* her, but he would wait for her to make a move. He could tell from the forced cheer in her voice that she missed her job, and he had learned his lesson from Eva not to hope others could change for you. Or even that they should.

Impulsive, stubborn, headstrong, outspoken. That was Grace, and he didn't want her any other way, except experience had made him cautious. If she made a leap into a relationship with him, he had to make sure that she looked first, for both of their sakes. And the boys'.

Her move was slow in coming. He had dropped off the twins yesterday for their usual Wednesday, and she had transferred them immediately into her vehicle for a day at the Calgary Zoo. She had dropped them off with a wave, and a quick exit. Of course, she had a right to her own life.

His phone rang. Mateo. "Good time to talk?"

"The mare can wait until we're through before she foals, I guess."

"That close?"

"In a day or so, I'm thinking."

"A little early." Mateo's voice had lowered in concern. He had still been on the ranch when Paintbrush had lost her first foal And even though she had delivered a healthy prizewinner fifteen months later, every pregnancy was now considered high risk.

Hawk looked over at Katz. "The baby probably wants out to see Blackstone's latest arrival."

"How's he working out?" Mateo's voice held an edge of deliberate lightness.

"Getting fat on carrots and apples. Dad has taken a shine to him."

"Then, he must be worth it."

"Time will tell."

"I guess Katz was a bit of a surprise, from what I hear."

"Yep."

"I told Grace to run it by you, but you know her."

"I do."

"Haley and I talked, and if Katz is too much, we can trailer him up here. I'll start on his training after the crops are seeded. And we can work something out with the mares going forward. I already told Grace that."

"And what did she say?"

"You haven't talked to her?"

He wasn't about to get into the state of his relationship with anyone, especially with the man married to Grace's sister. Mateo must already feel pulled in more directions than hair in the wind. "Just want to know what I'm walking into."

"She actually agreed to let it be whatever you and I decided." Mateo laughed. "She must not be feeling well."

So, she had listened to him. It didn't make him entirely happy. What was wrong with him? He didn't want her interfering with his life, but when she withdrew, he moped.

"Are the other horses a combined offer, then? You and her, like with Katzmobile?"

Mateo made a clicking noise, like to a horse. He also made it when about to unload his opinion which he'd done now and again as Hawk's hired hand. "Listen, for all Grace and I give each other the gears, she has a point about all of us coming together on the horses. You take good care of the horses, and we'll help out with whatever costs you got coming your way."

"How about I tell you what those costs are first?"

But Mateo didn't hesitate when Hawk told him. "Much what I expected. I'll transfer money in the next day or two."

The boys had left Katz's pen and were coming toward him in the barn. His dad didn't seem to have noticed, his attention fixed on the Blackstone's latest equine acquisition. Or maybe his mind had wandered off completely, while he just stood there.

There was his family before him, and yet Mateo was calling him into a wider one. He couldn't refuse, for the sake of the boys. And for the sake of the hope of a future with Grace.

"Thanks, Mateo. It means a lot."

The next morning, Hawk found Paintbrush pacing in her stall, her tail up, ready to foal. He felt the same rush from a year ago, not as intense as when the twins were born, but up there.

An hour later, his dad came in and shook his head. "She's not right." Her flanks were heaving, and she was in a full sweat, yet no progress.

"I'll give her another hour."

His dad gave a single nod and left. At the end of the hour, Hawk whipped out his phone and called the vet.

"I'm already on my way," Ryan said.

"How—"

"Grace Jansson called. She had gotten a call from Russell and contacted me for him."

His dad couldn't remember what he ate for breakfast some days, but still knew horses.

Between Ryan and Hawk, they worked to turn the foal. "I am not," Ryan said, pushing on the mare's flanks, "going to let you lose another one."

And he kept his promise. The foal dropped a half hour later. A male who immediately fell under maternal licks and nuzzles.

"I'll wait until both are on their feet before I go," Ryan said. "Grace will like the news."

She would.

"Useful neighbor to have."

"She is that."

"I have to admit that going around the ranches, you get their opinions on all kinds of topics, and that B and B came up more than once."

"Let me guess. No one was in favor."

"Somebody paints the fence a different color and everyone notices. Wait, what have we here?"

The foal was struggling to his deer-like hooves, the mare neighing soft encouragement. And then, one step, two, three and he had reached milk. Hawk experienced another rush, a tingly one that had come a year ago. Another special one. A winner.

Hawk took a picture and attached it to a text to Grace. Thanks for making the call.

Now, if she would just call him.

LEAVING HER GUESTS to relax in the living room, Grace drove over that evening, and with Amos and Saul, tiptoed into the barn.

"Are you sure it's safe for us to go in?" Saul whispered to Grace.

"I'm sure." After all, Hawk himself had sent her a text invite to say she could take the boys along with her. He had gone on the quad to repair fence in the pasture. Next week, Amos said, they would move the cattle to pasture. Meaning into her quarter of land.

There was the little beauty, tucked tight against her mother's side. The mare tensed at the sight of their peering eyes, but she didn't rise.

"It's okay, Mama," Grace said. "We just want to see your new baby."

"Rest up," Amos added. "You'll be having another one."

The mare's ears twitched, as if she had different thoughts. "How do you know this?" Grace said.

"Dad said so, and he's always right about these things."

Whatever Hawk lacked in confidence, his son made up for by the bucket. "Does the baby have a name?"

"Grandpa does the naming," Amos said. "And he said he doesn't know."

"And you can't keep asking him, Amos. It upsets him." Saul looked up at her. "We are not to upset him."

"Then, we won't. We have loads of time yet."

Despite their chatter, the foal's head had grown heavy and now dipped to the ground. "Is he okay?" Saul whispered.

"Just sleeping. How about you show me this roping you are practicing?"

Amos was gone like a shot, and Saul followed, after looking up at Grace for her permission. "Shoo, I'm right behind you."

Grace was trying, and failing, not to laugh at the boys when Hawk returned on his quad. He parked in an open lean-to and came across to where they were taking turns roping a calf dummy.

"The deal is," she explained to Hawk, "that whoever gets it roped first gets one more cookie than the other."

"Cookies? I don't think I have any on hand."

Grace lowered her voice out of the boys' range. "You do ever since I brought a batch over."

"Huh. Still chocolate chip and oatmeal?"

She nodded.

"And still about as big as your face?"

"More like the boys' faces."

"Huh." Hawk turned and headed for the barn.

She could have told him the foal was fine, but she also understood the urge to see for himself. But he reappeared immediately with a rope, much longer than either of the boys'. He started swinging the loop, and the boys started hooting as if he was a big-time country star. And wowza, but he looked it. Grace aimed for nonchalance as she leaned against the fence.

"So," Hawk said to the boys, "I hear cookies are up for grabs."

"You can't do it as close," Amos complained. "That's not fair."

"Move it away then," Hawk said, loop still circling.

The boys each took an end of the calf dummy and carried it off, placing it only about twice the distance from where it originally was.

"Easiest cookie you'll ever earn," Grace said.

"You want to up the ante?"

"Yeah, I place the dummy."

She thought herself clever when she and the boys tucked it behind a fencing panel, with only the dummy's fire-log head visible. She and the boys stepped away.

Hawk adjusted his footing and let loose. The rope uncurled through the air and snagged the head, as if drawn there by a magnet. The boys gazed at their dad as if he walked on water. Grace clamped her jaw shut. She wasn't behaving much better.

And from his lazy grin, he had read her mind. "Would you like to see that again?"

To their loud agreement, Hawk got the rope whirling above him. Like the boys, she fixed her sights on the dummy, so when the rope sailed around her shoulders and tightened at her elbows, she was completely unprepared. The boys laughed and pointed.

"Oops," Hawk said. "I missed."

"Some males around here obviously don't value my cookies," Grace said, trying to recover her bargaining power. The rope tightened a little more. Not so snug she couldn't wiggle free if she tried. Which he must know. Yet she chose to remain tied to him. Which she hoped he also knew.

"I got her now," Hawk said. "You boys run in and load up your plates."

They didn't need to be told twice.

"And don't forget I get one more than you two," he called after them.

"We should not leave them alone," Grace said. "Can we stop with the immature games now?"

"Nathan's inside with Dad. We're good." Hawk held the rope with one hand and took out his phone from the other. "I don't know. This looks pretty good."

"Don't you dare take a picture." She stalked after him, and Hawk gathered up the slack in the rope. With a foot of rope between them, he slipped his phone into his hip case.

She could make out every hair on his stubble, the faint laugh lines at his dark eyes. The way those dark eyes focused entirely on her.

"All right," she said. "You got me where you want." Or where she wanted him. "Now what?"

Hawk leaned against the railing. "Oh, I don't know. Let's consider the possibilities."

Laughter rippled through his words. Just like the Hawk of old. He didn't look the least tired or depressed, like when they met months ago.

"I could hitch you to the railing and go in for some bedtime milk and cookies. And I might remember to come out before I go to bed myself."

"Hawk, don't make idle threats. I know you will come back."

"Because I'm a decent guy?"

"Because of all the screaming I'd do."

"I suppose I could gag you."

If he tried that, she'd bust free. "You mean like what we did to Haley when she was nine, and we were old enough to know better?"

"Mateo found her, I remember. And I thought

I was safe because I was leaving to come back here the next morning. But he must've walked the mile from his place to yours, got into my room and emptied a fresh cow pile into my backpack."

"Ew. How did he get away with that?"

"I wasn't there." Hawk's eyes settled intently on her. "Remember?"

She did. "You spent the night in my room. We talked the night away."

"Almost. I fell asleep on your bed and stole back before anyone got up. That's when I smelled what he'd done."

Grace made the connection. "And that's why we couldn't find your backpack. That's why we found it buried in the garden the next year. We thought Mateo and Haley had done it. But you had!"

"Only thing I could do is pretend he hadn't gotten back at me."

"Is this what—" she gestured at her strung-up arms "—this is about?"

"I have been feeling as if I'm at the wrong end of the rope this past while with you."

She looked across to where the stallion had his gaze pinned to the mares in the far pen. "You called it. I'm pushy, and I like getting my way."

"You like deciding what's good for people, and then going full bulldog into delivering it, whether or not they approve."

"I have a hard time going halfway on anything. You included."

"I've always wanted what's best for the ranch since the day I was born. Question is, what do you want, Grace?"

"I consider our families connected, and I want what's best for us all."

"But what's in it for you, Grace?"

"Because I live here now. I need to make a fresh start."

"Couldn't you just find another job as a lawyer? Start up your own business around here? Why the ranch, Grace?"

It wasn't the ranch she wanted, but him and the boys. Except they came with the ranch. He should know that better than anyone else. "There's already a law office a half hour away. The market's saturated."

"Word is he's about to retire. Interested in buying him out?"

A legal business with established clients. Close to The Home Place. And to him and the boys. Except, was he testing her? Seeing if she would choose him over her career, again. There was only one answer to that.

She loosened the knot and wriggled free from the rope, but didn't back away. "I'm interested in you, Hawk. In your boys. In us finding a way for a couple of good things to build a life together." It felt so good getting that out.

Hawk lifted her chin, his dark eyes searching hers. She met his scrutiny full-on. She had nothing to hide.

"I really want to believe you, Grace."

"You can."

He smiled, more of a sad twist of the lips. "I saw the way your eyes lit up about the law office. You might want me, Grace, but you also want your old life back. You know how to reconcile the two?"

He had her. "Isn't this an 'us' problem, Hawk?"

He shook his head. "You know how long I waited to kiss you?" He didn't wait for her answer. "Since I was sixteen. Four years. That morning when I woke you were beside me, asleep. I was tempted to try for a kiss. I didn't in case you woke up and punched me in the face. And two, I wanted you awake for it. But I waited. Because I always wanted you to know that you could trust me."

Four years—since she was fourteen?

"Point is, I've always wanted you, Grace. There was a time when I'd given up on that dream and pursued others, but now we've got another chance. Only, you can't change who you are in order to make someone happy. Eva and I twisted ourselves into pretzels to do that, and only made each other miserable. I'm not doing that again, and neither should you, Grace."

The evening chill stole up her spine. "So…

you're breaking up with me before we've even got together?"

He gathered up the rope in even loops. "No, Grace. I'm not going anywhere. I'll be here, whatever you decide to do. I'm only asking you to be sure. For everyone's sake."

"But I don't know what that is."

Unexpectedly, he grinned and tossed the looped rope over a railing post. He wrapped his arm over her shoulders. "Whaddaya know? Grace Jansson is thinking before doing. Let's celebrate with cookies and juice."

She leaned into his warmth. "Might as well. I don't have a better plan."

HAWK RUBBED WILDROSE'S neck two days later as they took the east exit out of the barn. "Happy Mother's Day." She had last foaled three years ago, and he had kept her open since then for working on the ranch. He'd already given Paintbrush an apple by way of recognition of the day. Across the wide Eden Valley, the early morning sun spread down the hills and across the valley floor, spreading up to the Blackstone Ranch.

He often came here to set his day right along with the rising sun, and today, he would start with the most awkward part. He took out his phone and called his ex-wife.

Eva answered on the sixth ring, her voice low and groggy.

"Sorry to wake you," he said, though calling at a more reasonable hour didn't always guarantee her wakefulness, either. She never kept a regular schedule.

"That's fine," she said. He could hear the rustle of sheets as she moved about. "Are the babies okay?"

Eva still called them that, even to their faces. Amos would scowl and Eva would look hurt. Neither understood the other.

"They're fine. Only, it's Mother's Day."

Eva moaned. "And what would you like me to do about that?"

"I could bring them into the city for a quick visit, I was thinking. We could go out for a burger or an ice cream. I could stay with them, if that makes it easier."

"Oh, Hawk. To what end? To remind them their mom is absent every other day of their lives?"

"You are still their mom. That hasn't changed."

"No, but I wish for all of our sakes, it would."

That cut. He would never forgive himself for pressuring her into a choice she didn't want. She had loved him, and he used her love to persuade her to give him a family. Because then they would all be happy. "There's no chance, then?"

"No chance of what? That some future Mother's Day I will be bright and cheery, or that someday I will wake up and have the strength to be a mother? I want that more than anything else, and I'm getting help now. I'm seeing a counsellor and on medication. But I don't know how long it will take."

"Okay," he said. "I'll let it go. You doing okay?"

"Meaning, do I have enough money? Yes, I'm doing fine. I even have a part-time job now, so you can cut back on your payments next month."

A reduction in payments required courts and lawyers, and then, what if she relapsed? "Let's see how things go, Eva."

"You're probably right. I could slip off the edge at any moment, right?"

She had read his mind, and maybe her own.

"Listen," she said, "the best thing you can do for our boys—for all of us—is find them a mother. A real mother. And get yourself the wife I couldn't be."

His gaze sailed over the slight ridge separating his place from The Home Place. "I want the best for you, too."

"I know," she said softly, but with a hint of strength he hadn't heard before, "but I am responsible for making that happen."

She had released him from any lingering guilt, and in the new sun, his thoughts flew to Grace.

Not that he would show up at her place today with the boys. She probably had her B and B guests, and anyway, Mother's Day couldn't be easy for her. Even for him, and he'd had time to say goodbye to his mother. He couldn't imagine a sudden death.

It had been hard enough to come upon Miranda's body like that.

But hadn't Grace shown up for him when he needed help with the boys? What kind of person let her spend the day alone, remembering her mother?

If he was interfering, Grace could set him straight. He opened his phone again as he took his shades out from his jacket pocket and slipped them on. "What are you up to today?"

"Making an omelet for three fine moms who are here on a retreat while their husbandsare holding down the fort. And then I'm off for a hike. Up the ridge."

Short for "going to see her mother." He wasn't far off.

"Care for some company? Me and the boys. Dad, too, if he's up to it. We could take the horses up."

She didn't hesitate. "Sure, come in a couple of hours."

All four were at her door on the dot.

As they threaded their way through the trees, Hawk's dad turned in his saddle to Grace behind him, "There were Mother's Days where it was snowing. You couldn't see from here to Hawk." Hawk had chosen the lead position to keep ahead of the boys. "Remember that, Hawk?"

Hawk couldn't, not because it hadn't happened, but that he had never pinned the May snows to a specific date. "I remember, Dad."

"Not like today," his dad affirmed.

Today differed completely from any other Mother's Day Hawk had ever experienced. And it all had to do with the rider at the back. Grace was mostly silent as they switchbacked their way up the ridge. Probably thinking about her mother.

Her first words when they dismounted at the top were for the boys. "What did you two not do last time you were up here with me?"

"We didn't go past the trail by ourselves," Saul said.

"And what are you going to do this time, Amos?"

"I will wait for an adult to be with me," Amos said. He didn't even push it. "Can we have snacks now?"

She tapped her lip. "Hmm, give me something for them."

Amos looked around and darted off farther back down the hill. Saul hung by Grace's side, his eye on the backpack where the snacks were. That wasn't like Saul. A deal was usually a deal with him, and he didn't argue the point.

Saul took Grace's hand and tugged on it. She bent her head to him, and like a dating pro, he swept in with a kiss on her cheek.

Grace snapped straight. "Saul! You little trick-ster." But she was grinning, big-time.

Saul eyed her backpack. "I gave you some-thing."

She looked across at Hawk, her face glowing under her hat. "No arguing that."

She gave up the goods, and Saul sat happily down with what turned out to be a full-size cup-cake.

"Amos is going to howl when he finds out all it took was a kiss," Hawk said as she joined him. His dad had walked farther along the ridge, a long way from the edge, thankfully.

"But I'll have one more pretty rock for my col-lection. Besides, I think he would bring me a sack of rocks, if it meant avoiding a kiss."

"That's him. I get one hug a day, at bedtime."

"You poor cowboy," Grace said. Her voice was teasing, but then she stepped close beside him. "How are you doing?"

She glanced at the cairn of Miranda by way of explanation.

"Shouldn't I be the one asking you that?"

"I was always so wrapped up in my sad-ness, and then in Dad's and Haley's, that I never thought about what it must have done to you to... find her."

She stood as close to him as the other night, her eyes soft on his. "I'm sorry," she said.

"It was...a long time ago."

"Thirteen years, but some things you don't forget."

He glanced over at his dad who was riding his horse down the ridge. He would follow along the trail there and cut back where the hill opened into a gully. It was a good Sunday riding trail. Saul with his cupcake was going off to Amos, no doubt to gloat over his brother.

"Do you want to see where… I found her?"

"Only if it's not too much."

Normally, it was, but if it could give Grace some peace, he could do it. He took her hand, and they stepped to the edge. Thirty feet below, a rocky ledge jutted out of the rock face. "There."

"I was on Wildflower. You remember her?"

"Wildrose's mom. The horse that could read minds."

"Yeah. She stayed put, and I lowered down on the rope. I kept hoping that maybe she was just unconscious, but…" He couldn't finish.

Grace squeezed his hand. "Thank you."

Now that he had started, he couldn't stop. "The horse was farther down. Still alive, but in a full sweat. Both legs broken. All I could think about was Dad's rule—don't let an animal suffer.

"I climbed up using a rope, took the rifle back down. The thing is, I forgot what the rifle shot would do to Wildflower. She galloped away, not far, but far enough to pull the rope out of reach. No cell service, so I ended up walking through brush in the gully nearly a whole mile before I could climb back out and to her.

"By then it was pitch-black, and it was enough to come back with the news. We couldn't do anything about Miranda until the next morning."

Realizing his hold on her hand had grown tight, he released it. "Sorry. I guess it wasn't that long ago in my memory."

He looked away to steady himself, but then Grace closed the space and wrapped her arms around his middle, pulled herself tight against him. He didn't question it, and dropped his arms around her.

Holy. He ached to have her this close to him for the rest of their lives, but he couldn't force it.

Amos was steaming up the hill, slowed only by a rock the size of his hat. Hawk nudged Grace to look. Amos dropped his offering at her feet. "Saul gave a kiss and Dad a hug, but I brought the biggest and the best. What do I get?"

Before Hawk could cut in with a sharp word about manners, Grace crouched down before him. "I will grant whatever food wish you want."

Amos scrunched up his face. "Anything?"

"Anything that is within my power to provide."

"Then, I want hotdogs and potato chips and cookies and root beer. At The Home Place."

"All right, I can manage that."

"Today?"

Grace twisted to look up at Hawk. "Can you spare him?"

Amos shook his head. "No, with Dad. And Grandpa and Saul. All of us together."

"That's a pretty big demand," Hawk said, giving Grace an out.

Amos pointed. "And that's a pretty big rock."

Grace grinned. "You know, Hawk, your boys have me all figured out. Kisses and pretty big rocks are all it takes to win me over."

She was, he liked to think, dropping a hint like a rock on his foot. The trouble was he didn't trust that she knew her own mind. Patience, he told himself, still aching for her.

CHAPTER TEN

GRACE WAS OF two minds when Hawk called her a week and a bit later to ask for her help on cattle-moving day. She wanted to help Hawk, but working cattle was not her thing, and all that went with it. Like needles and castration clippers. Like separating worried mamas from their calves. Like tagging calves. She had only ever attended one at the Jansson Ranch. After that, she had been more than happy to let Haley and her mother and whatever hired help or neighbors they rustled up do the dirty work, while she cooked the huge, postwork meal dull as that was.

"Sure," she said. "I can watch the boys and barbecue steaks."

"The boys are at school that day, much as Amos disagrees. And I'll have a roast in the smoker for most of the day. I need you at the corrals, helping out."

There was never a better time to tell him that she chose a clean office over manure-riddled corrals. "All right. When do you need me?"

Hawk was up on Wildrose when she returned from dropping the boys off at school. Both Amos and Saul had pouted the whole way there, neither pleased that once again, they had been excluded from important ranch work.

In the far pen, Katz was on high alert, his gaze fixed not on the mares this time, but on the herding of cattle, the shouts, the dogs skimming the ground to get behind a straggling cow and calf.

Everyone wanted in on the excitement, except for her. But she couldn't let Hawk down. She had told him her interest lay with him, and now was a chance to prove it.

At the corrals, he tossed her a pair of gloves. Gardening ones with grips on the palms. They looked a few years old. His mom's, she guessed. Angela said leather gloves made her hands sweat too much.

"Irina is up at the chutes, tagging. If you could help with the gate."

To stand in one spot suited her just fine. Even if it was next to her father's girlfriend. Her dad had not returned in the past month. Or at least, not to stay with her. Haley reported that he had gone off on some mysterious road trip to a mountain lodge a couple of weeks ago, at the same time Amy said her grandmom was gone for a few days. Grace was tempted to ask straight up, except she wasn't sure she was prepared for the answer.

Irina avoided eye contact herself, and maybe it

was to get away from her that Irina asked if she wanted to take over.

"I don't know how to do it."

"Your dad never showed you?"

"More that I never showed any interest."

"Yet here you are today."

Grace couldn't help but look over at Hawk working the cattle. Irina chuckled. "I see. Anything for a good cause."

"It's not that." Not that, entirely. "I hate hurting them."

"Do they look bothered?" The ones released back with their moms didn't look rattled. They flicked their newly tagged ears and stood calmly beside their moms.

"How about I watch for now?" As in forever.

"All right." But that didn't stop Irina from showing her how the female part and male part of the tag fit into the clamp, and then how to grab hold of the ear about a third of the way or so from the headand one, two—snap. Done.

It couldn't be any worse than what Nathan was doing with the castration snips. Irina's phone rang. "It's Amy," she said and handed Grace the clamp. "Over to you."

"But—" She looked around. Nathan had finished with the calf and the day help was guiding the into the chute.

She fed in a tag and leaned over. "He owes

me big," she muttered. One, two and— The calf jerked as she hit home.

She sent it loose and pulled up the lever to let the next one in. Irina was still on her phone, and Grace refilled the clamp. When Irina got off, she waved to Hawk. They talked over the fence, and Irina left.

What?

"Her bull got into the neighbors'," Hawk said. "She has to deal with that."

"But you can't leave me here."

"Why not?"

"Because—" If she explained herself, he would give her an out, and she would have failed him. She gave her clamp a menacing chomp, chomp. "Fine. I always wanted to add bovine ear piercing to my list of skills."

After a twenty-minute noon break for everyone to bolt down sandwiches and pickles, Hawk and his crew resumed on fresh horses. Back at the chutes, Russell joined Grace at the gate after she said she needed someone there to back her up. It was also a way to monitor him.

"You want me to go get the boys?" Grace asked Hawk as she released the last calf.

Hawk shook his head. "Their aunt agreed to bring them out later. Along with her kids. I said we'd feed them."

Right, the roast.

Hawk tilted his head to her. "I was thinking baked potatoes."

She got his point. "I'm on it."

"Dad can show you where everything is."

Russell led her into the basement that served as an enormous storage room. Boxes were stacked to the ceiling and three deep. Tables, chairs, the old family couch patterned with a dusky brown-orange design of watermills now seated old lamps, a wall clock and pictures of horses. Curtains draped over more boxes and a TV. "This is from when I moved in a while back," Russell said. "Angela and I had a house in town. Hawk sold off some of the stuff and the rest we put down here."

A year of unpacked boxes? Then again, Hawk had worked himself to the bone to build a future. He didn't have the time to sort out old things. She spotted a set of boxes marked Clothes and then a name behind them. Dad, Mom, Hawk.

"Those go back twenty, thirty years ago. Angela thought they were too old and out of style for the secondhand shop, and she couldn't bring herself around to chucking them. Go without once, and you think twice about throwing things out."

He shrugged. "But I suppose you can't let things take up space." He snorted. "I guess that applies to people as well."

"Oh, Russell—"

He waved a hand. "Don't mind me. This way to the food."

But Grace hung back at the boxes. What if she used the clothes to make a memory quilt for Russell? The boys had started to piece together a few squares for their Grandpa's quilt, but they could incorporate new fabrics.

"Russell? Do you mind if I take the boxes? I'm always looking for quilting fabric."

He shrugged. "Have at 'er. I'll tell Angela you took them." He frowned at the boxes, as if seeing them for the first time.

"The food?" she prompted.

He waved his hand in annoyance. "Where it always is."

"Sure, of course, how about—"

"I'm going back upstairs." He pushed past her, she heard the floor creak above her as he crossed over and down the hallway to what she presumed was his bedroom. She quickly gathered up vegetables, and hurried back to the kitchen. She stepped into the hallway and from behind a bedroom door, she could hear Russell muttering.

Good, he was okay. Well, as okay as he could be.

From the kitchen window, she watched the dogs, hired hands on their horses and Hawk, now back on Wildrose, after an afternoon of rest, release the herd into the pasture that overlapped onto the home quarter, her quarter. It was a quiet enough event. The cows and calves were allowed to choose their pace, the horses and dogs only there to make sure that they headed in the right direction. The veteran lead cows set the pace, their young calves forced to keep up or get left behind.

This was the part she would have liked. Riding alongside Hawk, talking about the day, going over any problems. Not making supper. Gone from taking on city hall to figuring out how to get lumps out of gravy.

She caught herself. This resentment was what Hawk had warned her about. He was right. She did miss the law shop, and she had driven past the Diamond Valley law office, curious.

But she couldn't bear to give up on Hawk and the boys. Yes, there were working moms and wives the world over, but maintaining a law business was not a nine-to-five job. There were no half measures, just like with ranching. All-in or nothing.

She was taking potatoes from the oven when the crew filed in and used the mudroom to wash up. Hawk appeared with the boys, and Gemma with her girls, and directed them to the house bathroom. He turned on the tap at the kitchen sink and applied dish soap.

"Looks good, Grace. How can I help?"

"We need more chairs, and is there any way to make that table bigger or set up another one?"

"On it."

As if setting up a meal for a crew was an everyday occurrence for them, Hawk and Grace had the table set, serving bowls filled and roast carved in under fifteen minutes. Everyone took a seat. Except for Russell.

Hawk came from the hallway and gave a single headshake to Grace. Right, she would make a plate up later. "Time to eat."

Nathan reached for the bowl of carrots but pulled back when no one else moved a muscle. Grace glanced over at Hawk, who suddenly looked as if he had to shoot a horse.

"I guess we'll say grace first."

Grace remembered that it had always been Angela who said it at every meal. She had never seemed like the religious type, considering the language she got into when moving cattle. But saying grace was an ironclad rule, and the crew here knew that.

Hawk couldn't seem to push it out. Russell must have said it last year, and now he didn't even trust himself to sit at the table.

"Oh," Grace said. "I guess that's my cue." She bowed her head. "Heavenly Father." It was Angela's standard greeting. And then she pretty much ad-libbed the rest, covering gratitude for the weather, help and food. She finished with Angela's piece. "Bless this food to our bodies in the name of Jesus Christ. Amen."

"Amen," Nathan said ahead of the others, his hand already on its way back to the carrot bowl.

"Thanks," Hawk said into Grace's ear. "It threw me there for a bit."

"You're welcome," she whispered back. "I'm used to thinking on my feet."

"Grace, can you cut my meat?" Amos, beside her, asked.

"Say please," Saul said.

She cut both of the boys' meat, and when she turned back, Hawk was talking to one of the hired hands about where he would next be cowboying, as if the fact she was sitting in the spot Angela had always taken, occupying the traditional seat of the rancher's wife, taking on the role of grace-sayer, meant nothing.

Except, as she settled back into her seat, Hawk hooked his foot under her ankle and left it there for the rest of the meal, as if it was a natural thing to do. She didn't pull away, but when the cowboy turned to her and asked what she did when she wasn't at the corrals, she said the first thing that came to mind.

"I'm a lawyer."

She snuck a peek at Hawk, but he chewed on his meat as if she hadn't said anything surprising.

IT WAS DOXIE SUE skimming underneath the corral fence to Katz that alerted Hawk to Nathan's proximity. He turned as the boy joined him at the railing.

"Your dog going to give him trouble?"

"Hardly. She's just making her rounds for the night." Less for her to patrol since turning the cattle out to pasture two days ago.

"I always wondered. Back in November when you first came, I'd see you two walking around here."

Nathan looked to where Doxie Sue was drinking from Katz's horse trough. Ears perked, Katz snorted. Doxie Sue gave a dog grin and trotted off. "Yeah. It was hard to stay in one place then. I'm pretty settled now."

"Amy helping with that?" Hawk had promised Irina that he would keep tabs on the boy when Amy was over. *It's in both our interests that we make sure that boy can be trusted.* Other than coming from south of the border, where half the ranchers in this part of the country could trace their ancestry from, there didn't seem to be anything to fuss over. He got up, did his job and called it a night. He had to be the most boring young adult Hawk had ever met.

Another shy smile. "She is. That's, uh, why I wanted to talk to you. She has her graduation next Friday, and she has asked me if I would go with her. And I, uh, said yes."

Hawk smiled. At his graduation, Grace had been his date Though they had not called it that, because hey, they were just friends. But she had played her part and come in a tight, knee-length dress. Blue to match his shirt. Their moms had been talking, apparently. A sheath, Grace called it. He produced a wrist corsage, only because his mom had instructed him to do so. A pale white carnation will do, she said. But the florist had easily upsold him into a white rose with little, foamy flowers and a blue ribbon. Grace's blue eyes had widened at the sight. It was the best purchase in all his eighteen years, and she gave him the best night of his life.

"Have you got a suit?"

"I ordered one online. I used your dad's credit card. I paid him back right away but the thing is…as you know…" Nathan scratched his head "I was hoping…and I'm willing to work it off…"

"Spit it out."

"I was wondering if I could borrow your truck."

"You can't take Amy's?"

"She and her grandmother share it, and her grandmother wants to drive back right after the grad dinner, but we were hoping to meet up with her friends later. And then I would want to drive her back. Especially if there's drinking."

"And if you are drinking?"

"I don't drink. I don't do drugs." There was such bitter vehemence in his voice that Hawk believed him.

"And I take it you have a license?"

"I do."

Hawk hesitated. As much as he wanted to show confidence in Nathan, the truck was his means of transportation for the kids. He could point Nathan to his dad's beater pickup, but that wasn't the vehicle to arrive in for a date. "All right, then. Only condition is that I keep Doxie Sue as collateral."

Nathan stiffened and then relaxed as he registered Hawk's grin. "Agreed. This is the one time she's not coming with me."

The boy walked away with a definite lift in his step, drawing out his phone as he did. No doubt to text Amy the good news.

Oh, to be young and in love.

He remembered that time well, thinking that Grace might come to love him, too. It hadn't worked out for him then. Now Grace bowed her head and asked for the blessing, as all Blackstone females had done, and showed up to do a job he knew she didn't like. For him.

Yet she still called herself a lawyer.

He would have to wait to see how this all turned out.

"Do you want chocolate chip oatmeal cookies with your tea?"

"You could persuade me," Grace's former boss answered from the comfort of the leather recliner in The Home Place. George had called her three days after the cattle move to ask if she had an opening on Monday. He wanted to do something quick and special for Hilda. It turned out that it was their forty-third anniversary, and he had been on the cusp of forgetting. Grace hoped that his call meant that he had also forgiven her.

Hilda, in the chair beside him, smoothed her hand over one of Grace's quilts. A seascape one, inspired by her trip to the Caribbean a few years ago, back when she had more money than she knew what to do with.

"This is beautiful," Hilda said. "Who knew you had such talent?"

"I wouldn't call it talent," Grace said, "It's just sewing small squares into big squares until you have something you can sleep under or hang on a wall."

"You sound like Hilda here," George said. "She's always downplaying everything she's ever done. You know she sang in a band when I met her?"

"Oh, George. That was so long ago."

"And not so long ago. They fronted for the Stampeders. You know them?"

Grace vaguely recalled that the Stampeders was a Canadian rock 'n roll band from the '70s still played on classic rock stations. "Wow, that's a big deal." She set a plate of cookies on the coffee table, and George immediately helped himself.

Hilda tapped her husband's knee. "She's just

being polite. Our little band didn't make a recording. Everyone left for ordinary lives. I exchange texts with the lead guitarist about our kids and grandkids." Hilda smiled at Grace. "Raising a family became our business. Not like you."

George studied his cookie, as if counting the chocolate chips. Had he not told his wife about firing her?

"Your sabbatical looks good on you," Hilda said. "Will you still want to come back to the firm?"

George gave another hitch in his chair. "I certainly hope so. We would certainly miss your other talents at the office."

Okay, what was he trying to tell her? She would cover for him, if only to avoid a marital dispute.

"George was reluctant to bring you on at first. Since we are all family friends. But I told him to try you, and it has all worked out."

George had lied to Hilda to not disappoint her. He shot Grace a sheepish look.

"That it has," Grace said. "I am where I'm supposed to be."

Hilda frowned, and Grace hastily added, "For now. This has been a great experience."

"Well, I know the firm has missed your experience there. Right, George?"

"Just on one or two accounts," George said. "There have been some personality conflicts."

Rachelle.

Hilda laughed. "That's putting it mildly. Not everyone has your level of persistence, Grace, to get the job done."

It was only when Hilda left to pack that George leaned in to explain. "Rachelle took on a land-use litigation soon after you left. You remember that fellow with the housing development?"

At Grace's nod, George continued. "He had a friend with a similar problem. Stymied with housing permits and paperwork. He said that you were the one to talk to. Except you weren't there, and Rachelle was. She said she had worked side by side with you, that she knew the case inside and out... Anyway, I didn't question her too much. I am not in the office every day. But it turns out that wasn't the case?"

He raised a questioning eyebrow, and Grace said, "Rachelle helped out here and there, but really it was Keira who knew the most. Rachelle is bright, though. What's the trouble?"

George sighed. "The city brought documents to discovery that set her back. Hilda thinks I should ask you to assist Rachelle, but she doesn't know the history between you two."

"She also seems to be unaware of my employment status at the firm."

George gave another hitch in his chair. "She and your dad. Your dad called me back when it all...happened. He asked me point-blank if it was true that you were on a sabbatical or if you had done something to get yourself fired over."

"And like Hilda, you couldn't stand to disappoint him. I don't blame you. I did the same. Nobody in my family knows. Except for Hawk."

"Hawk?"

"My neighbor. Who Dad bought the land from. We're family friends. I guess you two never met."

"Different circles. So, he's not really quite family, then?"

"What? No, did I—" Grace replayed what she had told George, who, ever the legal wit, had not missed her slight slip. "I suppose I think of him as family." Despite his claims to the contrary.

"I'd like to offer you your position back."

Back. Back to everything that she had lost. Four months ago, this would have been a dream come true. But now— "Why the change of heart, George?"

George swept cookie crumbs from his lap, eyes down. "I—I may have overreacted. I lost a good lawyer that day. I should have considered other options, first."

"A suspension?"

"I hear from Keira you're calling it a sabbatical. That's a better term."

Grace looked out the front window to the hill that separated her place from Hawk's. His cows grazed there now, calves in tow. "It kinda feels like one. I think you gave me the break I couldn't see to give myself."

"And now you can come back. I know you sold your place, but Hilda and I have a little downtown apartment that's vacant right now. You could stay there—rent free—for the first few months until you find something of your own."

"But—I live here now."

George frowned. "But this can't be all that you had planned for your life. It's so different. And there's no need to get rid of it. You always planned to have both places, didn't you?"

"Yes, but that was before—" Before Hawk.

Grace gestured to the rise over which Hawk's spread lay. "I invested in the neighboring ranch. In horses, actually. Hawk breeds them. I committed to helping him see it through." She had done nothing of the sort. Why was she trying to talk herself out of the position she had once been ashamed to lose?

Man, she hated pacing the edge like this. She had never lacked direction as she did now.

"Can you see yourself coming in part-time, maybe until Christmas, and then we'll revisit it? By then, this case will have worked its way through the system."

"If Rachelle and I haven't clawed each other to death before then."

"She'll be fine. I talked to her."

"I can't imagine that went well."

"Her pride is secondary to the firm's reputation. My problem with you was internal."

"Look, I behaved horribly, George. I'm still pretty bullheaded. Ask Hawk."

"That man's name has come up an awful lot. How come you never mentioned him before?"

"Oh well, I moved to the city, we grew apart, he married and had kids."

"He's married," George said.

"Not anymore."

"So it is what I'm thinking."

"No—I mean—not entirely—"

A truck came up the lane. Hawk. What was he doing here? He drove past the kitchen window and parked. Grace turned to George. "Ah well, speak of the devil, here he is."

From where she sat, she couldn't see him approach the back door. George could, and his eyebrows shot up. "Well now, another piece of evidence to support my case."

Graceleaned in her seat to see what her old boss was talking about. There was Hawk, holding something unexpected.

Flowers.

THE LAST TIME Hawk had bought flowers was for Eva on the birth of the twins. She had stared at the colorful profusion and then had turned her head away, as if the sight offended her.

In the grocery store this morning, he had decided to give it another try. He couldn't say he wanted Grace to stay and then not demonstrate his sincerity. A different, smaller bouquet and for a different woman. But the reaction was only slightly more favorable.

Grace opened the door, her smile wavering. "Hawk. This is a surprise." She looked at the orange lilies as if they were weeds.

"I happened to be in the neighborhood." He extended the flowers to her. "I thought I'd give you more than my thanks for helping with the cattle."

She took them, glancing over her shoulder. "You shouldn't have."

"I know. I was halfway here before I remembered the boys broke your vase." He held up a pair of flowered rubber boots. "I had put these behind the back seat way back when. Castoffs from Gemma's youngest daughter. Four sizes too big and the wrong colors but I figured they'd do in a pinch for the boys. Eventually. In the meanwhile…" He'd never passed along so much useless information in his life.

She took the boots and the flowers. "Uh, come on in. I have guests."

He had seen the Lexus parked outside, but by then, he was already up the lane and he couldn't exactly retreat without it looking bad. The door was only half-open; she wanted him to skedaddle.

He edged backward. "Sorry to—"

"So, this is Hawk." An older voice boomed behind Grace.

Grace's eyelids fluttered, and she gave a faint gasp. Hawk had never seen her this uncomfortable since Miranda had caught her in a lie about her whereabouts with Hawk when she was thirteen. She opened the door wider to show a man about his dad's age. He wore pressed jeans and a crisp dress shirt and canvas boat shoes. He looked like a man deliberately dressing to appear casual.

"Hawk, I'd like you to meet George Davis. George, this is my neighbor, Hawk Blackstone."

George and Hawk shook hands. The guest seemed genuinely pleased to see him, so why was Grace so anxious for him to go?

"I'll put these in water," she said.

A woman came down the stairs, looking as pressed and neat in a pale yellow outfit as George did. "We need to get moving if we're going to keep our tee-off time." Her bright eyes skimmed Hawk.

"This is Hawk Blackstone, Grace's neighbor and investment partner," George said. "Hawk, my wife and minder, Hilda."

He smiled at Hilda, and wondered why Grace had shared their business arrangement with a guest.

Grace must have guessed he'd be thinking that. She had filled the boots with water and was arranging the daisies and lilies. She had her face down over a lily when she said, "George is my old boss from Calgary."

The man who had fired her. Yet now they were all smiles and looking cozy.

"What's this about 'old boss'?" Hilda said. "As in *former*?"

Grace's hands fluttered over the flowers. "I misspoke. This sabbatical thing throws me off."

George sighed. "Don't cover for me, Grace. A man's got to fight his own battles." He turned to his wife. "I fired Grace back in February. It was a mistake, and I just asked her to come back."

Hilda set her hands on her well-pressed hips. "Confessing to a lie is no way to celebrate forty-three years of marriage. At least, you did the right thing and brought her back."

Grace was leaving. Again.

She waved a bit of leafy branch. "I haven't agreed to go back."

He had a chance. The flowers were perfect timing.

"Anyway, you let me know soon what you'd like to do," George said and turned to Hilda. "Ready to go?"

"The suitcases are just inside the bedroom door," Hilda said and turned to Hawk. "Good choice of flowers. Showy but not imposing. Roses are a tad obvious."

"I was thinking that myself," Hawk said. "I don't want her assuming that I'm easy."

"Our Grace always did like a challenge," Hilda said. "I suppose it's a battle now between you and my husband to see who wins her devotion."

George returned, an overnight case in each hand.

"Let me see you off," Grace said, and to him, "There's coffee on the go. I'll be back."

Hawk watched the protracted farewell from the wide kitchen window, coffee in hand. He texted Nathan to say that he would be at least another half hour. He had a few questions that needed answering.

Grace's step on the old porch steps was heavy and she leaned against the door after closing it behind her. "For the record, he only made the offer about five minutes before you pulled in. I expected this to be an apology stay on my part, a kind of rebuilding of the bridge that I had blown up. I didn't realize that my old boss had other intentions when he accepted my invitation."

"Okay."

"And don't ask me what I'm going to do, because I don't know what to do."

She slumped at the dining table. He rose and poured her a coffee. Black.

"Thanks," she said when he set the cup in front of her. "And thanks for the flowers. You really didn't have to."

"I know," he said. "That's why I got them."

"Huh." Gone was the flirty Grace he'd carried to the door when she'd injured her ankle. Her renewed job offer had shoved aside any romantic notions about him she might have had.

"I take it he wants you to go back to work sooner than later."

"Yeah, I guess Rachelle—you remember her?—she has made a mess out of an account. The client is a friend to the guy whose case ended up getting me fired. Essentially, I'd be going in to clean up her mess. And after, to carry on."

Her voice was carefully neutral.

Stay. Stay here with me. He looked over at the flowers. One of the lilies had a broken petal, jutting out from the others.

"What do you think I should do?"

"I think," he said, "you should do whatever makes you happy."

Grace rubbed her thumbs over the stenciled letters on her cup, Quilters Patch Things Up. "Being a lawyer made me happy. Doing this—" she gestured around "—makes me happy, too." She paused. "Our—arrangement makes me happy. But if I go back to the city, something has to give."

Something and somebody. Hawk looked out the window of his childhood home, to the hills beyond. His cattle were there now, grazing. This year's calves tucked close or, as he watched, bucking in the late May sun. He kept his eyes on them as he said, "I'm the last one to tell you what to do. Look, you made a great life for yourself somewhere else. And this is my life. I'm not moving from here unless the bank drags me off."

She gave a thin smile. "You're not changing."

"That's who I am, Grace. I stay because land stays. You—" he stopped and looked up to the ridge. "You're the wind, Grace."

"Loud and noisy and creator of migraines?"

"Strong enough to knock a man flat." He could admit to that easy enough. It was the next part that choked him up. "And always on the move."

She twisted her mouth, not disagreeing. He reached across the table and pulled one of her hands into his. "I'm not going anywhere, Grace. That wasn't so great for us fifteen years ago. I'm hoping that this time, it's different."

He wished she would tell him she knew her mind, and that she was with him all the way. Kiss him hard and tell him don't be a fool. Instead, she nodded. "Okay."

Walking back to the truck, he turned to see her at the flowers, trying to tuck the lily petal back into place. *Leave it, Grace. What's done is done.*

CHAPTER ELEVEN

WHEN RACHELLE'S CALL came through, Grace was tempted to ignore it. "But that's not our style, is it?" she said to the cairn.

Grace had come to visit her mom to clear her mind. The wind ripping straight over the snow-tipped Rockies was trying its best as it whipped Grace's hair about, but not even the wind could wipe away an miraculously clear cell signal.

"Where are you?" Rachelle asked in response to Grace's greeting. "It sounds as if you are in a wind tunnel."

"Wait a minute." Grace walked down off the ridge and ducked behind the shelter of the boulder. "Better?"

"Better."

Grace braced herself against the hard rock curve and waited.

"How's your handsome cowboy doing?"

Really well without her, it would seem. It had only been a week to the day since their conversation, and he had acted neighborly and no more when he dropped off and picked up the boys. Saul had wondered about the flowers and Grace had only said that a friend had given them to her. It was true, and less messy.

"He's doing fine."

"Has he made a move yet?"

"Rachelle, is it really my love life that you are calling about?"

"It's just small talk."

Hawk's cattle were resting in the afternoon sun. The calves were gathered here and there in groups, one or two cows watching over the nursery while the others grazed farther afield. "Rachelle, we have never done small talk. We raced each other to the water cooler, rather than talk around it."

She laughed, and it sounded genuine. "We had so much fun together, Grace. You've got to admit it."

"It was, until it wasn't." It had taken months out here—and, as her gaze traveled to Hawk's place, other dreams—for her to realize it. "Neither of us are team players, Rachelle. First, I paid for it, and now you are."

"George didn't pull any punches when it came to my recent…performance review."

"He only gave me the big picture, but I know you—I know us—enough to fill in the details."

"I will tell you anything you want. You're still covered under the nondisclosure, right?"

"Yes. I don't think George would have said anything if I wasn't. But don't start. You know me well enough that if you go into the details, I will want to help, and George said he would give me time to decide."

"If we had time, I wouldn't be calling you."

Rachelle probably was under the gun. "Look, Grace, I'm out of my depth here. And the worse thing is I don't care. I mean, I understand that money and livelihoods are involved, and for that reason, I should care. But there's no justice involved."

Grace could have easily argued the point. Families and the pursuit of a fair living were crucial, but she got Rachelle's point. "You miss criminal law."

A cow walked her slow, ponderous way over to the nursery and nosed a calf.

"Yeah, I do. Except there was no money in it. I have just finished paying off my student loans. On to car loans and a line of credit."

Grace's father had supported her through her university training. Some of that money had come from her mother's life insurance. Another reason for the guilt over her firing.

But now she could sweep away her guilt. She could return as the glorious rescuer.

A calf stood, gave a shake and moved to the cow's full bag, its ears waggling, the yellow tag visible. Likely one she had put in. She had forged a life with Hawk, and he was as open to her as the land before her.

She couldn't give that up.

"I'll tell you what, Rachelle. I will consult with you on this case. You still lead it, but send me the files on the firm's email and I will review it. Okay?"

"I'd rather you took the lead, Grace, even though it kills me to say it. I'm willing that I pay you as the lead, too."

But that would mean driving to Calgary almost daily, that would mean giving up her days with Amos and Saul, that would mean telling Hawk that she had chosen career over him.

"You asked me how it was going with my cowboy? The reason I'm saying no to you, Rachelle, is because of that cowboy. Do you understand?"

"I've seen him. I understand the attraction."

"It's more than looks." She didn't realize until she had come back exactly how good-looking Hawk Blackstone was. She had always just seen him as Hawk.

"I know. Like I said, I've met him. If that's all you can do, I accept your offer. Be prepared for your inbox to start groaning under the weight of my emails."

Be prepared, Grace thought as the call ended, *to get even busier.* She rose and climbed to the ridge, and the wind slapped her across the face. Always on the move, Hawk had said of her.

"Not this time," she said. "I'm staying put."

Because she wanted it all—Hawk, the boys, her B and B—and her old career. Maybe if she only practiced as a consultant that would satisfy her lawyering itch. Maybe she didn't have to make a choice.

First, she had to prove that it could be done, before telling Hawk.

GRACE CAME EARLY the next Day, Wednesday, to pick up the boys so Hawk could get on the road to make the psychologist appointment in Calgary. His dad assumed she was coming, too, and grew agitated when Hawk explained Grace was staying behind with the boys. Grace switched gears. The boys were going on another road trip.

He wished she was sitting beside him now in the office, instead of in the waiting room with his dad and the boys. The psychologist had run the tests and was giving Hawk the depressing results.

"Early-stage dementia, you say?" He looked out the psychologist's fourth floor view of another brick building much like this one.

"Well into that stage."

"Can he remain at home?"

"For now, yes. But if it gets so he's not safe for your family or himself, then you will need to make plans. You will know."

Hawk didn't think he would know. He felt as

confused and uncertain as his dad must feel on a daily basis.

"He had an outburst about a month ago with the boys. Yelled at them. Which is not like him. And then he's having trouble naming a foal. Last week, he left a gate open." Doxie Sue's barking had alerted them to Katz head bunting the fence alongside the mares. That could've gone sideways fast.

The psychologist frowned. "I, well, I don't know about that…"

Of course, he wouldn't know. None of the literature on dementia addressed unusual behavior for a rancher.

"But anything that he wouldn't normally do is of concern. It's a question of severity and frequency." He paused. "Other than you, does he have any other supports?"

The woman out there with him right now. But how long would that be for? She'd mentioned her plan to assist Rachelle on the case, but that she wasn't taking the lead.

Hawk didn't believe Grace would take the back seat for long.

And even if she stayed, she hadn't signed up for long-term care of a dementia patient.

"I'm it. What can I do to help him?"

"I thought I could bring him in now and we could chat together. I would like to leave you with a plan."

The psychologist left to invite his dad in, and Hawk could hear his dad's voice rise in response. What now? His dad had seemed calm enough when he had rejoined them in the waiting room after the testing. Grace had sat beside him, their arms touching from elbow to wrist, even as his dad had stared blankly down at the gray floor planking. The boys had amused themselves with a box of Legos. No doubt a little freaked out by the formal setting, they had behaved better than he could have hoped.

The receptionist offered to watch over the boys, while Grace came in with his dad. The psychologist placed extra chairs and Grace took the middle one, Hawk and his dad on either side.

The psychologist pulled the pin fast on his diagnosis. His father nodded and then kept nodding as if his neck was on a spring.

Grace took a notepad from her bag. A large, leather one, the kind she might use in a courtroom. "I have a few questions, if you don't mind."

The psychologist invited Grace, in her casual clothing and braided hair, to ask away.

"What is the best diet for Russell?"

"I'm not sure. I'm not a nutritionist, but I would think a healthy diet is preferable."

Grace, Hawk noted, didn't even bother writing that obvious reply down.

"What therapies are available for the slowdown or reversal of the condition?"

"There are therapies to provide comfort and support. Studies are always underway, of course."

Meaning, there was nothing.

"Russell lives in the Foothills County. What services are there to support him?"

"I'm more familiar with Calgary and area."

"Diamond Valley, the town near us, is part of the Calgary metropolitan region."

"Is it? I didn't know."

Grace waited, her pen hovering above her still empty pad. Russell had stopped with the head-bobbing and now sat with his head lowered.

"I could check a few sources. I suggest you contact the health services there."

"You are part of the health services, and I am contacting you." She spoke with a kind of chummy humor. For his own sake, the psychologist had better not be fooled.

"I'll email you suggestions."

"Lovely." Grace took out a business card from her bag, her lawyer card. As she wrote her email on the back of it, she said, "I'm especially interested in any training caregivers can receive."

The psychologist looked at Hawk. "For you?"

"And me," Grace said.

Both Hawk and Russell turned to her. Grace didn't seem to register their surprise, but handed the psychologist her card. "Ignore the email on the front. That's my business email. The one on the back is my personal one."

She continued with a whole battery of questions about home care that Hawk would never have thought to ask. He might have taken it as a sign of her commitment to his father and him, but with her return to the firm, he was now just confused.

Between his dad and the boys, he didn't get a quiet moment with her for the rest of the outing. He resorted to a text, while the boys had a post-supper play in their corral.

Thanks for your offer to help with Dad going forward. But don't feel obliged. I know you are busy already.

She replied within minutes. I'd rather be busy in body than in my brain.

He couldn't exactly refuse her help, when his own dad stood to benefit. Okay.

How's your dad?

In his room with his photo albums. Your dad gave him the idea. He went outside and came back in and said he'd taken a picture of Picasso. I thought it was just him but then he tells me that's what he's calling the foal.

I like it!

Hawk's thumbs hovered over the phone. He wished she was here. Typing took too long and stalled his brain.

I like it, too.

After a quick wave of typing dots, How are you doing?

He couldn't unload on her when she was already doing so much. Okay.

Liar. Even knowing it was coming, it had to hurt. I feel all shaky inside.

The woman who had streamed out questions felt shaky? He typed, Maybe a little down.

Do you want me to come over?

Yes! If you want.

She pulled in ten minutes after he had put the boys to bed, and out under the early June evening, they leaned together on the railing and talked as he had not talked to anyone since he had roped her. They talked so long that finally he slipped his hand into hers and asked, "Tell me the truth about that night with Emmett. Why didn't you give us a chance?"

SHE LOOKED DOWN at their joined hands, her chest squeezed at how good it felt. "I was scared," she whispered. She shot him a quick look, and he raised his eyebrows. "I know, the great Grace Jansson scared, right?"

"Was it something I said?"

"It was the look on your face. Shocked, as if I kicked you in the gut."

"That's what it felt like."

"Kissing Emmett was easy," she said. "But you and me, if we had kissed, I don't think I would have had the strength to break away and become a lawyer."

"I wasn't against you becoming a lawyer. I was against you doing it without me in the picture."

"But, Hawk, back then, you filled so much of my picture." He frowned, as if he still didn't get it. She lifted her hand, palm to him, about six inches from his face. "You were like that hand. I had a hard time seeing around it."

Hawk took her raised hand and kissed her palm. She automatically closed her hand, as if capturing it. He smiled softly. "You know, you could have said something to that effect. I might not have felt like pile driving Emmett every time I drove past the bar."

"We didn't date, if that's what you're asking. I left for university the next week." Now it was Hawk's turn to tell the truth. "Then again, you could have visited." *You need to move on. He has.* Her mother's words.

"I might have, if your mom hadn't passed."

"How so?"

"It was two years after you had gone to university. An eternity back then. She was saddling up to go on a ride. That ride."

He swallowed. "She said that she'd asked you to come out, but you had 'made up a stupid excuse with a hole the size of a barn door,' she said."

"I didn't want to see you. It would have felt too…awkward."

"Miranda—your mom thought as much, but I remember her swinging into the saddle. 'But don't worry, Hawk, she'll come around. You'll see.'"

They both looked up to where a rim of orange light still lit the ridgeline. "Last words she said to me," Hawk whispered.

The ridge blurred and Grace blinked hard. "But after that, it seemed the hope kind of passed with her. You didn't comeback this way, and I made up my mind that I had better grow up and get on with living."

"Last time I talked to Mom, she told me I needed to get over it, because you had. I assumed she meant you were dating."

"I did date, but more because it was something to do on a Saturday night and all the girls I went with felt the same way. It didn't mean I was over you. But after your mom passed, and we still didn't see each other, I kinda put a foot down on my feelings. And now I guess I'm lifting my feet again."

"And here I am, with your boot prints all over me."

He grinned, and that gave her the courage to bring up another touchy topic. "I have to say it, Hawk. Eva doesn't seem like a natural choice."

"You mean she isn't a bit like you?"

"Yeah, I guess so."

"She isn't. I knew it wouldn't be easy, but that somehow made it more worthwhile. Opposites attract, and all that. I figured I could succeed with her where I'd failed you. But I couldn't pull her out of her depression, and with you, it's the opposite problem. I can't hold you back from taking on life, not that I care to. But it leaves us in an impossible situation."

He looked so defeated. She tugged on his shirt and he turned from his contemplation of the ridge to her. "Hey, if you couldn't make me stay, then no one could have."

His eyes warmed. "You're just saying that to make me feel better."

"If the truth makes you feel better, then yeah."

His arm slipped around her waist and she let him pull her close. It was an awkward embrace against his side instead of his front. "You still scared?" he whispered.

Her insides quivered and she couldn't draw a full breath. His lips were right there. She shifted to face him, sliding her hands over the plane of his hard back.

"To death," she said, and then kissed him anyway.

CHAPTER TWELVE

THEY HAD BROKE apart at Doxie Sue's barking as she and Nathan crossed over to the bunkhouse. Hawk had reluctantly let Grace go home. He'd expected to pick up from where they left off, after the weekend, when her guests left, but on Sunday, Mateo called and wondered if he and Haley could stop by during their two-day stayover with Grace. They were also trailering down two mares Mateo had picked up at a horse sale, suitable for Grace's trail riding.

Mateo pulled in two days later while Hawk was still wrangling the boys into pajamas.

All bets were off now that Ma-ta-to had landed. He hefted them both into his arms and mock-carried them to his truck. "I'm taking you back with me. I need help back on my ranch."

"You have to ask Grace first," Saul told him, limbs dangling. "She's expecting us at her place nine o'clock tomorrow morning."

Mateo turned to Hawk who was watching from the porch steps. "Your dad doesn't have a say?"

"Yes," Amos said, "but they team parent us."

"First," Hawk said, "I've heard of that term. Grace teach you it?" Did she really think of herself as a kind of parent to his children?

"She said it's for kids with two parents in different places."

Which should describe him and Eva. Hawk didn't know whether to be worried or hopeful at their distinction.

"I had better hold off taking you two back then," Mateo said. "At least, until tomorrow."

"Can we show him Picasso?" Saul turned to his dad.

"And then straight to bed."

"I will," Saul said and poked his brother who gave a reluctant commitment.

Mateo brought them back to set them on the porch steps. "Get socks and boots on. And then we'll go."

"Leave your pajamas on," Hawk added.

Mateo shot him a grin as they pounded back inside. "Team parenting, eh? We had that down when they were still in diapers."

Hawk lifted his hands, palms up. "No argument here. You couldn't wait until tomorrow to see the horses, I take it?"

Mateo leaned on the porch railing. "I came to get the inside scoop on you and Grace. You have no idea how much fun Haley and I are having at her expense."

"What is Grace telling you?" Long talks at fences aside, it might be useful to get some insight into her thinking.

"As if she would show her hand," Mateo said. "I was hoping you could give us leverage."

"Now, how would that help me?"

"Ah, so you are after her?"

The boys shot through the door. "C'mon, Mateo," Amos said. "He's out in the barn."

From there on in, it was all about horses, which suited Hawk fine. He didn't much want to talk about Grace yet, not with everything so new between them and it just as likely to blow away like the dandelion puffs at his feet.

The next day, Mateo arrived bright and early to saddle Katzmobile. The horse was sold as a performance cutter, but a horse behaved differently for every rider. As a treat, Hawk let the boys watch, which meant foregoing their usual Wednesday with Grace.

"I've been expecting your call," Grace said to him. "I've got Jonah and baby Jakob here to be an auntie to. Just don't let Mateo talk you into anything."

From behind her, Hawk heard Haley call out, "Like having a third kid. Trust me."

"Is there something that I need to know?" Grace said, clearly to her sister. "Sorry, Hawk, I got to go. Have fun."

Mateo certainly intended to. He had already

enlisted the boys' limited help to drag out the pulley system for training cutting horses. "You don't know what this is?" he was asking Amos. "You set it up along a fence and then you run a flag up and down it. The flag is the cow. And the horse chases it."

"A game for horses?" Saul said.

"And the rider. Here let's get this up." Mateo glanced up at Hawk. "This is fun, isn't it?"

He and Grace had kissed again, he had a promising foal in the pasture nearby, his boys were happy and healthy, and his ex-employee and now partner had come to share the day with him. Hawk lifted the other end of the pulley system. "I've had worse."

The pulley erected, Mateo saddled Katz, inspecting the stallion as he went. "Grace had a good idea, I admit."

"It was, though I can't say I liked the way she went about it."

Mateo eased the halter on Katz, adjusting the bit. "That's Grace. She barrels to the end, like a stampeding bull, because she thinks she knows best. It will get her in trouble one of these days."

Grace still must have not told her family about her firing…or her rehiring. Hawk pretended interest in the boys as they dared each other to balance on the railing with no hands.

Mateo interpreted his silence differently. "Of course, you hold a different opinion of her."

"I agree with you, and I hold a different opinion."

Mateo led Katz toward the corral. Hawk walking alongside. "She's not Eva," Mateo said quietly. "She won't come apart on you."

I was scared, Hawk. I was scared that I wouldn't have the strength to leave.

She was Grace, and that was trouble enough.

Katz and Mateo were a dream team on the flag. His dad came out and leaned beside Hawk on the railing, while Hawk was inside on the pulley. "I might be losing my mind, but I still know beauty in motion when I see it."

"He rides the tiger well," Hawk said and his dad pushed up his hat.

"You remember me saying that?"

"The day you came back with the first horse."

"I thought so," his dad muttered. "I thought I said that."

"Hold," Mateo called and Hawk let up on the pulley. Mateo came over. "We don't need to train so much as we just need to get acquainted. I can still get him in a few shows this season. I could even try for the Stampede. Only a month away but they might have a cancelation."

"What will you do with Risky B?"

"Show them both. The better they place, the more we can ask by way of stud fees, and Risky B's foals."

"You talk to Grace about this?"

"Can you see her saying no?"

He couldn't. "I say we show them as much as we can in the summer, then next April, Katz can cover Risky B. If she takes, then we can still show her over the summer and she can foal here. You can board Katz over the winter."

"Sounds good," Mateo said. "I'll start making calls to get them in shows."

Hawk saw a hiccup to their plan. "Two horses, twice the hauling."

"You bring Katz, and I'll bring Risky B."

"That'll mean days away from the boys and—" He broke off, aware of his dad next to him.

"And me," his dad said. "I can't be left alone with the boys anymore. I might leave them on the stove and boil them dry."

Mateo looked uncertainly between the two of them. Hawk wasn't sure how much Grace or Knut had divulged to Mateo and Haley, and out of respect for his father, he wasn't about to get into it. "I will need a few days heads-up, at least." Hawk said. "To arrange for care."

"Grace will help out," Mateo said. "She already does."

"The shows are usually on the weekend, Grace's busy time."

"If she sees it as you being part of the business she invested in, I'm sure she can be persuaded."

Persuaded into playing rancher's wife. "I don't like putting her in that position."

Mateo swung off the saddle. "You know you can't talk her into doing anything she doesn't already want to do."

"You should ask family first," his dad said.

"I was thinking the same thing," Hawk said. "There are people around on the weekend at Gemma's. The boys will have more fun."

His dad frowned. "I meant Grace."

Gemma had done more than enough when it came to her nephews. But to ask Grace… He wasn't so much afraid that she would refuse him, but that she would accept it out of obligation, and resent him for it later. That, he couldn't live with.

"I'll think on it," he said.

HOW INFURIATING.

Grace had invited Hawk and the boys for supper together at The Home Place, where Mateo dropped plans for how they were going to show both Katz and Risky B this summer. Her dad and Sadie had also come, but they had gone over to Irina's. Grace felt as if she had a teenage son ditching his family for his girlfriend.

"Who will cover for the boys?" Grace said.

The two men both dropped their gazes to their steaks and baked potatoes. "We haven't got that one figured out yet," Hawk muttered.

Grace raised her hands and pointed her index fingers to her head. "I'm sitting right here." She turned to Amos and Saul, Saul to her right and

Amos across the table at Hawk's right. "Your dad might need to be away a few days here and there over the summer. You okay to stay with me?"

Amos turned to Hawk. "Why can't we come with you?"

"Amos, you're brilliant," Grace said. "We can come along." It would be fun. They could take in the show. Do a little bit of touristy stuff, depending on where the shows took them, camp or grab a motel…

"What about your guests?"

Shoot, she had forgotten all about them. She was booked pretty well solid throughout the summer. Word had got around, thanks to her contacts in the legal community. "Let's not get the cart before the horse," she said. "We don't even have any show dates confirmed yet."

"Worse comes to worse, the boys can come up north to stay with me," Haley said.

"But that'll make you busy when you're already taking care of the outside work," Hawk said.

"Brock will handle that," Haley said.

"Which is to say," Grace said to Hawk, " we've got you covered. What I don't understand is why you wouldn't think we did."

"You got a lot on the go, Grace," Hawk said quietly. "And I don't want the boys and me making your life harder."

If by *hard*, he meant more purposeful, then

the Blackstone males were the hardest thing she had ever undertaken. All four of them. "Busy isn't harder."

"So it's all settled then?" Mateo said.

"It's all settled," Grace said before Hawk could answer, but Mateo turned to Hawk.

"I guess we have a plan," Hawk affirmed. He sounded more resigned than supportive.

She had promised Rachelle to forward case recommendations by that night, but she wasn't in the head space for legalese until she had sorted things out with Hawk.

The boys were camping overnight in the living room with Sadie, so Grace suggested they try out the trail mares while checking the cattle. Hawk shrugged his agreement but led the way to the pen where she kept the horses. He ran a hand over their backs and legs.

"Don't you trust Mateo's judgment?"

"Don't you make sure your tires are inflated before driving?" Hawk said as he laid the saddle pads on their backs.

"Who does that?"

Hawk gave her a dry look and reached for one of the two saddles in the shelter he had renovated when he'd fixed the fence two months ago in April. Mateo had brought down all the gear. When not annoying, her brother-in-law was thoughtful and generous, way more than she was to him. Which was annoying. "They come with names?"

Grace pulled down the second saddle, the weight yanking at her shoulders. "The one with the white patch on the haunch is Sage, and the bay is Willow."

"Good names." Hawk swung his saddle onto Willow's back and took hers. "You remember how to cinch a saddle?"

Not really, it turned out. One more thing to get on top of.

The sun was still high enough, light cutting up the west side of the pasture and daytime heat warming her bare arms and her denim jeans. Hawk turned in his saddle. "You want to get the horses into a trot?"

She would have been up for a gallop but changed her mind as she bounced, trying to catch the rhythm of the horse's gait. How had she gone full gallop when they were kids?

They slowed the horses as they began the climb across to the upper pasture behind The Home Place. Already her place looked tiny, the vehicles pulled up outside like toys. She thought she could see two figures moving to Irina's truck.

"Do you think that's Dad and Irina?"

"I'd say so," Hawk said without looking. He must have already spotted them.

"Great," Grace said, suddenly feeling grumpy. "Another wedding in the offing."

"But they've only been seeing each other for a couple of months."

"Dad proposed to Mom after only two months. I'm expecting the hammer to fall any day now."

"You don't like her?"

"I don't know her. Other than she kicked up a fuss about a dozen extra vehicles on the road a week and abandoned me to stapling the ears of innocent calves. Dad comes down to see Mom, and hooks up with Mom's friend. What's going on there?"

"I think it's called closure, Grace."

Something gentle and sad in his voice turned her to him. His lips moved as he counted calves. She'd not interrupt that process.

"There's probably more down by the creek," he said at last, and started that way, expecting her to follow.

He had always assumed she would follow and had always assumed right. She glanced down the hill one more time. Her dad was getting into the passenger seat beside Irina.

She urged her horse after Hawk.

Calves were bunched along the sides of the gulch, the majority along this side but a few peppy ones had crossed the shallow creek. Most were curled into tight, hair-covered rocks. A few stood quiet, staring curiously at the intruders.

Hawk's lips were moving again, and Grace

decided to join the game. When he looked done, she called over to him. "I got fifty-seven."

Hawk pointed across the creek. "Did you get the two under the bush there?"

She hadn't. "I guess that's why you're the cowboy. Is that all of them?"

He nodded.

"Then, you ready to tell me what's really bothering you? Why don't you want me involved in the business?"

"It's not that. It's—you, Grace."

Grace sucked in her breath. Word for word what George had said. "I'm pushy, right?"

"You said you cared about my family and I believe it. And you care about the ranch itself. And maybe about me."

"Correct on all points."

"The thing is, I care, too. You are more than this ranch, Grace."

"By *more*, you mean my career as a lawyer?"

"If you didn't want to do the work, you wouldn't have signed up for it."

He was right. Hadn't the sweaty work with the calves, in part, spurred her to take on the assignment? She'd come out tonight to give him support, to let him know that he could count on her. And he had pinpointed that she couldn't be held to one place. Nor did she want to.

"Look, you might be overthinking this. I'm ready to take care of the twins, because that's important work, too. I like to think that we are good for each other."

"You jumped on it, forgetting your own business here. And you might need to make some choices."

"What are you saying, exactly?"

"I guess what I'm saying is that you can't do it all, Grace. You're one person trying to be a bunch of people, someone for everyone. This whole B and B thing is for your mother, and she's been more than ten years gone. That's not fair to you."

She hadn't seen it that way. She had seen it as making peace. "But I can handle it all. I'll prove it to you."

"You will cut yourself into smaller and smaller pieces, and the thing is—"

He shifted in his saddle and looked away.

No way. "Finish what you start, Hawk Blackstone."

He slowly turned to her. "Because, Grace Jansson, I don't want pieces of you. I want all of you. That was the deal."

His dark eyes on her were like just before they kissed. Except he was a full body length from her and didn't look inclined to close the distance. "That's asking for a lot."

"I'm not asking, Grace. I don't want you to give up your life for me. I want you to feel that your life is with me. And the boys. You don't have to be everything to everyone, least of all to me."

She looked down and picked a brush bristle from the mane. She would give the mare a good brushing later. After her report to Rachelle, before babysitting the boys, between her B and B guests. She could handle this. "I don't," she whispered, "know how to be anything else."

His silence was reply enough. He was immovable. Like the land. And like the wind, she was going every which way, set to blow things apart. Including herself, if she wasn't careful.

GRACE SENT HER email to Rachelle and peered at the computer clock. 11:49 p.m. "Eleven minutes to get to bed before I turn into a pumpkin." Her mom used that line on her and Haley when they were kids. They'd never believed her, but neither did they risk it.

She sent a text to Natalia. Brock's wife felt more like a friend than family, probably because they both had lives outside the family. Natalia was a partner in a growing franchise business, had a family of two young ones, a cowboy husband and also traveled internationally. She had it all, and never had to choose.

Hey, Nats. I was hoping to get your input on something both personal and professional. Could we chat tomorrow?

Grace set down her phone, not expecting a reply at this late hour. Her phone buzzed.

Now is good for me.

"Aren't you supposed to be sleeping?" Grace said when Natalia picked up.

"I could say the same to you."

"I had work to do, and with Dad and Haley and the kids here, now's when I have peace and quiet."

Natalia laughed. "And thank you for taking them. I'm using the time to catch up on some paperwork. What's up?"

Grace didn't know how much to divulge to Natalia. She couldn't ask Natalia not to tell Brock, though she didn't think it would go beyond him. At any rate, she would have to risk it. She really couldn't figure this out on her own.

"I guess I want to know… Well, how do you juggle everything in your life?"

"*Juggle* being the operative word. I have gotten so used to dropping the ball, especially since Daniel was born. If it wasn't for Brock, I would have walked off the deep end long ago."

"You're saying that behind every successful woman, there's a good man." Was Hawk that man for her? It wasn't as if he had offered to help her out. Then again, she helped him because he was already going flat-out.

"In my case, oh yeah. Things coming hard and fast for you?"

"You could say that. The B and B is booked through most of the summer, I have the Blackstone boys twice a week, I bought shares in a horse, and the sabbatical with the firm is a wash because they need me to take on a case as a favor. And oh yeah, I promised the boys we'd make a quilt for their grandpa's birthday in November."

"Wow," Natalia said. "At least, you don't have to worry about taking care of a husband."

Grace hesitated for too long, because Natalia immediately pounced. "Or are the rumors about you and Hawk true?"

"We're not married or engaged." They had not even gone on a single date. That was just how busy they both were.

"Then, what are you?"

Two kisses and a few long conversations, that's what they were. "Not quite together and not quite apart."

"Ah, I remember those days with Brock. A bit…tense, then?"

"He's left it up to me to decide if we should be together. I know he still has hang-ups from his ex, so he doesn't want to push me into a relationship I'm nervous about, but he seems to think that I need to give up my career if we are to make it work out here with him and the family. And I don't want to have to make that decision. I want everything, like you."

"I have everything I want, but I still had to give up what I thought I needed. And as a guideline, everything connected to Brock and family I have kept my greedy hands on."

"Yeah, but Hawk is not like your guy. He can travel with you, and Mateo picks up the slack. I'm the one helping Hawk out. There's no time for just the two of us."

"So why did you go on sabbatical, Grace? It sounds as if you needed a break from the work. Could it be that in your heart of hearts you were already looking for a change?"

"I… Well, uh, maybe so. Maybe you're right."

"But then you took on more work. So, were you really?"

Maybe it was the late hour but Grace couldn't think fast enough. "The thing is that I was fired from the firm for good reason, and now I'm trying to make up for my past mistakes."

"Oh wow. That's the first I heard of that. I'm sorry."

"It's the first time anyone has heard about it except for Hawk."

"I won't tell, either. Besides, it sounds as if it might come out in the wash, anyway, if they came to you for help."

"That's what I'm hoping, but it's not a one-time deal on my boss's part, and tonight, well, I kinda lost track of time working the case. That speaks tons about how I still love law, right? I don't know what to do."

"Yeah, that's a tough one."

"Natalia, you're supposed to tell me what to do," Grace said.

"And if I knew, I'd tell you. But past midnight, I'll put it this way— Where do you want to be at the end of the day?"

With Hawk. With the boys. With an interesting case to tackle tomorrow.

She wanted it all and she could give it her all. She would find a way to strike a balance. *I'll show you, Hawk.*

CHAPTER THIRTEEN

HAWK MEANT TO drive past the house on his way out with Katz loaded in the trailer, but at the sight of Grace on the porch with the boys waving him off, he stopped.

One last goodbye.

"Did you change your mind?" Amos said.

"Can we come?" Saul said, finishing off the direction of Amos's question.

"Not a chance," Hawk said. "I came to make sure Grace is okay with me leaving you two alone with her."

"Why wouldn't she be?" Amos said.

"Exactly," Grace said. "Why wouldn't she be?"

Man, she looked good. Her light hair wrapped up in some kind of knotted bun, with a pink fitted shirt and her bare legs in denim shorts and sandals. All summery and fresh smelling. The knots in his stomach, all twisted up like her hair, eased off.

"I don't know. I feel guilty. Going off and leaving you to handle it all by yourself. A few hours is one thing, but bedtime is a whole other rodeo."

"First, I'm not alone. Nathan's here with his

trusty dog. Those two count for four people right there. Irina and Amy are also around."

"And there's us," Saul pointed out.

Grace winked at Hawk. "And there's the boys. Question is, how are you going to make out with only Mateo to help?"

"All right, then. I should be back late tonight."

"No, you won't. You're staying the night. Mateo booked the last room at the inn."

"He moves fast. Seems as if it were only a couple of weeks ago that we were talking about showing them."

"That's because it was. Two-and-a-half, to be exact. Now, hurry, go, we're fine."

"Go," Russell said, from the doorway. "Have fun, but not too much." He used to say that to Hawk when he was a teenager. Had his memory lapsed? And then— "Give Mateo my best."

Hawk let out his breath. Grace followed him to his truck.

"Don't spend all of your time thinking about me," she said.

Hawk took in her outfit again. Her toes were painted the same pink as her top.

He walked towards the back of the trailer, Grace following, until it stood between them and their audience on the porch. He kissed her, not for long but enough to kick up his heartbeat.

"I do nothing but," he said and then left quickly, while he still could.

That kiss carried him through the rest of the day, through a two-hour trip to Lethbridge and the show itself. Things were working out. He and Mateo had a strategy to keep the breeding program in place, thanks to Grace. His life had changed for the better since the boys had brought them back together. He could have a fresh start.

If she chose him. Because as much as she said she could handle it all, she couldn't. Nobody could. In the end, she would have to choose.

And it was on him to give her every reason to choose him and the boys. Something more than three kisses and a broken lily.

Mateo and Risky B in the arena were like two old-time partners. The cow—really a yearling steer—didn't stand a chance as they separated it from the others and halted its return, finally driving the yearling to a standstill. The audience sent up an appreciative applause, and Hawk drew in the sight of people giving it up for the horse he had helped bring into the world.

He spotted Grant Sears sitting with his wife, and an idea popped up. He stepped along the bleachers until he drew even with them. Grant looked up, first in passing, and when recognition set in, his mouth twisted down.

"Good to see you again, Grant." Hawk nodded to Deb. "Hello."

"I saw the horse you bought out from under

me was a last minute addition. I had to see what I got cheated out of."

"Just to be clear, Grace—and Katz's trainer—bought her. I was as surprised as you."

"Where is he being stabled?"

"My place."

Grant gave a grunt. "Even better deal for you. You got yourself a free horse."

"It's working out so far," Hawk admitted. "I'm anxious as you to see him perform. Mateo hasn't been able to get as much training in as he has with Risky B."

"That mare's a fine horse. Not selling her, is he?"

Grant's wife patted his knee. "Remember that you left your checkbook at home."

Hawk worked to keep his shrug casual. "Too bad. I was hoping we could do business. One-on-one."

"What did you have in mind?" Grant's words were out even as his wife placed a staying hand on his arm.

"Mateo and I are partners now." Grace, too, but he didn't want the mention of her name to rile Grant. "And we plan to breed Katz and Risky B. She would foal spring after next."

"That's more than eighteen months out," Grant said.

"But not unusual to be investing that far ahead."

"You want me to put money down on something that might not even happen?"

"Money held in reserve, Grant. I'm not here to rip you off. I'm here to give you an opportunity. See it as a kind of apology."

"An apology I pay for? How much?"

Hawk named a figure. "If you take her right at birth."

"I'm too old to work a horse all day long."

Music to Hawk's ears. "If you like how Mateo handles the horse, then we can come up with a different fee. He trains and shows. Sort of pay as we go."

"And what if I want him showing across the States, instead of around here?"

"Mateo shows into the States."

The announcer called in Mateo and Katz, and the pair entered the ring. Katzmobile was clearly up for the show, perhaps a bit too much. He had spirit all right. Mateo paced him back and forth a couple more times than he had with Risky B, and Katz seemed to relax into the job at hand. They split the herd and spliced off a set of five before working them down to one, and then it was game on, as the white yearling sought to return to the herd. Katz held him fast, but a sudden dodge left Katz back on his haunches for a split second too long and he raced across the arena to cut off the yearling in the nick of time. The cow gave up right after, but Katz had nearly lost it for them, and the judges would see that loss of control.

"He needs work," Grant said shortly. "How long has Mateo been working him?"

"Last two weeks, mostly."

"Huh."

Hawk didn't want him dwelling on Katz's less-than-stellar performance for too long. "As Mateo said, 'You can control the flame, so long as one's there.'" Mateo had said nothing of the sort, but it sounded better coming from a trainer.

Grant's wife watched Mateo and Katz exit the arena. "He has a wife and kids, and a ranch of his own, right?"

"They're…ambitious."

She fixed her gaze on him. "Like you and Grace."

Hawk dodged. "We all make for a great team. You could be part of it, Grant."

The horseman's mouth worked, as if he was chewing on a wad of tobacco. "All right, let's do this." He reached inside his jacket, and Deb leaned back.

"Remember, no checkbook?"

"No book," he said and pulled out a single blank check. His wife sank and Grant gave a rare grin. "You really didn't think I'd leave home without one?"

"READY TO GO?" Amos shoved his head between Grace and her computer screen, his thick, black hair going up her nose.

"Not if you keep getting in the way," she said,

pushing his head aside. "How about you and Saul go find Grandpa and see if he wants to come with us?"

She had promised them a trip into Diamond Valley for ice cream, once she had sent off an email to Rachelle. Her frazzled colleague had bombarded her with urgent questions, and the answers demanded careful consideration.

Grace heard the boys clatter down the porch steps of the Blackstone home and race each other to the corrals. She had a clear eye on them. Now for the first bit of peace all day. "The litigation between the parties," she muttered, rereading, "finds its precedent in the matter—" Her fingers and brain settled into the work, her thoughts finally coalescing after a day of keeping up with demands of twins who absolutely did not stop. They even vibrated while they ate.

"Finally, please instruct—" Truck doors slammed and Grace looked out the window to see Russell get in the driver's seat of his truck. The boys' heads barely cleared the dashboard.

"No, no, no, no, no."

The truck motor started and was pulling away as Grace yanked open the front door. "Russell, wait for me!"

But he was already heading down the lane. Shoot, shoot! Russell was having an off day. He had wandered aimlessly about the house, and once, she had found him standing in the lane, looking up and down. "I came to get the mail," he said when she joined him, "but I must have got the days mixed up."

Mail was no longer delivered but arrived at a community mailbox. "I hardly remember myself, Russell. You want to join me and the boys for lunch?"

And now he was driving down the same lane with the boys. There were no booster seats. At the end of the lane, she saw who she thought was Saul look out the back window at her.

The truck jerked onto the main road and Saul's head sank out of sight. Grace tore to her car. She would follow them into town, or maybe persuade Russell to pull over, and everyone could transfer into her car.

"Please, please be in your right mind."

No one had warned the kids not to get in the vehicle with Grandpa because Russell himself had said the day of his diagnosis that he wouldn't drive on the road, and he wouldn't drive with passengers at all. That had seemed enough. But she and Hawk should have warned the boys, regardless.

Hawk. She reached for her phone and then stopped. No use calling him. He could do nothing, and if she could get to Russell, there was nothing to worry about. Maybe there was nothing to worry about anyway. Maybe the Russell of old would surface for the next half hour and she would catch up to them at the ice cream shop.

She caught up with them at the bend before Irina's place. About two hundred yards ahead of her, she watched Russell brake for the bend and keep driving straight off the road and down into the ditch, stopping only after he smashed into the horse cairn.

Grace pressed on the gas and then slammed to a halt on the shoulder of the road, parallel to Russell's truck. The horse memorial was decapitated, the head in the ditch grass, and Irina's saddle of daisies and pansies hung in the truck grill. Russell sat slumped, his head on the wheel. She could see nothing of the boys.

"Please, please, please," she whispered and ran through the tall-grass ditch, the blades binding around her legs. The driver's door opened and Russell's leg flopped out.

"Russell!" She reached his side. He gave her a glazed look, and beyond him were the kids. Amos had one hand over his eye and another over Saul's mouth where blood outlined Amos's fingers. Saul stared ahead, as if his eyes were pinned open. Neither was crying. Shock, probably. Or ranching life had vaccinated them against the sight of blood.

"Are you okay?" Grace said. Stupid question when they clearly weren't.

"We hit here," Amos said, patting the dash-board. "My eye, his mouth."

She didn't see any bruising on their heads but— "Did either of you at any time fall asleep, even for a short while? Your eyes close?"

Amos and Saul shook their heads. "Why would we fall asleep," Amos said, "in the middle of an accident?"

"Do you feel dizzy?"

"No," Amos said and Saul shook his head.

"Feel like throwing up?"

Same response.

"Can you see okay? Nothing looks blurry?"

Negative. No point calling 9-1-1. The nearest ambulance was an hour away, and the injuries— thankfully—were minor. But she would run them to the clinic, just to be sure.

"You tell me if any of that changes, okay?"

"I forgot," Russell whispered. "I forgot I wasn't supposed to drive on the road." Wetness appeared in his eyes and he passed a hand over his face. "I thought I'd get the mail with the kids. We've done it before."

A quad gunned across the pasture from Irina's place. She cut the motor and yelled, "Don't touch the fence. It's electrified."

Grace waved to her in understanding, and Irina gunned for the fence box that housed the battery. At least, Grace assumed that was what she was doing. "Boys, did you hear that? Irina's fence is electrified. Stay in the truck."

Saul pulled away his brother's hand and fresh blood spilled from his lips. Oh God. Amos clamped his hand back over his brother's mouth.

"Hold tight. I've got a first aid kit in my car." By the time she returned, Russell was leaning on the truck box. From the way he sagged, Grace was pretty sure he wasn't wandering anywhere.

Irina brought the chugging quad up and turned it off. "The power's cut. How's everybody?"

"Conscious," Grace said. "Shaken." Herself included. "I'm just going to look at Saul's mouth." She took Russell's place behind the wheel. "Are you going to let me, Saul?"

She had to pry Amos's stiff hand away from his brother's mouth. Blood had dried around his mouth, even as more pooled inside his lip. She spotted a box of tissues on the floor of the cab and tugged out a few. She wrapped her arm around Saul and leaned him forward. "Spit."

It was a mess of blood and spit and...two teeth. "Wow, what a way to lose your loose tooth," Grace said, injecting more cheer than she felt. "Can I take a peek?"

Saul opened his mouth, and Amos, like he had with the computer screen, stuck his head between Grace and his brother to get the first look.

"You got two knocked out," Amos turned to Grace. "Did you see that?"

What she saw was a bruise swelling around Amos's eye. "You look as if you got in a fight," she said.

"Really?" Amos scooted to the side-view mirror to check it out, while Grace used the Amos-free space to lean over Saul's mouth. Two definitely gone, the gap there like a baby's.

Tears welled up in Saul's eyes.

"Don't worry," Grace said. "Those were your baby teeth. Adult ones will come soon enough, and they'll be bigger and better."

Saul pointed at the windshield. "We hit the memory horse."

A pansy with its purple-and-white face lay on the trunk hood. Irina stood beside Russell, both of them staring silently at the destroyed horse.

"Yeah, that happened, but what really matters right now is that you and Amos and your grandpa are okay."

Saul's eyes flooded with tears. "Grandpa forgot how to drive."

"Nobody quite knew that, Saul. It's not your fault, okay? Accidents happen."

Another accident she didn't prevent. And this time, she was in charge. She had thought she could handle her career, her B and B business, and take care of active kids and a disabled elder. One day in, and she had blown it. What if something worse had happened?

She sorted through the first aid kit to see if

there was anything to patch them up with. "Here, Amos. I found an ice pack." She cracked the plastic barrier to activate it. "Hold it against your eye. It will reduce the swelling."

"But I want it to get huge."

Hawk did not need to see his son sporting a big whopper of a black eye. "Trust me, you don't. Get it on there."

He and Grace had a split-second staring contest, with her having the advantage of two healthy eyes. Amos clapped on the pack, and then, because cowering before a brush with serious injury was not his style, he asked, "Can we get out now?"

Grace slid out and helped the boys down, though the little bale hoppers could handle themselves. It seemed important to have live contact with them.

"It's that bend. It's been nothing but trouble," Irina was saying to Russell, as the boys left the vehicle. She was leaning on the truck box, beside Russell. He was facing the inside of the truck box, whereas she was staring down at the horse head, its single visible painted eye staring back. She turned to the boys as they came out. "You two are having a bit of an adventure."

Amos lowered the ice pack. "I got a shiner."

Russell turned to take in his grandson, and he winced at the sight of the bruise and Saul holding the bloodied paper towel to his mouth.

"He lost two teeth," Amos reported.

Russell dragged a shaky hand down his face, and Grace quickly added, "One was already loose and the other is probably a baby tooth, too. That's all. They are both alive and well. Any damage to the truck?" Grace said, to distract everyone from the human injury.

Russell hung his head. "I hope it's totaled, so I never turn a wheel again."

Grace and Irina exchanged swift gazes. Nothing so robbed independence in the country as not being able to drive. Saul mumbled something behind his wad that only Amos deciphered.

"Saul wants to know if that means bicycles, too?"

It wasn't all that funny. Its humor only lay in its seriousness, but it broke up the adults, and even the corner of Russell's mouth cranked up.

"I suppose so long as the only motor driving the wheels is myself, I'll try it," he said. "If I even remember how."

Grace took his arm. "We can just leave the truck here for now. I'll take out the registration, and we'll lock it up. Tomorrow is soon enough to deal with it."

Meaning when Hawk got home. Russell picked up on her train of thought. "You'll tell him, then."

"Sure, I can do that," she said brightly, as if she'd only be passing on the normal day's events.

Russell pulled himself up straight. "I'm sorry,

Irina, for what I did here." He gestured to the broken wood and scattered flowers.

Irina shook her head. "It's about time it got taken down. I just didn't know how to go about it. So, thank you, Russell." She gave his arm a squeeze. "You always were a good friend to me."

Russell gave a nod that looked like a spastic jerk of his head and turned for Grace's car.

"Irina, if there's anything—"

"Go on. You have your hands full. I'm okay, but I think I'm calling your dad tonight."

Grace stretched out her hand to the boys. "Come on, boys. We're all going to the clinic to get checked out."

Saul mumbled something to Amos whose eyes widened. "Wait a minute. Does this mean we don't get ice cream?"

The next morning, Hawk rolled in shortly after breakfast, which suited Grace just fine. She had called him last night from the clinic after the three Blackstones passed physical inspections. She had confirmed that there were no signs of concussion, but she would monitor for signs as per the doctor's instructions, that Russell was completely uninjured, and that they were going home right after a stop at the ice cream shop. In typical Hawk fashion, he'd listened, asked a few questions and then spoke to the boys. Amos and Saul chattered on about the headless horse and bloody teeth and how the doctor didn't even know how to saddle a horse, and what flavors of ice cream they wanted.

"I'm so sorry," Grace said for what felt like the hundredth time when she took the phone again, and for the hundredth time, Hawk assured her it wasn't her fault.

But it was. Hawk had left his father and his sons in her care, and she had let him down. Now that he was back, she couldn't look him in the eye, and was glad when she slipped away and didn't have to try any longer.

Not that she could avoid him forever. He had texted her to say that he would like to come over in the evening, when Amy and Nathan could watch over the household. They had set a time, and she had come onto the porch to watch the laneway.

Instead, she heard the clip of hooves and the soft rattle of harness. Hawk had come through the backyard past the fence, past the two trail horses.

"Thought I'd combine business with pleasure," he said, dismounting Wildrose. "Checked on the cattle and the fence. Both are holding up."

"Good to hear," she called to him. "Do you mind parking your transportation on the other side of my lawn to avoid having to shovel anything she drops from her exhaust?"

Hawk obliged, giving her time to take a few deep breaths to steady herself. By the time he joined her, stretching his legs out beside hers, she felt a little less shredded. In fact, his presence went a long way to repairing her unraveled state.

"I had to resew a square twice today," she said. "I put it on upside down the first time, and sideways the second. The accident last night rattled me," she said in a rush. "And of course, here I am, stuck with bits of your dad's old clothes around me, cut and pinned and sewn together."

"I gathered that from the way you tore out of the house this morning." Hawk wrapped his arm around her shoulders and pulled her in tight against him. She should resist and not let him think that whatever they had going on could continue. But she softened against him, anyway.

"I'm sorry," she whispered. "I am so sorry. If I had been more careful, it wouldn't have happened. I should have been watching."

"You're not the first one who has apologized today. Dad, of course. I don't think he ate at all today. Even Amos and Saul apologized for not checking with you first. And then Irina called to say that she was just sorry about the whole mess, and that I was to call her anytime, if I needed help."

Grace forced herself to straighten away from him a smidge. "I'm the only one who should be apologizing."

"How do you figure that?"

He actually sounded confused.

"Do you know what I was doing when your dad drove off with the kids? I was answering an email from Rachelle. I was working when I should have been with the kids. Yes, I meant to follow them outside. Yes, I sent them to Russell, and I didn't think he would drive away. But the point was, they weren't my priority and they should have been."

"We all got work to do, Grace. It could've happened to anyone. It happened to me. Remember why we met back in March?"

"I do, and do you remember what you were doing when I called? Yeah, buying groceries for the family. Do you know what I was doing? Taking care of myself. I was more concerned about getting my reputation back than the welfare of your kids."

"You have spent days and days with my kids. I'm not going to let you beat yourself up about an event that came right in the end. By the way, Saul's teeth are fine. He should have two shiny white teeth in a couple of months. Ahead of Amos, likely."

"About the time Amos's shiner will disappear." Grace rubbed her arms at the memory of their little mutilated faces. "I don't know if I can do this, Hawk."

Tension entered his arm and corded around her shoulders. "How so?"

"You asked me to make a choice. And at first,

I didn't think I needed to. I could have it all, I thought. I ignored you, ignored my own instincts, and your family paid for my arrogance. I won't jeopardize the safety of your family again. You are right. I can't do it all. I have to choose."

"What if I told you I changed my mind?"

"I would tell you to change it back again."

Hawk smiled. "How often is it I ever change my mind about anything? You should call this a win." His arm tightened around her. "You're scared, is all. Don't make a decision out of fear. That's not you."

"I am only scared that I will do it all again. And the thing is, I really don't want to give up my law career."

"Then, don't. We'll make it work."

She twisted away. "How can you say that, Hawk? You were already stretched to the breaking point when we met. How can throwing my career and this—" she gestured to The Home Place "—little business here into the mix possibly work?"

His jaw set. "I don't know. It just will."

Except it wouldn't. His dad was only going to get worse and the boys would still be boys.

And what if—

"Hawk, do you want more kids?"

He looked at her warily. "I wouldn't call it out of the question."

Kids. Career. Side business. Ranch. Ailing parent. Grace shook her head. "No, Hawk. I can't do it. It's all or nothing for me. And I really tried all, so I guess—" she spread out her hands "—it's nothing."

CHAPTER FOURTEEN

NOTHING.

The word clanged in Hawk's brain as he rode back to the ranch in the falling light. That was what it had all come down to. Nothing. Back to pre-Grace times. Except now it was worse because there were traces of her everywhere. His boys depended on her for a place to go. His dad, too. And she was now part of his business. They might be over, but she remained wound into his life in a way that Eva, his own ex-wife, would never be.

He had thought she would be the one, because she had always been the one.

The fact of the matter was that they had both tried, and in the end, it wasn't enough. No remorse this time, the way it was with Eva.

Still, it was a short sleep that night, and Grace pressed on his mind like a hot rock the second consciousness kicked in. No. He had pushed his way through a breakup before and he'd do it again. It had rained the previous night, a rare peaceful one without a whole pile of thunder and lightning, and Hawk stepped with his cup of coffee onto the porch. The smell of rain and damp earth and grass, and everything with a sheen. Grace would get the same morning. He remembered the view from The Home Place. Through the trees and up the hill. The cattle would be up there. They both could see the same ones.

The front door opened on a squeak. His dad stepped out, coffee in hand. He walked over to the rain gauge perched out over the edge of the railing. "Three-tenths."

"Enough to keep the dust down for a day or two," Hawk said.

"Not enough for the pasture."

"Yeah. I'll talk to Nathan. We'll get them moved in the next week or so."

Russell took his chair. It was a padded office armchair on wheels. Not exactly fitting for Western porch decor, but then again, his dad never had cared for what other people thought. "If you find me trying to help, you have my permission to tie me to this chair and roll me off the stairs."

It was the first year his father would not take part in moving the cattle into the far pasture. "I hope it doesn't come to that."

"I'm saying it, nonetheless. And while we got a quiet moment here, I'm also giving you permission to boot me off the place."

His dad had his dark eyes locked on Hawk.

There was no confusion, only unflinching clarity. The same look he'd given Hawk when he had turned Blackstone Ranch over to him right after he'd married Eva.

"Dad, I can't do that."

"Yes, you can. You need to think of the boys. I'm a loose cannon, son. That accident was God's fair warning."

Grace had said much the same about her limitations. The accident had been about everyone finding out what they couldn't handle. All about giving up.

His dad leaned forward, the wheels rolling backward on the planking. "If I was a horse, you'd shoot me and that's the truth."

"Except you're not," Hawk ground out. "You're my dad and the kids' grandpa."

His dad sat back and then slapped the arms of his chair. "That's the truth. It isn't for a father to make his son choose between him and his own sons. I need to find a place to park myself. Away from you and the kids. You can all get on with your life, especially now—" he thumbed over his shoulder toward The Home Place "—that Grace is in the picture."

"That's—that's not an issue."

His dad shook his head. "I saw her at the accident. She was scared, and I made her that way. She's too good of a girl to go around worried sick about what I'm going to do next."

"Dad, listen. You don't need to worry about what she thinks. It just doesn't matter." His voice broke on the last word, and he looked down at his scuffed boots.

His dad rose from his chair. "Look at that. I'm wrecking your life, son. And I won't have it."

AMY HAD COME over late morning to watch the boys, which gave Hawk time to go with Nathan to check fence prior to moving the cattle. And she agreed to take the boys on Mondays and Wednesdays for the rest of July and August, with Gemma taking them on Tuesdays and Thursdays. In the fall, they would be in first grade, and with their aunt taking them after school, he would have the day care program largely handled.

He and Nathan had settled on Thursday next for the move. Amy would help, Nathan assured him. In fact, Amy came up more than once during their long afternoon together, which was something, given Nathan hardly ever said anything.

"You're going to be one mopey kid when she goes to university in a couple of months."

They were out behind the barn where it looked down over the valley, the spot where Hawk had come up with the stupid idea that Grace might want to become a mother to his boys. It turned out that Nathan did his dreaming out here, too.

"We'll make it work. She's less than two hours away."

The same distance he and Grace would have had to deal with at their age. That hadn't worked. Hawk didn't have the heart to tell him that time and space were enemies of the heart. He would find out soon enough, and who knew? Maybe they would be the exception.

"You have any plans to move with her? Get a job in the city?"

The boy flinched. "I have no plans to walk concrete. Unless... I mean, you still want me?"

"More than ever. That's the thing. I can't pay you much more than I am now. But I'm hoping that'll change in the next year or two. I'm working with Mateo to build up the horse breeding and the cattle. Maybe another thirty head or so next year. I was thinking we could settle on a number of cattle, and you could have a cut of whatever they sell for."

It was as if he'd handed Nathan the full check from the sale already. "Yeah, I'd like that. I could do that."

"But if something happens to a calf, that's not on me."

"I get it. That's life. I was thinking maybe, what with you building up the cutting horses, and I've seen it done and you've said yourself how useful Doxie Sue is and, well, maybe—"

"You got to break yourself from going tongue-tied every time you want something."

Nathan let out a breath. "I was hoping to go into the dog training business for cattle with Doxie Sue. I have some experience, you know. And I've heard where you can sell a trained dog for upwards of six grand, and even the ones that don't make the cut, there's still a market."

Hawk gazed across the blue-and-green sweep of Eden Valley. There was a vehicle twinkling jewel-bright far down the main road. Likely on its way to Kananaskis Country, the playground for urban dwellers. It had always given him a kind of perverse lift to know that he lived where urbanities dreamed of going.

"You're thinking of a package deal? One horse and a dog."

"One horse, two dogs."

Hawk smiled at the boy's enthusiasm. "One horse, two dogs, three hundred head of cattle."

Nathan grinned. "That's a perfect tagline."

"Now we just need a name for the company."

Nathan scratched Doxie Sue behind the ear. "Ah, we can just market it under Blackstone Ranch. I'm okay with that."

"That's not right," Hawk said. "You deserve to make a name for yourself."

"No. Makes more sense that I just ride on your name. Nobody knows me from that post there. I'd rather have the money than the name."

It made sense but not for a boy with his quiet drive. Hawk wasn't going to push him. It was enough that he had one good worker and yet another partner to add to his business.

A business partner, when he'd hoped for a life one.

"WHAT DO YOU mean we're not going to Grace's?" Amos gave Hawk a mutinous glare across the breakfast table. Monday breakfasts had become upbeat affairs as the boys anticipated a day with Grace, but today was decidedly different. Grace had not specifically said that the boys' regular visits were over, but he figured this was part of the "nothing" deal. His dad had taken his coffee and toast out to his porch chair and table, no doubt to duck the storm that was about to let loose inside.

Saul used his finger to spread the saskatoon berry jam on the toast. Hawk had opened up the special treat this morning to make the news about Grace go down easier. "Do you mean not on this Monday or all Mondays?"

"All Mondays."

Saul's finger punched through the toast. Amos let out a howl. "But why?"

"She's just got really busy, son. She's back to working at the firm and she still has her guests coming and she has her own family, too."

"But we're not a trouble," Saul said softly. "She said so herself."

"You're right. It's just that she can't manage all fronts, and something had to give."

"And now we only have Wednesdays," Amos said. He crunched on his bacon. He liked his bacon crispy and Saul like his soft. Hawk had made it exactly according to their individual wishes today.

Saul licked his finger. "I will have to work really hard Wednesdays on the quilt." He leaned closer to Hawk. "We're making Grandpa a quilt for his birthday."

Hawk swallowed coffee. He'd already gone through nearly a pot on his own and it wasn't even eight in the morning yet. "This affects Wednesdays, too."

Hawk braced himself for Amos's howl of outrage. Instead, his firecracker son hunched his shoulders and stared down at his bacon and eggs.

Saul gripped his seat, as if he might topple from it. "We're never going to see her again?"

"You just don't see her on regular days. You can still see her now and again, I suppose. Maybe for a horse ride. Or lunch. Something like that."

"How about half days? Like just the mornings or just the afternoons?" Saul must be desperate. He didn't usually wheel and deal. Amos's eyes hadn't shifted from his food.

"No," Hawk said. "That won't work."

"Why—" Amos spoke faintly "—why don't you like her anymore?"

More, why didn't she like him? Or why didn't she like him enough? "It's not that, son. I like her fine. She's a good person."

"You say the same thing about Mom. That's she a good person, but you don't visit her."

"That's because your mom wants a life separate from us. That doesn't mean I think she's a bad person. Lots of good people don't hang around me," he tried to end on a joke.

"So," Saul said quietly. "It's me and Amos she doesn't like anymore."

"Not at all," Hawk said. "She likes you both very much. Remember she took care of you with the accident? Remember she gave you cookies? Heck, she's the one who asked if you boys would come stay with her during the days I am away."

"But now she hates us," Saul shouted. "First Mom and now Grace. Why? What's wrong with us?"

Hawk stared at Saul and then at Amos who seemed to have shrunk further. It was as if his sons had switched personalities. "Hey. There is nothing wrong with either of you. Ever."

Amos still had his head down, but Saul faced Hawk. "Why don't they want us, then?"

Hawk and Eva had both agreed that the twins should never feel as if they had failed as children.

Blame me, Eva had said, *if the subject ever comes up. God knows it's true.*

"Your mother has...problems that make it difficult for her to be the kind of mother she knows you deserve to have. It's as if there is a part of her missing that's good with children."

Amos set his head on the table. "She's missing the mom part."

"Is Grace missing the mom part?" Saul said.

"Well, she's not a mom," Hawk said, "so that's different."

"So you're saying that she doesn't have the part, either?"

"I... I don't know, to be honest."

Saul dipped his head. "Me and Amos think she does. I've been with Auntie and she's a mom, and I've been with Irina and she's a grandma and Grace has the mom part."

"Her mom part is this big." Amos threw out his arms and then set his forehead on the table. Dramatic but effective.

Hawk had thought that the twins were reconciled to it just being Dad and Grandpa. They'd never really asked for more, and Hawk figured that their Auntie gave enough of the female warmth to round out their family life. Yeah, he had looked to Grace to become a mother to the boys, but he hadn't considered that the boys, too, were also checking her out as mom material.

"Tell me, months ago, when you went over to

The Home Place, was that because you had heard about Grace living there and you wanted to see if she…had a mom part?"

Saul looked over at Amos, but his head was still on the table. "The place had always felt like ours. And then she came, and it still felt like ours. We weren't looking for a mom part."

Amos lifted his head an inch. "Not at first." He lowered it back down.

Saul bit his lip and nodded.

It wasn't just losing Grace. It was losing hope for a mother who showed up for them. "Listen and believe me, it's not either of you. She's walking away from me. Blame me. The thing is, you two and me and Grandpa, we're a family package, right? There's no picking one but not the other. And I proved the deal-breaker. I was the one who was too much."

Amos's head shot up. "What doesn't she like about you?"

All the things that made him who he was. To give up any of them would lessen him, and oddly, lessen him in her eyes, too. But it wasn't just that. The fact of the matter was that he had no room in his life for hers, too. He could contribute nothing to her work life, and even her own family supported his ranch life, too. He brought nothing to the table for her.

He waved his hand and shrugged. "Oh, you know, I guess I'm a little too much ranch, is all."

Tears zigzagged down Amos's face, and at the sight of his brother coming apart, Saul's eyes flooded, too, and he clapped his hands over his face. "But, Dad," Amos said, "there's nothing wrong with that."

"I know, son. There is nothing wrong with any of us."

And that was the hardest part.

NINE O'CLOCK ON Monday morning, and Hawk still hadn't dropped the boys off. A full hour past his usual drop-off time. She checked her phone again for a missed call or text.

She gave it another ten minutes and then texted him.

Is everything okay? Just waiting for you and the boys.

Ten more minutes passed before her phone chimed a text.

They are with Amy now. I understood our previous arrangement is over.

What? She called him and he didn't pick up until after the fifth ring.

"That wasn't my understanding," Grace said. "I understood our arrangement, our—that we were over, but not the boys and me."

She heard a door open and swing shut, and he answered in a lower than normal voice. "I don't see how that would ever work, Grace. I get you care for the boys, and let me tell you this morning, telling them they weren't going over to see you, was rough. What if you are off next week to the city? At some point, you won't be around for the boys on a regular basis, and they might as well get used to it. If you don't want all-in, then it isn't fair that you pick what you want. Not fair to the boys and not fair to me."

He was right. Let's face it, getting close to the boys was the way she had hooked herself into Hawk's world. She didn't trust herself to keep her relationship with the boys separate from hers with Hawk, because it hadn't worked before. No, breaking with Hawk also meant breaking with the boys. At least, ending the same special closeness they'd developed over the summer. They would return to just being neighbors. She looked over at the quilt for Russell's birthday. She and the boys had cut up their Grandpa Russell's denim vest, and Grace had made good use of a flannel shirt she had remembered from a camping trip with Hawk. They hadarranged them into squares, and were ready to start sewing them together.

"Okay," she whispered. "I understand. Give my best to the boys."

Hawk sighed. "I'm not saying that to them now, not after I just got through the tears."

She had walked out on the boys as surely as their mother had, and left Hawk to patch their little hearts together again. And she could do nothing to make the matter better.

"Look, I know you are still part of the business, Grace, but I would really appreciate it if you kept your distance for the next while. Just let things cool down a bit. All right?"

There was nothing to do but agree. She hated Hawk had to pick up the pieces after a breakup she had initiated, but she needed to back off.

She was packing up the quilt squares when she looked out to see a horse rider coming down the backside of the hill from the Blackstone Ranch. Hawk? No, the sit in the saddle wasn't him.

A few more hundred yards, and she recognized Russell.

Had he wandered off with no one knowing? She got her answer when Russell dismounted at the horse. "Morning, Grace. Let me make a call before I forget."

He held his phone away from his ear and shouted into it, "I'm here safe and sound." He paused. "Yes, she's looking at me right now." He held the phone up to her. "Say something, will you?"

"Hello. I'm with Russell. I'm the luckiest woman in the world."

Russell grinned. "You got that?" he yelled into the phone.

He slipped the phone back into his jacketed shirt. "There, that's done. Nathan's a good boy."

Nathan? "I thought that was Hawk. Does he know you are here?"

"No, he doesn't. But I told Nathan to tell him if he asks. Hawk's got enough on his mind."

Not the least the fallout from her decision to leave him. "Can I get you a coffee?"

"I'd rather talk first."

"We can do both. Have a seat." She waved to the patio seat on the front porch.

"You know Angela wanted one of these sets for years," Russell said, lowering himself into one. He moved stiffly, as if cranking himself down like a machine. "And I said any old chair would do. Why fork out for a set? But I was wrong. We could have afforded it, and she deserved it."

She couldn't comment on Russell's treatment of his wife. They had been married for thirty-eight years, thirty-eight more than she had the courage to enter.

Russell tapped the wood arms, drumming up a fast tempo. "I want you to do something for me. Help find me a place that'll take me in."

This was sudden. And completely out of her wheelhouse. "Have you talked to Hawk about this?"

"This has got nothing to do with him. It's me taking care of myself and asking for your help to do that."

But she had given Hawk her word that she would stay away from them. "Fair enough. It's just that I don't want it to seem that I'm going behind his back."

"You're not. We're just doing what Hawk finds hard to do. Besides, you two aren't together, am I right?"

"We aren't. It's just that I don't want to cause any more trouble in the Blackstone household. I know that our breakup has disrupted things enough already."

"You, too, will get back together again, don't worry. He'll come around."

Practically the same words her mother had said to Hawk before the fateful horse ride. Grace squirmed in her seat. "I'm the one that started it all, Russell. I guess the ranching life isn't for me."

He gave her a sharp look. "It's because that accident scared the willies out of you, isn't it?"

She licked her lips. "Listen, it was building for a while and the accident just put it in perspective, that's all."

Russell studied her. "All sorts of perspectives out there, believe me. Some you can choose, some—" he touched his temple "—you lose control over. And today, I'm thinking clearly. By tonight, my brain could get scrambled again. Will you help?"

She didn't want to be the one shoving Russell into an extended care facility. But, if it would give him peace of mind, if it would help Hawk through this transition, then she really ought to help out the man who during the summers of her childhood had welcomed her into the very home she now lived in.

"All right," she said. "Let me get my laptop and we'll see what we can come up with."

CHAPTER FIFTEEN

GRACE DROVE RUSSELL to the extended care facility in nearby Diamond Valley. Except with no appointment, they only received vague answers and pamphlets. But Russell was "firing on all plugs," as he put it, and informed the staff he intended to visit with an old friend and offered a name. The two men visited, though since his buddy was deaf, they mostly shouted at each other.

"Now, let's go on a little walk," Russell said after a half hour, his voice noticeably hoarser. They still couldn't see much. Most doors were closed, and partly opened doors only gave a slice of a dresser, a mirror and a bedside table. But there was one unoccupied room, and they snuck in. A single bed, a dresser, a narrow built-in closet with plastic hangers. A window gave a view of a lawn and an outdoor patio, where an elderly woman in a wheelchair was nodding off.

Russell flattened his lips. "She was a grade behind me in school."

He pivoted and left. Outside, he scowled back

through the main glass doors into the lobby of the extended health care facility. "The rooms are a little small, aren't they?"

The room wasn't that much smaller than his current one at the ranch. It was just that he wasn't expected to actually live in it full time. "Hard to tell," Grace said noncommittally.

Russell blew out his breath. "Well, that's that. First step done."

"You want to go home, then?" Three hours had passed, and by now, Hawk probably knew that his dad had gone off with her. She was tempted to text him and let him know all was well. Then again, he could work a phone, too.

"I'm hungry. Let's eat. My treat." Russell didn't wait for her but headed across the lot. "Russell, I'm parked over here."

He rerouted himself. "See? It's starting to go. By night, I might as well check myself into that room."

The restaurant Russell chose was the local favorite spot. It served breakfast all day, and breakfast included steak. Russell nudged her elbow. "You see what I'm seeing?" He lifted his chin down the aisle to a booth at the back. There was Irina, and sitting across from her was a man based on what she could see—a shoulder in a plaid shirt. But then he presented his profile.

"Dad."

"I thought so." Not waiting to be seated, Russell headed straight for them, forcing Grace to trail behind.

"Knut, you lost again?" Russell spoke to her dad as if nothing of the awkwardness from their last meeting had ever happened.

Her dad turned at Russell's voice, and his eyes connected with Grace's. "Russell. Grace."

"I didn't see you at Grace's this morning. You just get in?"

Knut and Irina exchanged private looks. Very private looks. Wasn't this awkward? And it just got more awkward when Russell said that he and Grace had just come in for a bite to eat, and what could her dad and Irina do but invite them to sit with them?

Irina shuffled over for Russell and Grace slipped in beside her dad. Perhaps the two lovebirds had already eaten, but no such luck. Through the meal, Grace listened to her dad drop in various "we were planning on" and "we took in." How long had he been visiting Irina's without telling her?

"Sounds to me as if you've been logging quite a few miles on your truck," Grace said.

"I'm getting to know the road well enough," he said and winked at Irina, who colored right up. Grace's chicken salad tasted like straw, and before Russell could reach for the dessert menu, she asked him if he would like to go home.

"I'd like some apple pie first," Russell said. He had stayed remarkably lucid through the meal. Everyone easily smoothed over a couple of glitches.

"Pie and ice cream sounds good," Irina said, and turned to Grace. "If you prefer to go, we can take Russell home afterwards." Another "we." The new normal. She had to call Haley and get the update.

She was about to take her up on the offer when she remembered Russell's horse who was hopefully having a friendly get-together with Sage and Willow.

"You ride her back," Russell said. "Hawk can give you a ride home."

Except she had promised Hawk to stay clear of the place. On the other hand, he might forgive her if he knew his dad was having a rare day out with old friends.

She called Nathan and arranged for him to meet her out in the horse pasture beyond the Blackstone buildings. She would walk back.

But it was Hawk who came out to meet her. The wind was rippling his T-shirt as he stood next to a salt-block stand, hands shoved into his front pockets.

"I am trying to keep my promise here," Grace said quickly, as she dismounted. "I arranged for Nathan to meet me."

"I told him I'd take care of it. He has better things to do."

"Than deal with me, right?"

Hawk moved to adjust the stirrups on Russell's horse. Her long legs had fitted into Russell's well enough, but Hawk required extra inches.

At his silence, she said, "Your dad came to me."

"I know," Hawk said. "Nathan told me right after he got the call from Dad."

"I asked him if he had talked to you, and he said that he was taking care of his own business and would I help him. I couldn't refuse him, Hawk."

"I get that," he said and went around to the other stirrup. He couldn't seem to leave fast enough.

"He's having a really good day. The facility shook him up a little, but seeing my dad and Irina at the restaurant is making his day."

"That's good." Hawk was back to his old communicative self.

"How are the boys? The bruising and the teeth?"

"Good." He swung into the saddle. "Thanks for bringing back the horse."

That was it? He was just going to ride off. "Look, Hawk, I am trying here, okay? I understand we need space, but I can't help if our lives overlap now and again."

Hawk briefly closed his eyes. "You still want everything, don't you? My kids, my dad, my business—everything about me, except me. You walked away when we were young because I scared you. And now you're saying I'm too much to handle, but you still want to be in every part of my life. What's so wrong with me that's still got you running?"

"I'm not running," she said.

"Like the wind," he said, and rode away.

She watched him, his back straight and sitting right where he belonged. She began the trudge back to The Home Place. He might think she was the wind, but right now she felt heavier than stone.

THE NEXT DAY, Grace's dad invited her over to Irina's for a lunch before he headed north to the Jansson Ranch. It was so weird that her dad's girlfriend was at once his dead wife's good friend and her prickly neighbor.

"You sure you want me there, or are the both of you just trying to be polite?"

"None of us are too good at being polite, so I guess we really want you here."

She arrived to the sight of her dad pushing Irina in a wheelbarrow as she sat cross-legged and held on to the sides. Her dad was carting her over to a small pen fenced off with chicken wire, and as Grace walked up, she saw the couple dozen chicks inside. They were gaining the flat gloss of adult feathers, but they still had baby cheeping voices as they plucked the green grass. Her dad parked the wheelbarrow and held out a steadying hand to Irina as if she were in a carriage.

"Aren't they pretty?" her dad said. "Have you ever seen them so red? Pretty as a roan. Irina says the roosters get blue feathers."

Her dad had never given two hoots about chickens, much less the state of their feathers. He was just in love with Irina, and everything she loved. Something like she was with Hawk. Except she didn't love him. No, she did. But loving him was just too overwhelming.

A truck sounded on the gravel lane. "Amy," Irina said. "She brought the boys over to help with the chores. Something for them to do."

Grace wished she could disappear. She actually considered ducking behind the shed, but the twins would recognize her vehicle.

"Dad," Grace said in desperation, "I'm trying to avoid the boys. To not upset them."

"Why would you upset them?"

"Because of Hawk. We're not...together."

"Grace!" Amos tore toward her, Saul on his heels. Grace meant to greet them casually, but her knees gave way and she met them with a hug. They were both so bony and bouncy. Amos had a bit of egg stuck to his shirt and Saul sported a streak of purple marker up his arm.

Saul drew in a deep breath. "You still smell like cookies."

She smacked a kiss on his cheek. "You say the nicest things. Let me see your teeth."

Saul displayed the gaping hole. It seemed to have healed nicely. "And, Amos, your bruise is as blue as a rooster feather."

The boys shifted over to the chicken pen, sitting on their haunches to observe the pecking and peeping. Grace crouched, too, to observe the boys. Amos had picked up a cat scratch, and Saul had peeling skin on his ears from a sunburn. Amy finally said, "C'mon. The goat waits for no one."

Amos bit his lip. "But we want to be with Grace."

"Chores first," Grace said. "I promise I won't go without checking in with you. Deal?"

And they were off. A week away from them seemed like forever.

"Now," her dad said, "what was that all about?"

"Oh," Grace said, "remember how I used to babysit the kids a couple times a week? We got along well, but then things got busy for me and it just wasn't working out."

"You don't look busy," her dad said.

"I am," Grace said, aware of the scrutiny from both her dad and Irina. "I took time out of my hectic schedule to come here to see you."

"Grace Miranda Jansson," her dad said gently, "you look as if a breeze might break you to bits. What's going on?"

"I'll go make sandwiches," Irina said.

"Why bother?" Grace said. "Dad will just fill you in later. You might as well stay and hear it firsthand."

"But that means I get extra time with him before he leaves." Irina gave her dad a flirty smile. Honestly, it was all very sweet except for how it only highlighted what a mess her own love life was.

Her dreamy-eyed dad watched Irina walk to the house.

"In answer to your question," Grace said pointedly, "what happened is pretty typical. Hawk and I were moving into a relationship, but then Russell's accident made me realize I didn't have the guts for all this and told him so. Now we're back to just being neighbors."

"Irina said you handled yourself pretty well."

"Of course I'm good in a crisis. It's after it's all done. I'm still making quilts, and Mom has been gone for more than a decade, for crying out loud."

Knut looked off to the bend in the road. "I helped Irina haul the wood horse back here. She didn't want it there anymore. We both agreed that with people leaving us, there's no recovering. There's just making peace, and that's daily. She said everybody carries loss of some kind, and it isn't right to expect random drivers to take on hers as well."

"Look, Dad, I'm really glad for you and Irina.

I am, even though I sound like a grump. I'm jealous, okay? I wish I could find your peace."

"You still making that quilt with the boys?" She had told him about Russell's birthday gift during a phone conversation.

"I don't get to have them anymore. Hawk wants a clean break, and I don't blame him. The sad consequences of my decision, I guess."

Her dad watched a young rooster drink water. "Seems to me that making a quilt with the boys wasn't really about you getting over your mom. Sounds to me as if you were piecing something together with the boys."

Grace hooked her fingers on the chicken fencing. The bite of the wire suited her mood. "You might be right, but it hardly matters now. I'll have to finish it myself before Russell's birthday in September."

Knut studied his boots. "Hawk's just trying to protect them."

"Why do you think I got involved in the first place? I wanted to help as a friend and a neighbor, but when I wanted to pull back on us, he pulls the plug on everything. And I'm being the unreasonable one? I'm good for them. Why can't he see that?"

"I don't know that he doesn't see that," Knut said, "but he's always been sweet on you, Grace. This can't be easy for him."

"He doesn't need to worry about me banging on his door."

"I don't think," her dad said softly, "you got this far in life by not banging on doors. You just can't get scared by what's on the other side."

But she was scared. Scared of disappointing Hawk. Scared of not being there for those who needed her, and then not doing enough when she was there. And then when she had gone all-out in her work, her boss had rejected her anyway. And then she had run, too scared to tell others about her rejection.

Why are you running from me, Grace?

It's not just you, Hawk.

"Dad, I didn't go on sabbatical. George fired me."

Her dad lifted his arm into a hug, and she threw herself against him. "I called George back in February when you left," he said against her hair. "You taking a sabbatical so suddenly didn't sound right, but George didn't say otherwise, and I thought maybe you were looking for a break."

"I was scared that you would be disappointed in me."

His arm tightened around her shoulders. "I'm not disappointed in you, Grace. I'm sadder that you were too scared to tell me and held it all in-side."

Grace breathed in her dad's old familiar smell in his shirt. "I talked to Hawk about it."

"And was he disappointed?"

That talk had led them to their first kiss. "No."

Her dad eased his hold. "Well then. I guess there is a door you don't have to be scared to open." He looked at the house. "And there's another one. With sandwiches on the other side."

She didn't need sandwiches. But Amy would be along soon with the boys, and there was the sweetness of her dad and Irina to take in. "Then, let's bang away."

"YOU AND NATHAN are on to something with dogs," Mateo said to Hawk, as Doxie Sue darted after a straggling cow and calf. They were riding behind the herd as the nearly three hundred head and eighteen bulls moved from the lower pasture to the higher pasture. Hawk had postponed the cattle move for a few days so Mateo could be part of it. He had brought down the trailer to haul Katz back to the ranch for deeper training.

"Nathan says one good dog's worth three horses," Hawk said, his eyes on the twins. Off to his side, they were riding double on Greta, thrilled to be coming on their first ride, even if it meant staying well behind the herd. Amy and Nathan were up ahead, flanking the herd to keep them moving through the draw. "Cheaper, too."

"But trickier to ride," Mateo said, giving Katz a rub on the neck. "Unless, we're in the arena, isn't that right?" Mateo had wanted to test Katz in his outdoor element, and nothing wrong with an extra person on the drive.

"You know, Nathan's almost a worthy replacement for me," Mateo said, grinning.

"He's fitting in," Hawk said. "I thought I was doing him the favor by letting him work here, but I think I'm getting the better end of the deal."

"How's that going to work with Amy? She might steal him over to Irina's."

"I don't know," Hawk said. "I think Irina has her eye on stealing your help."

Mateo twisted in his saddle. "You mean Knut?" At Hawk's nod, Mateo said, "Haley and Grace had a long discussion about it the other night. And then they held a conference call with Natalia on the subject. Knut might make a move."

"Isn't he attached to his grandkids and being a great-uncle?"

"That's what I said, but apparently Knut promised Sadie trips down here no less than four times a year, each with at least one visit with the twins. He'll probably take Jonah and Jakob, when they get older, too."

Mateo's sons and Sadie running wild with his boys, just like him with Grace. "First I heard of this."

"That's just the speculations of three women and one girl. Though four pretty determined females." Mateo leaned to look past him to the boys. Even though they were mostly out of earshot, he lowered his voice. "So what's the deal between you and Grace?"

"What did she say?"

"Only that you two weren't together."

"She's got it right."

"And you're okay with that?"

"I guess I have to be."

Mateo snorted. "You don't have to be anything that Grace tells you to be. The only way I can handle that sister-in-law is to get right back in her face. You should know that."

"I don't like getting in people's faces. That strategy has backfired for me."

"And what did I say about that?"

"Grace isn't Eva. I know that, but I'm the same in both cases. I tried to make Eva fit my ideal. I'm not about to do that to Grace."

Mateo swatted his hat at a persistent horsefly. "You scurried down your burrow like a badger, Hawk. When has that ever worked with Grace? She takes on everyone when she figures the fight is justified. Haley, her father, me. I haven't seen her have it out with Natalia. Yet. We would worry about her mental health if she didn't."

Hawk thought of how she had gone head-to-head with the boys about everything from baths to coordinating tops with bottoms to applying sunscreen. She didn't let up.

But she had with him. Stopped dead in her tracks and walked away.

"She knows where I am," Hawk said.

"And you know where she is," Mateo said. "Take the fight to her."

Hawk didn't want to talk about this anymore. "We need to catch up." He called over to the boys. "You ready to kick it up a gear?"

The twins had only recently learned how to handle a trot, although Greta didn't care for the strain on her eleven-year-old heart.

"Are you ready?" Amos said to Saul behind him, and they were off. Sort of.

"How about you go on ahead with Katz?" Hawk said. "Let him show off. I'll stay back with the boys. We can bring in the stragglers. It'll give the boys something to think about."

Mateo seemed about to say something, probably to do with Grace, but Hawk pretended not to see and turned Wildrose toward the boys.

Greta didn't last more than ten minutes before she lapsed into a walk. "She won't do what she's told," Amos said.

"She's old," Hawk said, as he always said when the boys complained about Greta. "Be glad she's carrying your butts at all today."

"You can lead a horse to the trough," Saul said, "but you can't make her drink."

Amos twisted in his saddle. "What are you talking about? There are no troughs around here."

"It means," Hawk said, "that you can show

people the way out of their troubles, but you can't make them do it."

"That's not true," Amos said. "You make me and Saul do things we don't want to do all the time. Grace, too."

"I didn't mind doing things for Grace," Saul said. "They never lasted long. When can we see her again?"

"If she leaves for Calgary, you'll miss her even more."

"But we already miss her, and she isn't even gone. It doesn't make sense to miss someone when they are right here."

"I miss her cookies," Amos said. "And I'm sure they are there in the jar, too."

"I miss her riding with us right now," Saul said and offered his brother a slices of apple from his plastic baggie.

Amos took the biggest one and crunched down. "How can you miss her when she's never helped move cattle before? This is the first time for us."

"She's helped move cattle before," Hawk said before thinking. "A couple of times when we were older than you, about thirteen or fourteen." Hawk and Grace had been were up where Amy and Nathan were now, the summer heat sweating them up as they turned ornery cattle, calling each other out, egging each other on.

"So you miss her, too?" Amos said.

There was something in his voice, as if asking

permission to feel bad. His breakup with Grace was affecting them, even worse than with their mom. "Yeah, I do."

Saul stretched out his arm with the baggie. "Want one, Dad?"

He edged Wildrose over and took one. "Thanks, son."

"They're okay," Amos said, "but—"

"Not as good as cookies," Saul finished.

CHAPTER SIXTEEN

GRACE STEPPED OFF the elevator onto the carpeted hallway, turned the corner and kept moving, as much as her tight skirt and heels would allow. In the seven months away from the law firm, she'd forgotten how to walk in heels, and her toes and calves screamed at the unusual punishment. Still, the hot August sun had tanned her legs and arms nicely, and she'd worn a white sleeveless dress to show off a bit. First impressions mattered.

She couldn't fall flat on her face again. She and Rachelle had worked together via email, but Rachelle had suggested a face-to-face with the client. "I really need him to see that you are on board," Rachelle said.

Grace pushed open the mahogany doors with the name of the firm in a steel-and-brass installation mounted on the nearby wall. There were already two clients waiting, but neither seemed to be the one Rachelle was representing.

"Good morning," she said to the receptionist

who looked new. "I'm Grace Jansson. I'm here to see Rachelle."

A familiar face popped around the corner. Keira. "Grace! No one told me you were coming."

"Rachelle asked me to come in. I'm here for a meeting."

"Oh." Keira's smile dimmed. "This isn't a social call?"

Grace had been so focused on making a good impression at the firm that she'd forgotten that Keira had never seemed to care about that. "Not right now, but um… How about I take you for lunch?" There, quick recovery.

"Great, I'll see who else wants to come."

Was she expecting Grace to pay for everyone? If that was what it took for her to get their forgiveness, then fine. It wasn't as if she planned to buy any more horses.

"And I'll go see Rachelle."

"Right, she's in—" A look of pain crossed Keira's good-hearted face.

Grace wrapped her hand around the strap of her computer bag on her shoulder. It felt a bit like taking hold of reins. "At the end of the hallway, on the right?"

Keira gave a half laugh. "Yeah, that one."

Past five doors, past colleagues she had composed apology letters for and then discarded because they had come out either flaky or formal.

A door opened on her left, and out came Devon with his perpetual frown.

"Oh, sorry," he began and then recognized her. "Grace. Wow. Good to see you. I've been meaning to call you." His excitement looked genuine. "Any openings at your place? My fiancée and I are looking to get away."

"I'll text you my website," Grace said. "No weekends available until September, unless you want to come out in the middle of the week. Lower rates and it includes a trail ride."

"Horses? I'm in. You still have my number, right? Text me the earliest date. Better yet, call."

A second door opened. "Is that Grace?" Out came Diana. The twenty-three-year veteran of the firm had guided Grace through her earliest cases. The apology note to her had not gotten beyond the opening.

Diana wrapped her in a hug. "Oh my gosh. Keira said you were alive and kicking, but look at you with a real tan. And did the sun do that to your hair? You look gorgeous."

Did they all suffer from amnesia? Didn't they remember that her bullying had damaged their corporate team? Only the promise of a lunch together, with coworkers vying to pay for her, extracted her from their clutches and down the rest of the hallway to Rachelle. She waited outside her door, her arms crossed, her mouth upturned in a slight smile.

Grace recognized that smile from their Zoom meetings. It came just before she pointed out something Grace had overlooked. "You didn't expect to run the welcome-back gauntlet."

"I'm not exactly back. I'm just…here." Grace took a seat across from Rachelle who swung into the deep leather chair that had once been Grace's. It was the same chair that she had specially bought for herself when given the promotion.

"You look good in my chair," Grace said. "Honestly."

"It feels as if I'm sitting on tacks," Rachelle said.

"It's a big seat to fill," Grace said, for the fun of it.

Rachelle narrowed her eyes. "Oh really, Grace, you're not as fat as you think you are."

That was a good comeback. Grace waggled a finger. "You want help or not?"

Rachelle flipped open a folder. "Yes. I worked on this mess until two in the morning . What do you think?"

Grace barely had time to jot a couple of notes before Rachelle's computer dinged that the client's arrival. "Okay, I'll go get him." Rachelle stood and pointed to the empty seat. "You take it. Please. It'll look better."

Maybe there were tacks in the seat, because it didn't feel as comfortable as it used to. And when the client's damp hand met hers, Grace could barely stop from squirming. He was nothing like the one Grace had successfully defended. Her client had talked about keeping promises. This one talked about how to get out of them. What had Rachelle been thinking by taking on this sleazebag?

Once the meeting was over and Rachelle had shown him out, Grace popped out of her seat and back into the harder chair. The office door clicked open and Rachelle entered. "Well, what did you think?"

"I think he's scum, and if there's any justice in the world, they will toss our case out."

Grace expected Rachelle to come back firing. Instead, she dropped her head into her hands. "I knew it. We're hooped. I'm hooped."

"Rachelle, this is not like you. Why?"

Her reply came muffled through her hands. "Because his case was like yours. And if I could win this one, I would have earned this stupid seat of yours. And yes, I know, it was not a good reason, but it was what I thought I had to do."

Rachelle dragged her hands away from her crumpled face. "The fact is that I've always envied you, Grace. You are so good at everything you do. After getting fired, you sailed out and opened up a B and B the next day, and that took off."

"It was not exactly the next day, and my dad bought that land for me. I have had lots of help you didn't get, Rachelle, and yet you are in my seat."

"And who's the complete wreck here? No one knocks on my door and wonders where we should go for lunch. You, you even landed a cowboy with kids to boot."

Her perfect life according to Rachelle. "Not exactly. That went…sideways."

"How?"

"Despite what you think, I'm not good at managing everything. I decided that I'd rather reestablish my career than take on the responsibilities of man, kids and ranch."

Rachelle's crumpled face widened into shock. "Are you out of your mind? You gave up all that for—" her hand swept around the room "—for this?"

"I missed it." Except now that she was here, it was the people she missed the most, and her good name among them, which, apparently, if their warm greetings were anything to go by, she had not lost.

Rachelle shook her head. "You shouldn't be here. You should be back at your home place, begging that cowboy to ride double with you forever. There are loads of ways to scratch the lawyer itch."

Like taking over from a retiring lawyer in Diamond Valley? "Not as easy as you think."

"Yeah," Rachelle said, "but remember that you make hard things easy."

MISSING GRACE. It could be the name of a cheesy show, but it described the state of the Blackstone household through much of August. Saul drew pictures of a tall, yellow-haired woman with big blue eyes. Amos drew pictures of cookies and grids that he explained were quilts. Russell kept setting out an extra coffee cup and then muttering, "I thought she was coming over." As for himself, he wasn't sleeping well, and he kept looking at his phone for messages. What did he expect? He'd told her to stay away, and wouldn't you know it, she was actually listening.

Only Nathan didn't seem perturbed. He came in for meals, especially if Amy was over babysitting, and Hawk usually hauled the boys somewhere to give them a few minutes together. Nathan didn't spend too long with her, and rejoined Hawk soon enough. Once given the green light on dog training, Nathan had come up with new projects from renovating an old granary to working up the lawn south of the house for a vegetable garden. He didn't have to, Hawk thought, but the boy seemed driven to prove his place.

It was during one of those downtimes after lunch that Hawk had the boys in the side pasture with Paintbrush and her foal. Doxie Sue had joined them, finally comfortable after all these months to let Nathan out of sight.

"Don't chase him," he told Amos, who was trying to pet Picasso.

Amos kicked the dirt. "But Saul got to touch him."

"Saul didn't stomp over as if he owned him."

"But we do own him."

"Only on paper," Hawk said. "Mostly they are partners."

Amos didn't seem to buy it, his mouth turned down as he watched the foal high step back to his mama's side.

"Hey," Saul said. "Company."

Sure enough, a wide truck, dark gray and kicking up road dust, rolled up the lane. No one he recognized. Doxie Sue tore away toward the vehicle, barking. Her barking of general announcement with her tail up changed suddenly as the driver and passenger emerged. Her barking ceased, her tail went into a brisk wag, and she scampered over to the passenger's side. Out stepped Grant and Deb Sears. Why were they here?

"I know that lady," Amos said. "She gave us pretzels and cheese crackers at that horse sale. She and Grace are friends."

As if his longstanding relationship with the Sears counted for nothing, one he'd had to repair after Grace's stunt at the horse sale. Grant got right to the point as soon as Hawk was in hearing distance. "Deb wanted me to call, but I figured you could kick me off the place if you didn't want me here."

"Of course not, Grant. Good to see you."

"I got kind of curious about where that horse of mine was going to be raised, so I thought—"

"Grant, tell me, do you recognize this dog?" Deb had rounded the hood, Doxie Sue at her heels.

Grant's face lit up. "It can't be. Doxie Sue?"

In response to her name or to Grant, Doxie Sue came right over and slipped her head under Grant's open hand.

Grant frowned at Hawk. "You bought my horse, *and* you took my dog?"

Before Hawk could answer either charge, the door to the house opened and Nathan stepped out. He stood on the porch with his feet apart and his hands shoved in his pockets. Amy stood behind him, waving her arms about, as if not knowing what to do with them.

"Nate!" Deb said. "That you?"

Nathan walked slowly down the porch steps. "It's me."

"Have you lived here the whole time?"

"More or less."

Grant turned on Hawk. "And you didn't have the decency to tell us?"

"He didn't know," Nathan said. "I didn't tell him I came from your ranch. I just said I came from Montana."

Hawk felt much like when he was on a horse set to spook. Grant and Deb looked genuinely perplexed. Amy still looked as if she were trying out her arms. She *knew*.

It made sense that Nathan shared his secret with Amy. Had Grace known? No, she would have told Hawk. He could always trust her to be honest with him. He wished she were here right now. In this episode of *Missing Grace*…

"Amy," Hawk said. "Aren't you planning to take the boys down to the creek?" The low waters of late summer created a quiet wading area behind The Home Place. He and Grace had spent many a lazy afternoon there when kids. During much better times.

Amy seemed reluctant to move.

"I'll see you later," Nathan said to her, with its implied meaning of "I got this."

"Sure. Come on, guys. Time to pack up."

Amos and Saul knew where the real excitement lay, and hesitated. Hawk pointed to the house. "Git." They shuffled off, their heads coming up when Amy mentioned snacks to pack.

The door closing behind them, Hawk said, "That'll give us a good quarter-hour to square this away. Nathan, what's going on here?"

"I didn't lie to anyone."

"You stole my dog," Grant burst out.

"She's not your dog. She's mine. Her mom was mine. You sold all her pups, and they were excellent dogs. They had potential, but you wouldn't let me train them. I gave up half a month's salary so I could keep her. You remember that. She's mine."

"That is true," Deb said quietly. "But, Nathan,

you just…left. You sent a text, so at least, we didn't call the police. It was just cold. You'd been with us, since you were a boy."

Nathan scuffed the dirt. "Eleven. I came with Mom when I was eleven."

"And we gave you a place and covered expenses when your mom's wages couldn't."

"She hated every minute there," Nathan mumbled. "It's why she left. Her and her loser husband."

"Ranching's not for everybody. But it's the only thing we got to offer people," Deb said quietly.

Wasn't that the truth? It was the only life he could offer Grace. And she hadn't wanted it.

"You liked it," Grant said. "You were on the horses and out with the dogs. Why did you leave and come right to another ranch anyway? What's this one got mine doesn't?"

"And don't say 'Amy,'" Hawk said. "You didn't know her before you came here."

Nathan looked at him, and then blinked and turned away, as if Hawk was a bright object. "You, actually," he said.

Grant sent Hawk another blistering look. Hawk raised his hands in defense. "Listen, I came to your place once years ago. I don't think I even remember seeing you there."

"I was just a kid then." Hawk didn't point out that the fifteen-year age gap still made him a kid.

"I was out in the barns when Grant introduced you and I picked up on the name, Blackstone. That was my mom's name before she married my dad, you see."

"What? You think we're some long-lost relatives?"

"We are. I told Mom to ask you about them, but she said what was the point of that and that *Blackstone* was common enough. And then I heard you tell Grant about how your people came up here from Montana, because it was a big family and the boys went off in all directions. But there are no Blackstone Ranches down in Montana anymore, so I thought maybe, you were the last of them, so I thought… I thought I'd go check you out."

"It's possible." His dad had come out onto the porch and was listening in. "Granddad talked about coming up from Montana. It wasn't even Montana then, just wild country. Here, there were Mounties and the law. He could lay claim and not have to worry about another rancher shooting him off the property. I'm not saying it is. I'm saying it could be." His dad turned to the door. "Let me see if I can find a few pictures."

Another Blackstone. Hawk faced Nathan. "Why didn't you just say that to me day one?"

"Because then he'd have to admit that he ran off," Grant said. He frowned at Nathan. "I could have made proper introductions, given you a reference."

Nathan touched Doxie Sue's head as she sat tucked against his leg. "Because you would have made me leave her behind. And that wasn't happening."

"Oh, Nathan," Deb said, "I wish you hadn't thought the worst of us."

Grant leaned against his truck door, embossed with the Sears brand and the company name, Sears Cutting Horses. "I might not have been the most…benevolent of employers, but I didn't think anyone would have chosen to run off."

"I suppose I could have handled things differently," Nathan mumbled.

"I'd say," Hawk said, which the best he could come up with. Grace would have so much to say and to so many people.

"But things seem to have worked out," Deb said, looking around at the corrals. "You seem to have met a girl."

"Amy," Nathan said. "We're actually getting married."

Hawk must have made gulping noises, because everyone, including the dog, looked at him anxiously. "Did this all happen when I was out with the boys?"

"No, it's been a couple of weeks."

A couple of— "Does Irina know?"

"No, we were keeping it a secret."

"Then, why did you tell?"

Nathan looked sideways at Deb as if she were another, overbright object. "It's hard to keep secrets from you, Deb. Another reason I had to leave so quick."

Amy came out onto the porch, wrangling boys and bags ahead of her.

"They know," Nathan said to her. "About us."

She closed her eyes. "Now we'll have to tell Grandmom, for sure."

"We'll do it, tonight."

"Know what?" Amos said.

"They're getting married," Hawk said. "To each other," he added just so everything was clear.

"Oh," Saul said. "Does Grace know?"

"I don't think that—"

"We'll tell her on the way from Irina's," Nathan said. "She'll want to know."

"That Grace who bought the horse out from under me?" Grant said.

"That Grace," Deb said, shooting her husband a warning look, "who operates a lovely B and B close by and might just have a room available tonight. If we ask nicely. Hawk, you wouldn't happen to have her contact info, would you?"

Deb had given him an opening. "I'll tell you what. Let me call her."

"AND I HAVE to sit on this for how long?" Grace squirted window cleaner onto the front of the dining room window and applied elbow grease. Fly specks always stuck as if glued on.

"At least, until tomorrow," Hawk said through her speakerphone. "Do you think you can hold on?"

He spoke dead seriously, so seriously she knew he was joking. Had he forgiven her? Was this out-of-the-blue call his way of reaching out to her?

"No guarantees. I may call up random people just to get the news out of my head. I mean, wow."

"Yeah, not every day you discover your hired hand is some cousin. Dad's gone off to find old pictures to show Nathan."

"So he believes it?"

"It's so bizarre it must be true." Hawk paused. "I don't mind if he is. He makes a good fit here, and if he's family, all the better."

"The Blackstone legacy grows."

"And then their marriage joins the Blackstones and Sandbergs together."

"They're so young," Grace said. "And they haven't known each other for a full year. How do they know what's good for them?"

"I'm sure Irina will have the same questions."

"And you don't? No words of wisdom as Nathan's older, experienced cousin?" Grace stepped back to examine her work. There, all little fingerprints gone. Those boys. She blinked at the sparkling surface. Empty and boring.

"They are young," he said quietly, "but that doesn't make them wrong."

He was talking about them fifteen years ago, wasn't he? "Who am I to talk? Thirty-four, and I haven't figured anything out." There, an admission that maybe with him, she had got it wrong.

"I got two years on you, and I'm no better."

So, he was admitting to uncertainty. Was that an opening for her?

"Hawk, I was thinking—"

"Not the only thing—"

They both stopped at the overlap of their voices. "Go ahead," he said.

"No, you. You called." She just needed a moment to settle her nerves.

"Any room at the inn? Grant and his wife were looking for a place to stay."

He hadn't called to shoot the breeze, to connect, to talk her back into his life. Grace swallowed. "He's not still sore with me about buying Katz out from under him?"

"He's gotten over it. I think. Maybe sleep with one eye open tonight, just in case." Again dead serious.

"A cancellation came this morning, so send them over when you're done with your visiting. How long, do you think?"

"Not until later. Maybe after supper. He's here for the horses."

"What? You're not selling them, are you?" It was none of her business but—

Hawk breathed out. "I guess I never got around to telling you. He bought first rights to buy the foal from Katz and Risky B, if that happens. I arranged that at the show, just before Dad's accident. Then after the accident—"

Right. They broke up, and that had sucked the air out of their business partnership, too.

"Mateo knows. I assumed he would have told you. I'm sorry."

"It's okay, Hawk. I didn't keep you in the loop about buying Katz. Let's call it even. You've got enough on your plate, what with the Nathan drama now."

"Yep, meanwhile back on the ranch…"

The conversation was teetering back into the familiar. Now or never, she thought.

"I went to—"

"I suppose I—"

Another stop. "Your turn to go first," Hawk said.

Grace found a fingerprint she had missed. Beside it, she smeared her thumb against the glass. "I went to the office the other day," Grace said. "Rachelle wanted me to go over that litigation. It was the first time I had seen everybody."

"And how did that go?" His voice was neutral. Because he really didn't care? Or cared but couldn't show it?

"It went well in a way I didn't expect," she said. "I was hoping for a way back into the firm through this case, and to gain back their trust. Only they were all excited to see me. They seemed to have forgotten, or it mattered less than I thought. They took me out for lunch and it was like old times."

"Good to hear." Still neutral.

"George was there, too. You remember him?"

"Yep."

"And I mentioned that there's a lawyer retiring in Diamond Valley, and George asks if I want to open up a second office and I said that it might be too much, and then Diana—she's been with the firm the longest—says that she's looking to go half time, and how about we share hours? And I said that I would think about it."

Several beats passed before Hawk said, "Don't keep me in suspense, Grace. What did you decide?"

"I haven't. It would give me flexibility. I could choose clients. Still be a lawyer and run the B and B and—help out. What do you think?" Her grip on the bottle was so tight it hurt.

"Sounds as if you're the one with a full plate. Not sure if there'll be room to…help."

"I plan to close the B and B over the winter, and the firm will handle the setup of the office. I will have loads of free time. There are only so many quilts I can make. I like to be busy. I think… I think I found a way to have it all. If you like."

A burst of voices rose from Hawk's end. "Hey, they are all back from the tour of the yard. I should probably go."

"Okay." She waited for him to say something about how they could talk later. Then again, she had offered herself up before and then pulled back. Why would he believe this time was different?

He would have to be an idiot to try a third time, and she would have to be an idiot to expect him to.

CHAPTER SEVENTEEN

Two WEEKS LATER in early September, Grace stood beside her mother's cairn. "Happy birthday, Mom. Fifty-eight today."

The sky was in vast motion. Wind stretching and building clouds. A stiff breeze battered at her windbreaker. She had better come off the ridge soon, before the wind knocked her off.

"One misstep is all it takes," she muttered to herself and her mother. To lose your life. To lose your chance. The way she had with Hawk. He hadn't called back. Amos and Saul had come over a few times on quick visits, once when Knut was down with Sadie. Amy delivered them, never Hawk. She could have a piece of the boys, but not him.

And she had kept busy. August was her record month for the B and B. If she could pull it off this season, then each should get easier. She already had a few bookings for next season. This week, George would sign off on the Diamond Valley office. Her business life, as always, roared on.

She came down from the ridge to lay her head just below the cairn and stretched out her arms and legs to gaze starfished up into the churning sky. She would lie here for a few minutes and then head back.

Her first Friday night without guests. Weird. She had nothing to do and nowhere to go. "Mom, I really blew it."

Her cell phone buzzed. Hawk.

"You alive?" he barked.

What a question. Wait, his binoculars. Was he watching her? She pushed up onto her elbows. "Yes."

"Then, tell the boys to turn around and get back. Now."

"What?"

"Look at—" His cell call dropped. It was a wonder he had even made the connection. She sat up and looked toward the ranch. There, coming across the browning pasture were the boys on the back of Greta. And it was no gentle walk. They had her at a full trot. And they were bareback with just the halter on.

Hawk's number flashed up again but then dropped before she could swipe it open. Never mind, she knew what to do.

The boys were still coming at a full trot, so she hadn't far to go down the hill before they met. Saul held the reins. They were pale and they must be freezing in their T-shirts.

"All right, what's the panic?"

"Dad had the binoculars," Amos said, "and he saw you on the ridge and he said that you were going to fall off—"

"He said," Saul interjected, "that you had better get off before you fall off, but he wouldn't let us see."

"Then he sets them down and goes back in the barn. We look—and you were just lying there!"

"We call him and he looks and he says you're okay, that you are just lying there. But who lies there for that long?"

"And you decided to check things out for yourself."

"It was mostly Saul," Amos said. "He needed help getting the halter on, and then I came, too."

"You lost your mom," Saul said quietly. "And I didn't want to lose…you."

"Oh, Saul." She stripped off her lined jacket and settled it around Saul. Then she took off her sweater and pulled it over Amos's head. She was down to her shirt and the stiff wind bit at her skin.

"Listen, I am okay. And I deeply appreciate that you two risked life and limb to come to my rescue. But we all need to get home, okay? There's a storm coming, and your dad is worried about you two."

"He's going to kill us," Amos said.

Saul nodded. "Probably." He opened his fanny

pack and took out three store-bought cookies, and handed them around. Grace couldn't say no.

"You shouldn't have come up here by yourself," Amos said. "It's dangerous."

"It is, if you're not careful," Grace said. "But I wanted… My mom's birthday is today. And I wanted to check in."

"Are you going to leave something there?"

"We should put up another rock." He moved to slide off Greta and Grace pushed him back up.

"Not today. Go home."

Saul leaned over and handed her a cookie from his baggie. "Here, give it to your mom."

"Sure, I'll do that. Now, git before I'm in trouble with your dad, too."

She watched the backside of Greta and the boys recede back toward the ranch. Greta wasn't losing time. Down by the corrals, she thought she could make out the lean frame of Hawk.

Well, that little drama was over. She thought of polishing off the cookie herself. No one would know. Unless Hawk had those binoculars trained on her.

Anyway, she couldn't lie to the boys and some cruising raven might appreciate the handout. She retraced her steps back up to the cairn.

"Here, Mom, a cookie. I'll see you again. Miss you."

She stood and turned to leave. Her boot caught

on the rocks gathered during the summer visit with her dad. She stumbled, her arms windmilling.

"No!"

Her last thought before tipping over the edge was that at least the boys hadn't seen her go.

BUT HAWK HAD.

He threw down his binoculars and raced for the quad parked next to the barn.

"It's out of gas," Nathan said, coming out of the barn. "What's going on?"

Hawk pivoted, and wolf-whistled to call Wildrose over. "It's Grace. She's fallen off the ridge." His breath caught. He couldn't say more, and he didn't need to. By the time he saddled Wildrose, Nathan had crossed to open the far gate. "I left the binoculars down by the corrals," Hawk said on his way through. "Keep an eye up there in case I need help. And watch the boys."

They weren't more than five minutes away on Greta. "I don't care what kind of lie you come up with. Don't tell the boys anything."

Nathan nodded and Hawk only slowed when he drew alongside the boys to tell them to stick with Nathan, and then he set Wildrose into a full gallop. He couldn't have lost her, not like this. She had to be okay.

But accidents happened all the time. A mother. A daughter.

Why not Grace, too?

I think I have found a way to have it all. If you like. But he hadn't believed her. Or his luck. It had seemed more real that she would leave than that he, too, could have it all. And now, right before his eyes, she had vanished.

Please, not for good. Wind tore at his clothing, had taken his hat long back. Wildrose's breathing came in hard, jolting pants. *Let her live, let her be alive.*

"Come on," he urged. They were approaching the steepest part now, and Wildrose slowed. Hawk could run just as fast, but he needed the mare in case he had to lift Grace up.

"Grace!"

Was it the wind or his own wishing, but was that her calling to him?

He couldn't take it anymore. He halted Wildrose and swung off, making for the ridge.

There she was, thirty feet below him on the same ledge where he'd found her mother. Kneeling, her face turned up to him, dirt all up her front and on her face. Alive.

"You were spying on me with those binoculars," she said, the wind whipping away her voice, so her words arrived in pieces to his senses.

Hawk looked at the roiling clouds and took a long breath. Then he turned to the ranch and gave a wave and a thumbs-up signal. That should be good enough. "I apologize. How about I forget what I saw and head back to the ranch?"

"Sure," she said. "And then explain that to your boys."

He squatted. "You really think that I would only haul your butt up because of what the boys might think of me?"

"Okay, you have a conscience. Could demonstrate it at your earliest convenience?"

Hauling up a living being who could brace herself and help the process was a sight easier than...before. He uncinched the rope from her middle and gathered it up. His hands were shaking as bad as she was. Cold pebbled her arms, and her bottom lip was trembling.

He wasn't aware he'd moved to her, but suddenly she was flat against his chest, his arms wrapped tight around her. And he had no thought of letting go anytime soon.

"What happened?"

"My foot caught, and I slipped. I mostly slid and grabbed at whatever until I landed on the ledge."

"You hurt?"

"Major grass burn, bruised ribs and I grabbed a thistle on the way down, so my hands feel as if they are on fire. The whole front of me feels on fire."

His front did, too, but for a different reason. Wildrose whinnied, her ears flicking. "Hold on, we'll go soon."

"There's a storm coming," he said into her

hair. Her very prickly hair. He tugged out a sage-brush twig.

"I had noticed that. Can I bother you for a ride back to my place?"

That would require moving, loosening his arms around her, and he wasn't ready for that yet. "I saw you go over and my heart stopped beating."

She didn't say anything, her arms folded against his chest.

"I have pretended with you, Grace. I pretended it was up to you, if you wanted to make a go of it with me."

Her reply came muffled. "You said that you wanted to be with me."

"Sure, I said it. But what happened when you got scared and left? I got scared, too. I didn't go after you. I nodded my head and let you go."

"That was the deal."

"That was a rotten deal." He rubbed his hands up and down her back. She was cold, and they should go. But he wasn't going to let her go until he had finished.

"You know why I look for a missing calf, even though I've got hundreds? Part of the reason is money, but a bigger part has to do with not letting a creature suffer. What I did to you was let you suffer because I didn't want to take responsibility for you."

She shuddered against him. "That's a tad dramatic."

"No, I was always great at taking on responsibility. Unless it came to us. I let you go and called it giving us freedom, the right to choose. I could have compromised on everything else, except you. I should have chased you, Grace. Fifteen years ago and when you broke it off after the accident."

She lifted her dirt-smudged face to his. "But you said I was like wind and couldn't be caught."

He could feel her ribs under his hands, her heart beating against his chest. Grace, alive and in his arms. "And yet here we are with a storm about to break. I'm not letting go."

"It wouldn't matter if you did, because I'm not going anywhere."

Her mouth was inches from his. "I've got one more thing to say."

Her blue eyes widened. "Say it."

It was the most natural thing to say in the world. "I love you, Grace Miranda Jansson. You were always my best friend. Now you're my neighbor and business partner. And I aim to make you my wife one of these days."

Her arms slid around his neck. "Make me, you say?"

There was that same light in her eyes that had him since he was five. "Is that a dare?"

She ran a finger down his cheek. "Yeah, it is. I love you back just as hard, Hawk Blackstone. If you accept the dare, I'll make sure you win it."

Hawk grinned and lowered his head, getting a head start on the challenge.

Meanwhile, back on the ranch, Nathan hastily lowered the binoculars. He had done that as soon as Grace was in Hawk's arms, but Amos and Saul insisted he keep checking, just in case. Not that he'd seen much with Hawk's checkered back bulking up the view.

"Can we look now?" Amos said.

"Is Grace still okay?" Saul said.

Nathan pocketed the binoculars and spun them toward the house. "She's very okay. Your dad's okay. He'll bring her home soon."

EPILOGUE

GRACE OPENED THE door to The Home Place, bringing with her the rush of the April winds.

The stink hit her. The cake. She raced to the oven. "Haley!" she yelled. She opened the door and out billowed a wave of heat and smoke. The wedding cake, a simple form cake Grace had popped into the oven two hours ago, looked like a giant charcoal briquette.

The smoke detector shrieked, and her sister pounded down the stairs, carrying baby Jakob in her arms. Jonah peeked out at his aunt from behind the safety of his mom. "Jakob's teething and Jonah bumped his head—"

Grace tilted the pan to her.

"Oh. I'm so sorry." Haley opened her phone. "I'll call Mateo."

"He's busy enough helping Hawk get the chores done so they can dress for the wedding," Grace said, waving a towel under the detector to clear the smoke and shut off the noise.

"He'll know what to do," Haley said with quiet confidence.

There was only one thing to do with this cake. Grace flipped the smoking brick out the back door for whatever hardy wildlife was up for the challenge. She lifted her gaze to the ridge. Through the bare branches of the early April trees she could make out the cairn on the ridge. "I hope you can come, Mom."

Hawk had the solution. "He said there's an extra package of cake mix left over from the boys' birthday in October that hasn't expired," Haley said. "Natalia's whipping it up."

"She's a godsend. Thank God Brock married her."

"Yeah, she's the good sister we never had."

Grace snorted. "Hey, it's not me that nearly burnt the house down. Come on, let's get the decorations up. There's less than two hours to go."

A frantic two hours it was. Texts flew back and forth between The Home Place and the Blackstone Ranch, the load lessening once Natalia and Sadie arrived with Irina and Amy. Between swapping out toddlers and babies, the women arranged hair, and wiggled and zipped into dresses. Haley caused another minor emergency when her dress, perfectly fine two months ago, couldn't accommodate her baby bump. Grace opened seams and basted in quilting fabric. For the same reason, she would be opening the seams on her own dress for Nathan and Amy's wedding in late August.

The men pulled in, and Grace heard them assemble in the living room. She picked out Mateo's and Brock's voices. George, who had a special one-day license to act as marriage commissioner, and the single female voice of his wife, Hilda. Nathan spoke with her dad and Russell.

At the top of the stairs, Grace cocked her ear to Russell's voice, deep and raspy. It sounded strong and centered. She had plowed through mountains of research, and had instituted a new diet and mental therapies for him. Russell still lived at the ranch, and could keep a routine easily enough. Last week, when Irina came over for last-minute alterations on her dress, the topic had turned to Russell.

"You have saved his life," she said flatly.

Surprised, Grace pricked her thumb on a pin. "You are…okay with me, then?"

Irina played with the spill of blue faille. "I have grown okay with the entire world, since your father came along." She looked up at the ridge. "Though I will never compete with her, I suppose."

Grace repeated something she had overheard Hawk tell Amos about a school rivalry with another boy. "No competition if you don't enter."

Irina released a long breath. "You're right. Wise words."

But now, among the rumble of voices downstairs, she couldn't make out the speaker of the wise words. She peeked out the upstairs window to the driveway below. His truck was missing. Where were he and the boys? She couldn't do this without them.

Just as she turned from the window to fetch her phone, in he rolled. She allowed herself the quiet pleasure of watching him and the boys assemble themselves. For the quick dash to the house on the cool spring day, the boys just wore the suits she had bought them in early November for a similar occasion.

He was wearing her favorite shirt. A dark, bright blue under a black suit jacket. Nothing more satisfying than a cowboy dressed up, holding a cake server. He glanced up at the window and pointed her out to the boys, and they waved as if she had just arrived back from a long trip. The boys ran to the house, but Hawk lingered and shot her another look she understood. She touched her lips.

"Are we ready?" Natalia said quietly. The five women glanced at each other, and then at Sadie and the babies.

Irina gave a brisk nod. "Let's do this." They lined up and proceeded to the living room.

The men and boys were already in their assigned places, so it was only a matter of the females settling into place. Amos and Saul opened a spot between them on the ottoman for Sadie. Jonah followed her and sat at her feet. Haley sat beside Mateo with Jakob on Mateo's lap. Beside them, Amy nestled next to Nathan. Brock and Natalia with baby Daniel took one end of the second couch.

Hawk sat at the other end and Grace claimed the open spot next to him. He drew her left hand into his lap, the one with the wedding ring. True to his word, Hawk had proposed marriage in early October and they'd married in January in a ceremony not much different than this one.

"Did you tell Haley?" he whispered.

She shook her head. "I want to tell Dad first."

The news of a grandchild due in the fall would be her special wedding gift to him. Then together, they'd tell Russell.

Her dad stood near the fireplace, his eyes on his bride who came to stand beside him with the bouquet. They both looked wonderstruck.

"Welcome," George said, "to another special gathering."

And there had been so many in the past few years, Grace thought, as she glanced around the room. Mateo and Haley, then Brock and Natalia, Hawk and herself. All of them happily married. What were the chances of that happening?

And for her dad, to happen twice in one lifetime?

Hawk laced his fingers in hers and squeezed, her ring hard in their hands. He knew the odds. She squeezed back, and along with her family, attended to the words of abiding love.

* * * * *